THESE PEOPLE

and other stories

JUNE BASTABLE

Published in 2015 by FeedARead.com
Publishing Copyright © June Bastable

A CIP catalogue record for this title is available from the British Library.

For my offspring:

Sarah and Jonathan

FOR BARBARA

HAPPY READING

LOVE

JUNE xxx

[signature] x

Also by June Bastable in FeedARead books:

Some People

Credit where it's due…

I wish to pay tribute to those authors whose humour has stimulated me, viz: Alan Bennet, William Trevor, Victoria Wood, Dorothy Parker, Muriel Spark, Stan Barstow, Angus Wilson, Kingsley Amis, S J Perelman and Keith Waterhouse.

I also applaud my writer friends and literary groups for their great ideas and, of course, the laughter.

My heartfelt thanks to:

Kate Murphy-Nutt *for the photograph*

Pete Williams *for the layout*

Sheila Kara *for her patient listening/feedback*

Steve Morrell – *Leeds-based artist/actor/director for his wonderful paintings which inspired my stories "All She Ever Wanted"; "The Akimbo Arms" and "Christmas Punch"*

In a fair number of these stories, we make a return visit to quirky Quagmire Village, encountering characters you will recognise from Some People, e.g. Mrs Veronique Frobisher, the doctor's wife; Miss Dorcas Gorringe, the librarian; her mother, Mrs Gorringe; Miss Jocasta Fontenoy, the schoolteacher; Percival and Dorinda Catchpole, licencees of The Akimbo Arms; Max and Pandora Bellchamber of The Quagmire Inn, and many more familiar faces, plus quite a few new personages who have chosen, sometimes mistakenly, to make their home in that corner of the English countryside.

Other tales are set in some of the places I love…

CONTENTS

CONTENTS /continued

CATSPAW COTTAGE

For years, Kitty Bast had pictured herself retiring to a West Country seaside cottage and, as her sixtieth birthday approached, she put her Edwardian villa on the market and began to plan her future well away from the London rat-race.

Catspaw Cottage, situated on the outskirts of Quagmire Village, was the first house viewed by Mrs Bast, and she had immediately fallen in love with everything about it, even the price, which was well within her means. After that, no other property could compare and when her plans finally came to fruition, she was able to take up residence in the home of her dreams.

The garden fronting Catspaw Cottage was stocked with hollyhocks, honeysuckle, roses and lupins, a joyful sight to any city-dweller's eyes. Mrs Bast had little experience of horticulture, but she looked forward to learning and had bought green gloves, green gumboots plus an assortment of gardening implements.

And Quagmire Village itself provided an idyllic setting: thatched roofs, village hall, two pubs, library, post office and Victorian pier, with the nearest town, Quorum Thisbé, lying some ten miles distant.

Mrs Bast was busy during the first few days of settling in, ensuring each piece of furniture was in its correct place, hanging new chintz curtains, determined to have everything in keeping with such a quaint cottage.

'Set for life, that's what I am,' she thought happily, polishing the brasses arranged around the timber-framed inglenook. 'Now I can relax and look forward to a comfortable retirement with no money worries: all I have to do is enjoy myself.'

During the second week, the chairwoman of the Village Hall Society knocked on the door. She came bearing a bunch of flowers and a tin box of biscuits from Harrods. 'Hello – I'm Veronique Frobisher, the doctor's wife,' she beamed, 'and I should like to welcome you to Quagmire Village on behalf of the other residents.'

Kitty Bast, caught on the hop in her dusty pinafore and cotton bandana, was nevertheless pleased. She invited her visitor in and made coffee.

Mrs Frobisher was keen to impart information on the various village activities, including a horticultural society with its associated Quagmire Annual Flower Show, which Kitty Bast immediately agreed to join. 'I shall definitely come on Tuesday,' she promised.

The first meeting went well, people seemed friendly, and Kitty Bast picked up several tips to help her tackle the job of caring for her garden. The other members thought she had taken on a huge task, saying that the previous owner had employed Mr Laidlaw, a reliable local odd-job man, for the heavy work.

Suddenly, one of the ladies laughed and said, 'What a coincidence that you bought Catspaw Cottage – Kitty is short for kitten, and Bast is the name of the ancient Egyptian goddess: you know, the one with a cat's head.'

Kitty Bast had never heard of the Egyptian cat-headed goddess, but agreed that she had felt a strong attraction to the cottage, not only for its quirkiness and the beautiful garden but for a strange, almost spiritual, sensation she had experienced when first viewing the property.

'Perhaps it was meant to be, that you would come and live in Catspaw Cottage,' remarked Mrs Frobisher. 'Are you a cat-lover?'

Kitty Bast was rather spooked by this. 'No, I don't like cats at all – I am actually allergic to them.'

'Oh dear,' trilled the doctor's lady, 'you'll have to get used to all the moggies hereabouts – we have lots of them roaming around.'

The following morning she was in the garden, weeding and dead-heading, when a cat, loping along the top of the fence, stopped and stood staring at her. Mrs Bast shooed it away, but then found a pile of droppings in a flower bed. 'Drat,' she said aloud, removing the offending deposit.

The following day there were two feline offerings, this time in the herbaceous border. 'Well, what a nuisance,' she thought. 'I must ask the society's advice at next Tuesday's meeting.'

Each day that followed was worse in the cat droppings department. It appeared to her uneducated eye that it had to be more than one or two animals leaving their little gifts after dark. She couldn't wait until the Tuesday but telephoned Mrs Frobisher for her advice which was: *try scattering orange peel – cats just hate citric acid.*

Fortunately, Mrs Bast had some oranges in the fruit bowl; she took three and distributed the peel in strategic places around the garden.

The cat activity increased! They avoided the orange peel and deposited their offensive bequests elsewhere. 'This is spoiling my lovely garden,' she moaned, lifting the receiver to telephone Mrs Frobisher.

'Cats don't like thorny twigs, brambles, that kind of thing,' Mrs Frobisher said confidently. 'Gather some from the hedgerows and scatter them around: that should do the trick.'

Kitty Bast did as directed, carefully placing spiky branches and twigs in the offending areas, and went back indoors.

Later that same day, standing at the kitchen window overlooking a walled courtyard at the back of the cottage, she was thinking about the problem, hoping that the latest ploy would have some effect, when she was startled by the appearance of a large black cat on the sill outside. She tapped on the window and the cat leapt down, only to be replaced by a ginger tom which gazed at her inscrutably, pawing at the window.

She telephoned Mrs Frobisher for Mr Laidlaw's number, but the aged handyman had no useful advice to offer. 'Um, sorry, missus, we never 'ad no worries like that when Mrs Fleabane were alive. She 'ad a cat, d'you see, which might well 'ave kept the others away. Get yourself a moggie, that's the ticket.'

With a sigh, she thanked the old man, fervently hoping the cats would eventually be put off by the brambles under their paws. If that failed, she planned to buy a cat scarer, a contraption with movement sensors. This battle had become an obsession, a fight to the death!

That night, Kitty Bast found sleep difficult and lay awake into the small hours. All this worry was spoiling her joy in Catspaw Cottage...

She fell into a doze but was awakened by noises outside the house: cat noises! She opened the bedroom window and threw a glass of water into the darkness. Loud maiowing, spitting and caterwauling followed. 'Good, I must have hit the target,' she thought, getting back into bed where she tried to sleep but then became aware of feet, or more correctly, paws padding around above her head. 'It can't be,' she thought, 'how on earth could they get into the attic?'

The next day was a Tuesday, and at the horticultural society meeting she related all the latest happenings regarding the feline problem.

'Well, no-one else is having a particularly troublesome time of it,' commented Mrs Frobisher, and the others looked askance, nodding in agreement.

Various remarks followed: Could it be an over-active imagination? – Perhaps you're having an extreme reaction to normal events – You'll have to get used to things being a little different in the country – They're only trying to be friendly, those cats – Have you seen the doctor? – Perhaps you're a bit overwrought, what with the move etc...

Kitty Bast was taken aback, and when she overheard someone refer to her rather unkindly as "the catwoman" she realised there was not much empathy or sympathy to be had there.

Mrs Bast left before the meeting ended and walked a short distance to the post office to buy stamps.

As she entered, all conversation ceased. The short queue of people turned and smiled, but appeared uncomfortable. Had they been talking about her? Or had they not? Was she becoming paranoid?

'Has it all been a mistake, this move to Quagmire?' she wondered sadly. She could never have imagined it would all go so terribly wrong! And why could no-one understand her plight? She wasn't being unreasonable, surely. Why didn't the neighbourhood cats bother the other villagers to such an unacceptable extent? It was all unsettling and very strange.

Mrs Bast contacted a local builder to check the attic. Mr Armstrong arrived and went up the loft ladder for a thorough inspection. 'No, missus, I can't see anything up there, only cobwebs and a few spiders,' he laughed, pocketing the £30 fee.

She was obliged to keep her lovely new chintz curtains closed at all times, day and night, against cats' peering eyes. And then the animals began throwing themselves against the back door.

'Why are they torturing me,' the frantic woman wondered. 'What do they want with me?'

One terrible night, the sound of paws padding around above her head increased, and she heard claws tapping at the window. Groggily, she sat up in bed and to her utter shock saw a hundred pairs of yellow eyes staring at her through the gloom. She screamed as the animals leapt upon her, scratching at her face and neck: Kitty Bast fainted dead away.

When she regained consciousness, it was almost daylight. She sat up and looked around, dazed and uncomprehending, gradually focusing on her reflection in the dressing-table mirror opposite.

Cats of all breeds frolicked around, on the bed, the furniture and the floor. They nuzzled against the woman's body as she, mesmerised by her newly-grown whiskers, furry face and pointed ears, smiled triumphantly at this, her successful reincarnation.

'I am Bast, the cat-headed goddess made flesh,' she purred. 'Home at last – in Catspaw Cottage!'

FIVE MINUTES TO MIDNIGHT

'Chop chop, Bernard, come along, it's almost midnight,' Clarissa Vertigal, swathed in grey silken lace, was calling across the room. Bernard turned from his deep conversation with a pretty female guest and regarded his wife with some irritation. 'Yes, I know! I know my duties – plenty of time, it's not five to twelve yet.'

'Well, please drag yourself away from Phillida and, chop chop, get a move on, we can't spoil it for the sake of a few minutes.' Clarissa left her seat and moved towards the ornate antique fireplace. 'Friends,' she said, addressing their guests, the cream of Quagmire Village society, who were chatting and laughing, bursting balloons, kissing under the mistletoe and generally having fun on this particular New Year's Eve.

'Friends, attention please – your charming host, otherwise known as my dear husband, will now go outside and wait for twelve midnight!' Everyone cheered and looked expectantly at Bernard.

'All right, I'm going, I'm on my way, although it's pretty chilly out there for hanging about, but nothing is too much trouble if it pleases my darling wife.'

Bernard wrapped a thick red muffler, a Christmas present from Clarissa, around his neck to much cheering and laughter and good-humoured catcalls of "good old Bernie boy" and "do as you're told, old lad".

'He'll catch his death,' someone remarked, 'it must be ten degrees below.'

'Bernard will listen for his cue,' continued Clarissa, unfazed, waving her purple cocktail cigarette in the air for emphasis, 'which will be, as you all know, the church clock striking midnight, and then he'll come back inside, letting in the New Year and bringing a lump of coal for good luck.' Everyone cheered again.

'But,' added the controlling wife, 'he will of course go out the back way, via the kitchen, thereby keeping the cold air out. And he will re-enter this way by the French windows here.' Further cheering and good-humoured, slightly drunken, guffaws followed as Bernard exited the dining room.

He took measured paces along the stone-flagged hall, passed through the large warm kitchen, entered the utility room, and opened the back door where a blast of cold air and wet snowflakes greeted him. 'My God, you wouldn't send a dog out on a night like this,' he muttered. 'But that's Clarissa all over. She has to keep the tradition, no matter what; has to be the perfect hostess, doesn't give a damn about me at all.'

Bernard stepped outside into the kitchen garden and surveyed the scene. In the light from the house he could see neat lines of vegetables, a wooden shed and a wrought iron bench. The obedient husband fetched a piece of coal from the shed, and sat down on the bench, oblivious to the dampness beneath his thighs, a fine snow settling on his head and shoulders.

He took out a cigarette which was quickly discarded, being too wet to light.

'Everyone knows I'm hen-pecked,' he thought. 'They all snigger about it behind my back, I'm well aware of that. But what can I do about the situation now after all these many years: it's been allowed to go on far too long.'

Then he sank into the luxury of his favourite reverie, which was How to Kill Clarissa – or, what was more to the point, how to murder his wife and get away with it scot-free!

Yes, if a perfect crime could be arranged, and Clarissa was got rid of for good and all, he was absolutely certain that Phillida would agree to marry him, after a respectable period of mourning of course. *Yes, that young lady really does fancy me, although she pretends not to, but that is how a lot of ladies go about things – they show no interest in a man, purely because it inflames his passions all the more.*

Bernard took out another cigarette and tried more than a few times to light it without success. Finally, he threw it away, feeling irritable, his indigestion bothering him again, probably caused by all this stress.

His thoughts ran on, fantasising about how his life would be without Clarissa. He could never demand a divorce when she held the purse-strings: all the money was hers, all in her sole name, so he dared not go down that path and come out of it penniless. He had no wish to have to go out to work again, having grown used to a life of leisure, well, apart from being a body servant to Clarissa and a figure of fun to all their friends – *her* friends.

She was such an irritation to him, her peremptory attitude, and a fondness for bragging that the marriage contained neither dogs nor children as she held both in equal abhorrence. All her little habits like drinking and nagging, got on his nerves, and time was running out – he would never get these years back.

How wonderful life would be if Clarissa were gone, leaving him free, wealthy and in a position to propose to Phillida. They could have a new beginning together, a fresh shot at happiness, buy a dog and have a child, preferably a boy whom he would like to name Osbert Jolyon.

And if Phillida decided to turn him down, well, more fool her – with all that cash in the bank he could easily find someone else, someone probably more beautiful and pliable. She wasn't the only pebble on the beach, the silly girl! Yes, that's what he could do with, a beautiful and pliable woman but one with a bit of spirit, to make life exciting again.

But how could the deadly deed be done? How could such a perfect murder be effected, without leaving traces, hints, evidence of his guilt? Yes, it was good to have something pleasant to think about in his too few solitary moments.

In the meantime, out here on the bench, his indigestion was proving bothersome. He knocked on his chest with a knuckle and took out another cigarette but sat there without trying to light it. Presently, after gazing into space for some seconds, he returned to his wonderful reverie of life without Clarissa, until the church clock began to strike the midnight hour.

Bernard leapt to his feet; *can't be late bringing in the New Year otherwise Clarissa would never let it drop, she would go on about it ad infinitum.*

He made his way round the house towards the dining room, avoiding a trailing bramble, and gripped the handle of the French windows. It did not turn. Oh damnation, the door jamb has swollen, he thought, another job for me, I must get that seen to tomorrow before Clarissa has a tantrum.

He began rattling the handle and knocking on the glass. There seemed to be no strength in his fingers, probably through hanging around outside in the freezing cold night air.

He squinted through a chink in the curtain and, strangely, the room appeared to be in darkness apart from one blur of light. Are they having a joke, he wondered irritably. 'Let me in,' he called urgently.

Nothing happened! No-one came to let him in. Bernard was frantic with impotent anger! How dare they do this to him? They treated him as his wife's jester, her buffoon! He loathed all these childish pranks that Clarissa and her friends were so fond of playing.

Returning to the rear of the house, he almost tripped over the rogue bramble. Damnable thing, he thought, it wasn't there this morning! Bernard was suddenly incandescent with rage. Someone must have sneaked out and put it there! But thankfully, the kitchen door stood slightly ajar – he must have forgotten to close it. So, Clarissa's stupid friends hadn't gone as far as locking him out completely!

He walked through the dark utility room and kitchen, paced his way down the stone flags of the hall, and arrived at the dining-room door which stood ajar.

A strange scene met his eyes. The room was in darkness apart from glowing embers in the grate. Through the gloom he could barely discern a group of people sitting around the oval table, their eyes closed and fingertips touching.

'I feel something in the room,' intoned a voice. 'A presence is amongst us! Is anyone there? Knock once for "yes", twice for "no".'

Bernard was outraged! How far would these people go in order to tease him, play cruel tricks on him? He felt for the light-switch but his fingers were too numb. He tried to speak but his lips were frozen and he could not shape the words.

Moving towards the fireplace, hoping to thaw out a little, he noticed a calendar on the mantelpiece which displayed the date: 31st December 1980. What was this, a further joke they were having at his expense? Bernard's fury increased – he was perfectly aware that the day was New Year's Eve 1950.

'Hello, Bernard, I've been waiting for you,' quavered a familiar voice close by. A strange scent of foul dankness wafted towards his nostrils.

He turned, startled, and through the gloom beheld a silver-haired crone clothed in mouldering grey silken lace. She was holding out withered arms to him, her fingernails long, green and rotting...

'I'm glad you've finally let in the New Year after all these years,' laughed the phantom through blackened teeth. 'Now we can spend eternity together – so come along, Bernard – chop chop!'

BEST FRIENDS

Oh Bertha, I'm so relieved to find you in. I hope you don't mind my turning up out of the blue? But I simply had to get away – I couldn't have been more annoyed, I was almost at screaming point.

So I made a lame excuse and just left them to it, absolutely! Can't help it if there were hurt feelings but, anyway, that lot haven't *got* any feelings and they're all *probably* pulling me to pieces as we speak – I've seen it happen so many times.

Honestly, those females, they're so damned shallow. All they're interested in is clothes, diets, parties, on and on ad nauseam! Utterly spoilt, the lot of them, no purpose in life other than to pamper themselves!

It's such a relief to see you, Bertha darling. I really, really needed desperately to talk to you, my only true friend! Oh, yes, you are, the only one on the absolute same wavelength as me.

But the dratted meeting was supposed to be about arrangements for The Quagmire Autumn Fayre; well, yes, I *do know* you *know that*, dear, but as you can guess,

23

all they yapped on about was clothes, particularly Veronique Frobisher, that new outfit she was wearing – I wish you'd been there – it's that latest Shubette model, you know, the one with caped sleeves, like a bat.

Actually it looked absolutely vile and really horrible on her in that vivid acid yellow. It made her look washed-out, such a pale woman at the best of times in spite of all that makeup she ladles on with a trowel, but I didn't say so, of course – I pride myself on being the soul of tact and anyway I'm far too kind-hearted to say what my true opinion is, even though I'd had a couple of sherries (I could feel my cheeks flushing but I don't think anyone noticed), so I just nodded with my usual forbearance, and did my best to grin and bear it.

But really, I did begin to imagine that outfit might suit me in black. What do you say to that, dear? Or blue? Yes? No? Yes? Well, we could go shopping in Quorum Thisbé tomorrow morning if you like – call in at Shubette's boutique. Then we can both try the dress on, see how it suits us.

Yes, I'd love to put one over on that Frobisher woman – the two of us turning up looking a million dollars instead of a dolled-up mess like her. I wonder whether she'll be at the Bellchambers' luncheon-party on Thursday! That would be really marvellous if we turned the tables on her then, wouldn't it? In front of all the others – aha ha!

What, dear, no, no I won't have a sherry, thank you: as you very well know, I hardly drink at all and I've already had two this morning – well, if you're having one then, but just a teeny weeny, tiny, teensy one, darling.

Thank you, yes, that's right, well, a little more, perhaps, yes, all the way up to the brim, if you insist. Cheers! Here's to our friendship, dear – you're definitely the best pal I ever had! Absolutely! The only one who understands me – we're on the same wavelength. Have I ever told you that?

Do you know something – if it weren't for you I would go absolutely mad – I'd have no-one to discuss the deep and important things in life with.

And, I must tell you, this morning they were going on about this new taste-free diet that's all the rage. I couldn't have been more irritated and absolutely annoyed!

As you know, I never diet myself, so why did they think I would join in, and anyway I couldn't have got a word in sideways if I'd wanted to. They get so worked up about it, as if it matters. They're all stick-thin, as you know.

By the bye, I meant to tell you that cucumber is very good for losing weight – did you ever hear about that? Apparently digesting cucumber burns up more calories than the actual food itself. So you're bound to lose weight. Try it, darling. No, no, no, not that you need to lose weight, not at all, not in the least.

And if I'd been able to get a word in edgewise this morning, I should have shared that information with those stupid women, but no – it was just terrible, darling, the absolute rabble going on – my ears were literally ringing and I simply could not wait to escape.

Oh I wish you'd been there but I do understand why you didn't want to be on the Quagmire Village committee – you were very wise. People did mention about your not taking part – what, no, no, please don't worry about that, don't get upset – I absolutely put them right on that score, dear girl. It's a free country, I said – more than once or twice – when they kept on about it! Honestly, these women are like a bitch with a bone – they won't let it drop once they get their teeth into it! But I took your side and told them to calm down and get on with the meeting – well, I tried to but I simply could not be heard – it was like being in the zoo. Don't worry about it though, darling – it's simply not worth bothering about, really it isn't.

You should have been there this morning though, because it was so irritating and annoying that it was almost funny! I kept thinking I must tell Bertha about all this and I tried to remember every little stupid thing they said – absolutely nothing worthwhile or useful to the world. They're so empty-headed and it's always the same old, same old. Not like us, darling, with our deep and meaningful conversations.

There was one thing that Dorothea Loomis mentioned, though, something about dancing keeping her slim. We ought to join a class, darling, it's on Tuesday mornings. Burlesque, I think it was she had signed up for. You can dress up for that, too, feather boas and black corsets, stuff like that – absolutely! You'd enjoy that, wouldn't you, darling? You like dressing up. No, not that you need to lose any weight, not at all, absolutely, definitely not, not in the least. But it keeps you fit, as well, so I might enquire about it and book us in. It's on Tuesday mornings…

Oh, and I forgot to ask what you'll be wearing tonight? The Plunges always invite the smartest people – I might wear the purple lace with the taffeta peplum. How about you? Oh, the red satin? We-e-ll, darling, not sure about that, it does show every slightest wrinkle when you've been sitting down. What? You hadn't realised that? Oh, dear, well, what about your black velvet? It covers a multitude of sins – no, no, darling, not that you have any "sins" to hide, no, no, believe me, not at all, absolutely not.

I might change my mind and leave the purple lace – I'm actually thinking of having my dressmaker remove the taffeta peplum – and yes, now I think of it, I could do with giving my green silk with the floating panels an airing – I haven't worn it for a couple of months and never at one of Amelia Plunge's dinner parties, although some of the other guests might remember seeing me in it and have a good old gossip about it. Too bad – they're so shallow, they like picking holes in other people: not like us, darling, we live and let live, and anyway why should we care what the others think?

Oh, and I nearly forgot to tell you – Sophia Granville-Twigge wore that awful frock this morning, she looked an absolute horror – you know, that puce number, the one with the silver piping and slung hip-belt!

Really, darling, these people *just do not know how* to dress, do they?

I wonder what she'll be wearing tonight – if she's had an invitation, that is. I somehow doubt it though, because Peregrine and Amelia Plunge are people of discernment, they have great taste, although, actually, Amelia doesn't always come up with the goods, but I suppose everyone is allowed one or two mistakes. Hmm, I was thinking of last time when she wore that gold lamé two-piece with the frogging! It didn't do a thing for her – she should never wear shiny material with those hips; it literally highlighted every ripple. Perhaps I should tip her the wink about cucumber and burlesque? What do you think?

By the way, I believe she's had a chinlift – those dangly earrings simply do not hide the scars. And you know me, darling, I literally *never* gossip, but strictly *entre nous*, Amelia told me in confidence that she's having an affaire with one of her husband's business contacts. How awful of her when Peregrine spoils her to bits! No gratitude, these people, but I'm not one to criticise, so I let them get on with it! But remember, you heard it here first!

Hmm? Yes, please, Bertha darling, just a teensy weensy tiny little bit more, merely a spoonful! Mustn't risk getting squiffy so early in the day – I hardly drink much at all, as you know!

And well, I must ask you before I forget, what do you think of that rumour about Carlotta de Wyke?

What, you haven't heard? My goodness, you should have come this morning – they were talking about it in great depth, and apparently she's gone under the knife, too! Yes, it's either a face-lift or a nose-job, she hasn't said which, so it could be both!! We'll be able to tell as soon as she emerges from her self-imposed exile, won't we! Haha! I've heard these things can go so drastically wrong – so here's hoping! What? Oh, no, dear, I was only joking!

No, honestly darling, I wouldn't wish that on my worst enemy – and, as you are well aware, I couldn't hurt a fly but some people get what they deserve and Carlotta is one of those women who should! Although, I am quite fond of her, really, to be honest…

Hmm, what was I saying?

Oh, yes, actually, hmm, going back to the Plunges, I heard that Peregrine has booked himself into rehab next week – he's describing it as a health spa, but you and I know different, don't we, darling? Ahaha! We shall have to be very careful what we say tonight at dinner. But then, we always are, aren't we, dear? Yes, the soul of tact, that's us, quite definitely!

Erm, well, yes, please, dearest, perhaps another teensy tiny top-up, except – *oops*, I nearly fell off the chair – help me up, dear, that's right – goodness, and I've hardly had a thimbleful at all today – *ha ha ha…*

Now then, where was I…

Ooh, *ha ha ha*, yesh, cheers, and here's to our friendship, Bertha dahling – you're the besht pal I ever had! Did I ever tell you that? Yesh, you're the only one who undershtands me, who I can talk to about real life, about things that matter in the world – we're on the *wame savelength*, oops, *ha ha ha*, I mean "*shame wavelength*"…

Hmm, jusht to the brim perhapsh, yesh, don't shpill any, darling, ah, that'sh right, dahling, no, no, don't shlop it over, or I shall have to lick the table – *oops, ha ha ha*.

And do you know shomething, darling heart? You're the besht friend I ever had! Absholutely and definitely! Have I ever told you that?

SAVING FACE

The Quagmire Events Committee whooped with joy when I managed to secure Freya Tumbrill to come and open our Christmas Fayre. Miss Tumbrill's only stipulation, apart from an above-average fee, was that she might be allowed to bring along a stock of her latest lifestyle publication entitled "The Positive Woman".

Came the day, the great lady swept from her limousine, draped in mink and sporting a felt busby hat in bright red with a feathery fall cascading down one side. Her chauffeur, appearing quite short in comparison, brought up the rear carrying two large boxes. 'This coat is actually fake fur,' she announced brightly to the welcoming committee.

The usual generous hospitality was on offer, but Miss Tumbrill refused all food and drink, maintaining that she never ate before a speaking event and drank only "Adam's Ale" as she termed it, taking out of her copious handbag a bottle of what appeared to be still water.

The village hall was crowded with folk, mainly women, anxious to see this paragon of virtue and healthy living, a veritable guru on lifestyle and how to grow old gracefully. Many admirers had already obtained copies of her latest tome in readiness for the widely advertised book-signing.

After spending several long minutes in the dressing-room, Miss Tumbrill appeared on the stage to enthusiastic applause and, with much graciousness, began to speak in a voice like plum velvet.

'I should like to begin by thanking the committee for inviting me here, and also my thanks go to so many kind personages for turning up on such a cold and frosty afternoon – I do believe we are actually full to capacity! Yes, yes, you can show your appreciation if you wish – come on, ladies, let's hear it for the dedicated organisers!'

Miss Tumbrill paused for the ripple of applause, before continuing: 'And another important thing to mention is that my personal assistant-cum-chauffeur here, Mr Oliver Bodfish, has set up his little table and there will be copies of my book "The Positive Woman" hot off the press, available to purchase, and which I shall, naturally, be most pleased to personally sign for each and every one of you here present. My book would make a wonderful Christmas present for anyone – yes, I would say even for the lovely men of your acquaintance, as they might, at this late stage, begin to understand the female gender a tiny bit.'

A wave of laughter swept around the hall and some women began to clap and cheer.

'Please, I beg of you, ladies,' resumed Miss Tumbrill, 'save your applause for the end, partly because you may not agree with everything I say and partly because I am constrained by tight timescales.

'Now, what I recommend to those married women amongst you is that you live by your husband's law, his rules – you promised to love and obey and this you must do – that is, until you find out what he's really like – then you can chuck him out!'

Miss Tumbrill held up one hand, stemming the ensuing hilarity. 'I *was* joking, of course, ladies – I myself have been married only the twice and, sadly – or not – both my husbands ran off with an actress, different actresses of course, well, "actress" is what they called themselves anyway, but I did learn a lot from all this, which was the old adage: remarriage is the triumph of hope over experience, and so I have remained happily alone ever since in what I like to call "single blessedness" or even "blessed singleness", whichever you prefer, it's all the same to me!

'But I don't want to bore you with my personal affairs – no, what I came here to say is that to remain healthy and, as you will read in my latest book "The Positive Woman", the best food is raw beetroot, not the pickled kind, but raw, straight out of the ground – and do *not* trouble to wash it as the earth clinging thereto contains many vitamins and peripheral minerals, otherwise known as trace elements, which help to keep us healthy and free from disease.

'And also, dear friends, as stated in my book "The Positive Woman", you must avoid meat, dairy, chocolate, tobacco, drugs *and* alcohol. These things, we never, ever touch. They are so ageing and will shorten your life. And also, I would add, that after the age of, say, 40, we ladies must decide whether to save our figures or our faces: that is, without resorting to surgery!'

At this point, a man's voice could be heard calling out from the back of the hall, 'And which did you choose, Miss Tumbrill?'

There was a communal gasp and a turning of heads. Miss Tumbrill raised one hand and said calmly, 'Oh, I see, a person here present thinks he is some kind of humourist? Well, before we continue, would a committee member escort that wag out of the hall, please, or at least gag the wag?'

At this, there was much laughter followed by deafening applause from the admiring audience.

Miss Tumbrill patted her hair, and projected her beaming smile around the hall before continuing with her talk: 'No, no – I forgive him, the brute – let him stay. But as I was saying, before I was so rudely interrupted, too much dieting is very bad for visible parts like the face and neck which show every little sag and loss of flesh. For myself, I prefer to *save* my *face* because, as you can see, I could never be called skinny – slim, or almost slim, I'll allow if you must, yes, but never skinny.

'And whilst I'm on the subject, I must mention my next book, my forthcoming book which is presently a work in progress, and, as you might have guessed, it is to be entitled "Saving Face" wherein I let you into my secret, and so that you don't have to wait to read it, I can tell you now! Oh what lucky ladies you are!'

Miss Tumbrill paused theatrically and cast her eyes around the room, before continuing.

'Yes, I have a trick I would like to share with you, my friends. I know we're not all blessed with perfect features, but, as long as you don't look like the back of a bus, as the saying goes, you can make yourself appear beautiful to others. All you do is close your eyes and think of your best feature, then picture yourself looking lovely, see yourself in your mind's eye as Marilyn Monroe, Greta Garbo, Bette Davis or whoever, but *not* Joan Crawford as she was a right dog, in my humble opinion. Then, out loud, you repeat, "I am beautiful, I am beautiful". Come on ladies, do it now with me, close your eyes and say it.'

The female section of the audience, with a good deal of embarrassment, did as instructed and for the next twenty seconds or so there was a drone of feminine voices echoing around the hall.

'Yes, that'll do for now, ladies,' Miss Tumbrill barked. 'I can see we're embarrassing the few men who have turned up, ha ha. I do apologise to them, but must mention that it will work for the male sex, too, if only they can overcome their tiresome inhibitions; and "handsome" should be used instead of "beautiful" of course, ha ha! But don't forget to look out for this new book, entitled "Saving Face". It will be appearing on the shelves of all good bookshops by March of next year.'

Miss Tumbrill glanced at her diamond-encrusted wristwatch, then across at her chauffeur who nodded. She swept the audience with an incandescent smile, displaying perfect dentition behind scarlet lips, and took a deep breath before adding: 'Well, I could go on, but I'm here to open this Fayre and so I announce the Fayre duly open – I shall be available for signing after a short break for meditation, which, by the way, is covered in my next publication "Saving Face". I thank you! Oh, and before I forget – always be kind to each other – that's my watchword in everything I do.'

Miss Tumbrill swiftly disappeared from the stage to thunderous applause. 'Give me ten minutes – for communing with my muse, you know,' she said to me, slamming the dressing-room door behind her.

A queue quickly formed at the chauffeur's table, and fans began to chat enthusiastically amongst themselves. But after twenty minutes, I began to feel a mite concerned at the length of time it was taking the authoress to reappear and, overcoming my trepidation, I knocked on her dressing-room door. There was no reply, so, gathering my courage, I went in.

Miss Tumbrill was slumped before the large mirror, her busby hat on the floor, wig askew on her wispy head revealing recent stitch marks along the sparse hairline. A half-bottle of whisky was clutched in one hand, the remains of a pork-pie in the other and a partly-smoked cigarette had burned itself into the edge of the dressing-table. I touched her shoulder gently.

'Oh, crap,' she yelped, jerking awake, licking the chocolate around her mouth.

'It's time for your booksigning, Miss Tumbrill,' I ventured, timidly.

'Huh? Oh, gahd, I must have dropped off: eating makes me so-o sleepeee.'

'H-have you finished your meditating?' I enquired, shocked by her disgusting appearance.

'Huh, meditating, my fanny,' she grimaced, rootling around in her handbag and bringing out a fold of white powder. 'This will sort me out in no time – I must save face in front of my public, or should I say those *gullible half-wits*. Tell my husb… I mean, chauffeur, that everything is under control. Now, get on with it and leave me alone!!'

As if experiencing an electric shock, I jumped to do her bidding and turned towards the door, but she called me back, her voice rasping in her throat.

'Hey, Mrs whatever-your-name is, I *like* you – so here's a personal word of advice at no extra charge: don't do as I do – do as I say, and you'll live a long and healthy life!'

By now terrified of the monster before my eyes, I gasped and hurried out, forcing a beaming smile onto my face, on a mission to reassure her army of devoted fans that the great lady would reappear in their midst very shortly!

THESE PEOPLE

Hilda Parslow, widowed these many years, regularly strolled to the pedestrian precinct on Quagmire Village High Street as a matter of routine. She liked to get out of the house whenever possible and, since retiring from the bank, her time was her own to do with as she pleased.

Most days, strolling along, maybe window shopping, she would suddenly pick up speed, smile and give a slight shake of the head, hurrying past the man crouching outside the bookshop with his stock of magazines. She often wished to browse inside the bookshop but felt too afraid to run the gauntlet of the homeless man's pleading look and reedy voice announcing his wares. To each person who ignored him he would nonetheless give his usual call of "God bless you, have a good day" – and to women passers-by he would add "sweetheart" or "darling".

Sometimes, other shoppers would stop and speak to the man, handing him change or buying his magazine. He must have been in his forties, Mrs Parslow decided, and she couldn't help wondering how he had ended up on the street, whether he had a family somewhere and where he slept at night. Surely they had hostels for these people? You didn't see many homeless types in Quagmire Village.

Once, she saw a woman stop and hand a carton of soup and some bread to him. He looked up, smiling, thanking the lady excessively, and Mrs Parslow noticed that, in spite of his missing teeth, he must have been handsome, once upon a time.

What a sad world it is and what kind people there are, ran through Hilda Parslow's mind as she hurried along to the warmth of her comfortable home on the outskirts of the village, a slight feeling of guilt intruding upon her sense of well-being.

The weather suddenly turned cold. Nevertheless, Mrs Parslow ventured out to meet her ex-colleague Joyce Glossop for their regular Tuesday afternoon chat over coffee and cake.

Mrs Glossop was also retired and both ladies enjoyed their leisure hours with nothing much to do, but still there seemed to be a lot to say, Mrs Glossop doing most of the talking. This day, as they walked past the homeless man, she interrupted her usual self-obsessed monologue to observe in a loud voice "these people make £300 a week, you know – begging". Hilda Parslow squirmed with shame, her cheeks flushing at her friend's rudeness and lack of sympathy, but she did not make any comment in response.

At about four o'clock that afternoon, the sky had darkened and fat flakes of snow were drifting down as the two ladies left the café. Mrs Glossop was driving home, but Mrs Parslow refused a lift as she wished to call at the village greengrocer's on her way back. They pecked cheeks and parted.

Scurrying along the pedestrian precinct, Hilda Parslow pulled her fur-lined hood around her face against the snow, which was now falling thick and fast, carpeting the ground. She suddenly saw ahead the homeless man crouching in his usual place against the wall of the bookshop. *In this weather, too*, she thought, hunching her shoulders as she hurried on past to the strains of his usual "God bless you, sweetheart; have a good day".

Before reaching the greengrocer's, she had a change of heart and backtracked to the bookshop. The man looked up at her with his bright blue eyes: he smiled and said, 'Hello, sweetheart, how are you?' Mrs Parslow scrabbled inside her bag and took out some change. The man beamed and handed her a magazine, thanking her effusively.

She felt brave enough to say, 'But where will you sleep tonight? Is there a hostel locally? You shouldn't be out in this weather.'

'No, darling, there's no hostel. If I make enough selling these I can go to Mrs Thirkill's – she's a kind landlady, lets me have half-price bed and breakfast for the night. Otherwise I sleep in the church porch.'

Mrs Parslow gasped. 'What? You actually sleep outside in the freezing cold?'

'Yeh,' he grimaced, 'that's where I kipped last night. I have this sleeping bag – it's not too bad.'

Shocked to the core, Mrs Parslow thrust a five pound note at him. 'Here,' she said, 'I hope you'll have enough by tonight,' and, to the sound of his effusive thanks, she swiftly took her leave.

The next day she returned the magazine to the man. 'I've read this,' she said, 'you can have it back to sell on again.'

'Good grief,' he beamed, 'what would I do without people like you, Mrs er – what was your name again, sweetheart?'

'You can call me Hilda,' she smiled, nervously.

'Hello, Hilda – I'm Derek,' he said, 'very pleased to make your acquaintance.'

After that, she often went for a chat with her new friend; they spoke of many things: art, philosophy, literature, music – he was obviously educated or at least widely read and intelligent. She was never courageous enough to ask how he had taken the wrong path in life and ended up on the street or, indeed, what his line of work had been, if any.

In addition to buying his magazine, she took him food, a warm scarf and sometimes small amounts of cash although he always protested at this – and he would never say whether he had collected the necessary payment for Mrs Thirkill's establishment or not.

All through the following year, the summer days and a golden autumn, Hilda saw Derek several times a week. She looked forward to hearing his opinions on many subjects and, in return, he seemed extremely interested in what she had to say and allowed her to say it, unlike her friend Joyce Glossop.

Then suddenly it was winter again. During that freezing November, Hilda worried about Derek. She continued to go out regularly, stopping for a chat, buying the magazine, taking him comforts: even a cup of soup was gladly received.

One morning she saw through the window a world obliterated by snow. She felt feverish, a sore throat coming on, and decided to stay in, hoping that Derek would have enough money by tonight for bed and breakfast. Surely he wouldn't have to sleep outside in this awful weather, surely people other than herself would see his plight and take pity on the poor soul.

That evening as she sat watching the ten o-clock news, there came a sharp tapping at the window. She pulled the curtain back but could see nothing unusual. Then it came again, a loud knocking, this time on the front door. She sighed, wondering who it could be at this time of night and went to peep through the spy-hole, recoiling in shock at Derek's grizzled face peering back. *How does he know where I live?* she wondered, suddenly afraid and panic-stricken.

Leaving the chain on, she opened the door slightly, calling in a low tremulous voice, 'Derek, what is it, what's wrong?'

'I missed you today. Hilda. Is everything OK?'

'Nothing to worry about, Derek, it's only a cold coming on; it was nice of you to enquire but I'm just this minute on my way to bed.'

'Hilda,' he grated urgently, 'let me in – I have something to tell you, a secret.'

'No, no,' she whispered, 'I really cannot let you in. What would the neighbours think? How on earth did you find where I live?'

'I followed you home once – I'm sorry about that, Hilda. But you are the kindest, most caring person I've ever met – we have so many interests in common. Please let me in – I have something to say to you.'

'You can't come in, Derek, I'm not dressed or anything. You'll have to tell me here.'

'Oh, sweetheart, I can't tell you on the doorstep. I'm dying of cold out here!'

'Look, Derek, stay there a minute and I'll get my purse – I'll give you enough money for Mrs Thirkill's, just for tonight.'

'That's not why I came, sweetheart,' he said sadly. 'Mrs Thirkill's place is full – I was sure you'd let me in – I could clear the snow for you, do your odd jobs – don't turn me away – I promise I won't touch you.'

"Touch"! The very word sent a frisson of horror down her back! Just the thought, the image conjured up of his hands on her body, and their whole friendly relationship melted into the snow.

'See here, Derek, I think you've got this all wrong. I was only trying to help you – I can't have you staying with me. Wait just a moment and I'll let you have enough money for a hotel if Mrs Thirkill really can't take you in tonight.'

Mrs Parslow left the chain on and, shaking with nerves, went to fetch her purse, silently vowing that this would be an end to it – *these people, taking advantage of one's kindness!* In future she would avoid that part of the High Street. If he called again, she would complain to the police.

When she returned to the front door, Derek had gone, leaving only deep footprints in the thick snow all the way down the path.

*   *   *   *

On the local news the following morning, there was an item concerning the body of a man, identity unknown, who had been found, frozen to death, in the porch of Quagmire Village church.

THERE'LL BE SOME CHANGES

Cyril Neesham perched on the edge of his mahogany desk, one foot swinging nonchalantly to and fro. His audience of two men and two women sat on wooden chairs arranged in a semi-circle. There was a glint in his eye – was it of determination or even domination?

'You'll be wondering why I've called you in so early on this damp Monday morning,' he began.

His audience shifted uncomfortably. 'Yes, we're all agog,' remarked Janet Greely acidly. 'I got soaked to the skin setting off in the pouring rain, as you can no doubt detect from all the squelching.'

'Well, I'm sorry about that, Mrs, er, Janet; this chat won't take too long, and Dulcie will be bringing in coffee shortly. I have a few ideas to impart to all you loyal, long-serving employees of Mandrake Modes.'

Mr. Pomphrey cleared his throat and grimaced. 'Bad news then, is it?'

'No, no, not at all, Dennis – in fact it could be to your advantage. The thing is, this company needs to move forward, into the Swinging Sixties and, since Lord Peckover brought me in as MD to update the firm, it is incumbent upon me to initiate several changes, both on the factory floor and here in the office.'

'What kind of changes,' asked Mr Bonechurch, nervously. 'Do you mean invoicing, that sort of thing? I know we have many late payers, which does make life difficult, to say the least. Why, at times, I've actually gone round to various customers demanding immediate settlement of our, erm…'

'Not only the accounts, Robert,' interrupted Mr Neesham, 'although they are of course very important, and I'll come to that in a moment – but in the styling and designs of our clothing range and how they're marketed. We are simply too old-fashioned to make any headway in these modern times.'

'I hope you don't make too many changes, Mr Neesham,' Miss Gribthorpe squeaked. 'Our garments appeal to a particular type of woman and we wouldn't wish to upset our loyal customers. Some of them have been with us for years.'

'Aha, got it in one, Florence – that is entirely my point! We need to start aiming for the younger set: after all, the civilised world has moved on from the Frumpish Fifties, and our old customers are, sadly, gradually dying off. No-one wants to wear those old pinafore dresses and dowdy cardigans any more – well, not for much longer. Our net profits are down on the past two years and Lord Peckover is depending upon us to improve things, otherwise, who knows, the whole company could go kaput, and we wouldn't want that now, would we?'

Mr Pomphrey raised one index finger. 'Excuse me, Mr Neesham, but how do you propose to suddenly get us to change our designs? No-one here knows the first thing about high-street fashion.' Everyone nodded their heads in agreement.

'Well put, Dennis – I couldn't have expressed it better myself. And the answer is – we need new blood in this establishment: highly-qualified, creative people who will take Mandrake Modes forward into a rosy future! Just think - this could be the making of us as a respected and lucrative company.'

'And what will be our role in all this?' asked Florence Gribthorpe, smoothing the skirt of her tweed pinafore dress. 'Are these highly-qualified youngsters going to walk all over us and take our jobs?'

'Dear me, Florence! What an idea! They will have to be shown the ropes, of course, and that will be your collective role, all four of you, because I myself know nothing about design, marketing or accounts. I am in a merely organisational capacity and will have to report our progress to Lord Peckover on a regular basis.'

'And what, I wonder, will be our role once we have shown these newcomers how the place runs,' queried Robert Bonechurch.

'Aha, you've hit the nail there, Robert, old boy,' nodded Cyril Neesham encouragingly. 'Some of the recruits will, perforce, be graduates, and we don't want to end up with far too many masters and not enough slaves, do we? Ha ha ha! There will be, I envisage, some entirely new posts created together with various adjustments in job-titles, seniority, etc.'

'Do you mean to say they will be appointed on a superior pay scale?' demanded Janet Greely.

Cyril Neesham pursed his lips. 'First things first, Janet – and, oh, here's Dulcie, our loyal retainer, with coffee. Just put it down there, Dulcie – now come and help yourselves everyone, and don't forget these delicious biscuits, courtesy of our caring benefactor, Lord Peckover.'

The elderly foursome gathered around the tray, grim faces downcast.

'Please take your seats again because I have more news to impart,' announced Mr Neesham through a mouthful of crumbs, 'the most important being our change of name. Lord Peckover feels that "Mandrake Modes" is boring and old-hat, and, therefore, we have decided on "Fiesta Fashions" as being more modern and likely to appeal to our target customer-base.

The foursome looked at each other. 'Change of name?' they echoed.

'Yes, but please do not panic,' Mr Neeshum said, with a false grin. 'We have to compete with those so-called boutiques in Carnaby Street, and Lord Peckover thought "Fiesta Fashions" would hit the spot. We plan to have all the latest "gear" as the modernists call it, including the mini-skirt, ex-army uniforms, great coats, tights of all shades and patterns, large hats, statement belts, even duffel coats which seem to be *de rigueur* these days. It will be a mixture of the bohemian and haute couture, if you can picture it.'

His audience of four sat in stunned silence. Loyal retainer Dulcie broke the spell and began, 'you'll notice that the firm will be branching out into men's ready-to-wear apparel, too…'

'Yes, yes, Dulcie, don't go into too much detail just yet, but, OK, of course, perhaps I should explain that we do indeed plan to include designs for the other fifty-percent of the population, i.e. men – or should I say, *young* men!'

Florence Gribthorpe dabbed her thin nostrils with an embroidered handkerchief, jerkily returning it to the sagging pocket of her cardigan. 'Well,' she said, 'this is all too much to absorb in one go, I must say. But what about our existing customers? They depend upon us.'

'Oh, they'll be all right, Florence – they've lived through two world wars. Our niche clientele will definitely be the youth of today! The economy is booming, youngsters have money to spend, and spend it they jolly well will.'

'And our catalogue?' queried Dennis Pomphrey. 'Will that continue?'

'Catalogue, you call it, Dennis – pooh, it's more of a pamphlet, our present merchandise being so limited and, quite frankly, the format of said publication is flat and unattractive.' Mr Neesham grimaced before continuing. 'We plan to go for a really glossy, thick, proper catalogue which will be widely advertised in every available media. That will be one of the new posts: Advertisement Responsibility Special Executive.'

'I see,' shrilled Janet Greely. 'So where does that leave me? My role will be completely changed or replaced. Is that correct?'

'We'll go into all the niceties later on, Janet,' Mr Neeshum frowned. 'Don't worry about it – you will be well taken care of, all of you will, believe me.'

'And don't forget the kinky boots,' piped up Dulcie, the private secretary.

'Please Dulcie, I fear that is simply too much information at this early stage. But well, yes, I admit it, we will be branching out into footwear, and, as Dulcie so rightly said when she gave the game away, it will be extremely fashionable footwear, like, for instance, the so-called kinky boot.'

'And the shop on Beak Street…' Dulcie began.

'Dulcie, *please*!!' Mr Neeshum said sharply, 'I shall get around to the minutiae very very soon, but not just yet awhile.'

'Beak Street?' his audience repeated.

'Oh well – if you must! Beak Street is adjacent to Carnaby Street, and the overheads there are much less expensive, e.g. rental and rates, etc. And the little place is just a narrow sliver of a shop, one up, one down, but with an attic and basement for storage, plus it could, of course, be run with just two or three part-timers.'

Mr Neeshum's elderly audience turned their heads this way and that, exchanging grim glances.

'So, how many new people are to be recruited?' asked Robert Bonechurch timidly.

'This we have yet to decide,' came the reply. 'But you will be apprised of all the details in due course. For the present, you have much to think about, so I shall now draw this meeting to a close. Thank you all for your time this morning and also your input, which I shall, of course, convey to Lord Peckover with all haste.'

As the foursome shuffled out, muttering to each other, Mr Neeshum smiled inwardly: yes, one had to be ruthless, cruel even, in order to thrive in this cut-throat business, and it was going to be an easy matter shifting this load of dead wood long before more Draconian measures were brought to bear, like, for instance, moving them all to the mail-order room.

*   *   *   *

Mr Neesham sighed and looked across at ageing Dulcie, busying herself with the coffee cups: *hmm, a young, blonde-haired dolly bird with long legs will definitely be a pleasant upgrade from that raddled old blabber-mouth,* went through his mind, and, with a self-satisfied smirk, he allowed his fancy to take flight...

DUMB WAITER

Sam was working as a waiter in a Soho bar when in walked Suzie. *It must be jelly 'cause jam don't shake like that*, he couldn't help thinking, as her bare dimpled shoulders quivered in his general direction. His knees trembled as he eyed the upper slopes of her busty substances which were squeezed upward and inward, partly overflowing the tight bodice, putting him in mind of whipped cream and whetting his appetite in more ways than one, oh yes!

'Hey, you catching flies or do you always talk with your mouth open,' the object of his affection cooed, leaning forward and resting her elbows on the counter, thus allowing Sam an even better view of her lavish upholstery.

'Nah, I, er, oh, sorry, ma'am – what can I get you, a cocktail, a Pimms No. 1 – an engagement ring, a marriage certificate?' he managed, huskily.

'Cor, bleed'n hell, you're a fast worker,' carolled the girl demurely, patting her blonde hair. 'I'll have a port and lemon, ducks, if it's any business of yours.'

'Have this one on me,' crooned Sam, still leaning on the counter admiring the view.

'Well, OK dearie!' smirked Suzie. 'And make it a large one while you're at it.'

Sam rushed to get her drink. 'Say, why not sashay your cute assets round to my place tonight? And bring your toothbrush.'

'Yeah, OK, sounds all right to me – never could resist the romantic approach,' Suzie smirked, busily plumping up her hair. 'I think our relationship has matured enough over the past fifteen seconds or so.'

'You're right there, doll-face – we go back a long way in modern day terms! And, by the bye, here's my address, but let me take a picture of you on my mobile, just in case I don't recognise your face next time.' Sam handed over a hastily scribbled piece of paper with a shaking hand.

'Likewise, I'm sure,' said Suzie, delving into a bejewelled tote bag and bringing out the latest edition Blackberry. 'Say cheese! And number 3, Pigeon Yard is where I hang out – you should drag your Calvin Kleins over there, just in case I forget all about you: I've got a memory like a bleed'n sieve.'

'OK, babe – 3 Pigeon Yard it is. Shall we say eight o'clock on the button? I can take time off – no problemo. You should be flattered – I don't usually skip a whole night's tips for just any old dumb broad, ya know, kiddo. By the way, what's your monicker? – we haven't been introduced.'

And so it came to pass that Sam turned up at Suzie's pad that evening a little before eight, only to find 3 Pigeon Yard was a lurid massage parlour labouring under the name of "The Wow Factory" as proclaimed by a discreet banner festooned across its façade. He rang the bell and was shown into the fur-lined hallway by a lynx-eyed minx who seemed to be expecting him. 'Please to go up, sir – madame, she awaits you.'

Sam was thinking, *uh huh, what have I let myself in for*, when the sound of a gunshot ricocheted from the upper floor – kachow, whrrang, ping, ping, kachow!

He raced up the red velvet staircase and burst open a purple satin-quilted door to find Suzie, a smoking automatic in her hand, standing over the prone figure of a man – he was as dead as a taxidermist's skunk.

'Hi Sam,' giggled Suzie, 'silly thing, look what I just did. It went off in me hand – here, take it,' and she coolly handed the gun to the dumbest waiter in the civilised world who stood there opening and closing his mouth, something on the lines of a landed cod.

Sam was still staring at the shooter clutched in his mitt when the lynx-eyed minx appeared in the doorway and commenced bowing in a friendly fashion.

'Lola, this is Sam – Sam, Lola,' announced Suzie. Lola and Sam bowed to each other repeatedly. 'Nice place you got here, ma'am,' said Sam politely, remembering his manners.

'Would you wish I call police yet, madame?' Lola queried. 'I give you alibi, as previously arranged.'

'Yeah, call the fuzz, Lola,' Suzie said, 'we don't want this vile body left hanging around, it'll begin to pong, and I'd hate to trip over it in these fluffy pink high-heeled mules. But on second thoughts, just give me an hour with this sucker, I mean, gentleman – I'm in the mood for lurve and the guy deserves his reward before paying the price.'

As Lola bowed out of the room, Suzie draped herself over the red velvet couch and patted the seat, the rolled gold bracelet on one swinging ankle glinting in the pink lamplight filtering in through red muslin curtains. 'Come over here, Sammy, but first, close your gob and lay that pistol down, babe – honestly, what are you like? Men get so bladdy passionate that they can't help but bladdy kill each other.'

Sam could hardly believe it! He'd been set up – it was a goddam honey trap he'd walked into. Did this witch think he'd just got off the boat, did the trollop think he was still wet behind the ears? Him, a man of the world, carry the can for a slut he'd hardly said two words to – a slag he barely knew?

Blow that for a game of soldiers, he thought, I'm outta here, but, we-ell, I could just hang on for a bit, might as well cop a fondle of the slapper's soft furnishings, otherwise I've had a wasted journey *and* lost about ten quid in tips.

But first, he thought he'd try playing hard to get. 'Why should I take the rap for you, babe?'

'Because I'm worth it,' came the husky reply.

And so it came to pass that after an hour of heavenly acrobatics with the pneumatic and versatile Suzie, Sam had no idea at all of making a quick escape – he could barely remember his own name or what day it was, and when the police arrived to investigate Suzie's allegations, i.e. that out of insane jealousy Sam had shot his love-rival, who also happened to be the local pimp, he offered no evidence in his own defence.

Later, as the police were leading a love-struck, handcuffed Sam down the red velvet casement towards the Black Maria parked outside, Lola entered through the front door carrying a parcel wrapped in newspaper.

'Here, madame,' she called to Suzie who was standing on the landing dabbing her eyes with a lace hanky. 'I hungry, you hungry, we both hungry – fish and chips for supper, as promised.'

'Cor, bleedn' hell,' laughed Suzie, suddenly dry-eyed. 'Don't bother setting the table, Lola gal – we'll have it straight out of the paper with our fingers! Come on, then, get a move on – I'm that starving I could eat a scabby donkey.'

Sam suddenly came to a halt in the fur-lined hallway and called back over his shoulder, 'Suzie, all I ask is that you wait for me – will you do that?'

'Spread out, little boy, you bother me,' his beloved screeched, outraged. 'I hear you knocking but you can't come in! You should know by now I'm too hot to handle for soft guys like you. Now get out of town – this ain't Liberty Hall, you know.'

'Right ho, Suzie, fair enough,' said Sam. 'But, in that case, all I ask is that you come and visit me in jail – give me something to look forward to – oh, and wear that corsety bodicey whatnot that shows all you've got.'

'Well, I might do that thing: I hate to miss a chance of showing off my assets to a wider all-male audience,' cooed the lady coyly, 'although I don't usually go for murderers or burglars – or losers: they're a real turn-off – or is that just me?'

ONLY YOU!

'Of course you are,' he said, jingling the coins in his pocket and moving the curtain slightly to give a better view of the street scene. 'Of course I do…don't be silly!'

The girl on the sofa wriggled uneasily before speaking. 'But then why do you still see Ruth and Felicity and all the others?'

The man turned to face her. 'You know I always stay on good terms with my old girlfriends,' he said.

'Hmm, "old" is right,' the girl replied, 'well, as far as Ruth is concerned – she's ancient, at least ten years older than you.'

The young man smiled. 'Age brings wisdom, Dora dear, and experience.'

Dora grimaced. 'But I need a commitment from you, Jerry. I feel so insecure with all these other females flapping around you all the damn time.'

Jerry came over and sat by Dora on the sofa. He kissed her passionately. 'Isn't that commitment enough?' he murmured, when they came up for air.

'Well, not really,' replied the girl, huskily. 'You probably still kiss the others just as nicely. I've seen how physical you are with them. It's horrible when I know you belong to me.' She began to cry quietly.

'Oh, here we go again.' Jerry yawned. 'Don't be so jealous when there's no reason for it. You're too possessive when there's no need. Let's go to bed and I'll really prove it to you.'

'Ooh, you disgust me,' Dora sobbed. 'Is that all you want me for? You can get that from any number of your old girlfriends, I'm sure.'

'Well, I hope we're not going to have another tantrum like last week,' the young man said extricating himself from her octopus embrace. 'You promised all that was in the past.'

'No, no, honestly Jerry, I'm not going to make a scene, really I'm not. It's just that I can't bear to see the others fussing around and having to watch them fawning all over you. I need a commitment – for instance an engagement ring would let the whole world see that you are mine and not theirs!'

'An engagement ring? All in good time, Dora, but not at present. Why spoil our relationship? We have a good thing going; that is, when you can stop ranting on about Ruth and the others. I enjoy my circle of friends too much to drop them.'

'But we see them, with or without their husbands, everywhere we go. This is the only place where we can be alone. I'm sick of having to look at their silly giggling faces! And then there are all these reminders everywhere, the ornaments, the curtains, this sofa, your clothes, even your bedding – all chosen or even bought by one or another of those floozies.'

'Look, Dora, can't we talk about something else. It's getting a bit tiresome, to be frank.'

'Jerry, if you'd tell them to get lost, we could discuss other matters, like our future together, for instance. But as things are, it's playing on my mind.'

'You're obsessed and possessive, that's the trouble, Dora. Can't you just accept me as I am, a chap with a wide circle of friends?'

'But I want a husband and a family, Jerry. We'd be so happy together, in a little house with two children. Think of it, darling – can't you just see it?'

'Lord, no, my sweet, not just yet. We're both too young for that kind of thing, the marriage estate: oh no, the thought of all that responsibility. Look, can't we just go along as we are for the present?'

'If you tell me I'm the only one, and that you love me,' Dora pleaded with tearful eyes.

'Of course you are, of course I do,' Jerry smiled. 'Now, let's go lie down.'

Hand-in-hand, they made for the bedroom and were soon under the satin sheets ('*Ruth's satin sheets*' thought Dora), entwining their bodies in increasingly intimate fashion.

Just at the crucial moment, the bedside telephone rang, shrilling through their mindless passion.

'Oh, God, let it ring,' Jerry growled, intent on more immediate matters.

'No, no, you must answer it,' Dora insisted. 'It might be important, one of your old girlfriends, it could be Ruth, Sadie, Felicity or goodness knows who!'

'Oh, Lord, we're not back on that again,' Jerry sighed, turning over and picking up the receiver.

'Yes, who is it? Well, hello there. How are you? Yes, yes, I'm fine. Yes, of course you are, of course I do. Silly thing! Hello? What? Well, I'm devastated to hear that. No, can't today – so sorry. I'm just getting ready to meet my father, in town you know. No, no, if you come over I shan't be here – it'll be a wasted journey. Look, why don't I ring you later tonight or better still in the morning? Yes, yes, of course you are, of course I do. Well, bye for now darling. Kiss kiss. Bye…'

Dora sat up in the sumptuous bed and stared straight ahead with glassy eyes, dumb with rage.

'Well, come on darling, where was I when we were so rudely interrupted?' Jerry laughed, grabbing Dora by the waist. She struggled out of his grasp. 'So! And who was that, pray? Ruth or Felicity or Sadie, or maybe one of the others?'

'Oh, dear,' Jerry sighed. 'If you must know it *was* poor old Ruth. She's having problems with her husband. Wanted to come over and discuss it, get my advice.'

'I see,' said Dora, her face like stone. 'She uses you as her confidant, it seems. But why tell her you were getting ready to meet your father, of all people? Why couldn't you say you were with me? Are you ashamed of me, Jerry? Sometimes I think you are.'

'No, of course I'm not ashamed of you, Dora. Good grief, here we go again.'

'But why didn't you just come out with the truth and say you were with me?'

'Oh, I don't know, Dora. Why does anyone say anything, it was the first thing that came into my head rather than explain that we were in bed together. It didn't seem right to say that to poor Ruth when she's so upset over her old man.'

'Well, it's nothing to be ashamed of or embarrassed about, being in bed with me when we are practically engaged. You said I am the only one that you love, Jerry; yes, you did, not fifteen minutes ago.'

'I meant it, Dora! There's only you. Now where were we…?'

'No, I don't feel like it now, Jerry. I'm going to get dressed. I need a drink.'

'OK, my sweet, let's have a dry martini, and then perhaps we can get back in the mood and carry on from where we left off.'

They dressed quickly, and Dora went to the bathroom to tidy her hair and makeup. Just as she was satisfied with her repair job, the telephone rang again. She listened from the hallway as Jerry picked up the receiver in the sitting room.

'Hello? Oh, hello darling. How the devil are you? What? Yes, not bad, not bad, all the better for hearing your voice. Oh really? No, no, I can't today, I'm afraid. No, don't come over – I'm really tied up, you see.

No, it's business, darling, all that boring stuff. Yes, of course you are, of course I do. Don't be silly. How about if I ring you later or better still in the morning? OK, OK, yes darling, kiss kiss, bye for now, byeee.'

Dora froze and she remained standing, rigid as a marble statue in the hallway. Through a red mist she heard Jerry calling to her from the sitting room. 'Dora, where are you? Still prettifying yourself? Come and get your martini, let's drink a toast…'

Jerry suddenly appeared in the doorway. 'Come on, sweetness – I know you're annoyed again, but please hear me out.' He put his arms out to her, 'Come on, Dora, you can make it.'

Dora's legs felt stiff, but with an enormous effort she managed to make a move towards him. Then the telephone rang again, shrilling through her nerves, her very being. 'I won't answer it this time,' he said, embracing her unresponsive body.

'Oh, I've had enough of this,' she shrieked, pushing him away. 'Answer it, why don't you! I'm off! And just don't try to contact me because I shall be out. I've had dozens of invitations from other men, you see! I never told you before but they're clamouring to take me out!' She picked up her bag and coat and swept out of the flat, slamming the door behind her.

'Oh, rats,' he thought, 'what a stupid airhead dimwit of a girl.'

Then, smirking, he turned to the telephone, picking it up in one smooth and practised movement.

'Hello, who is it? Oh, *Sadie,* darling. Yes, I'm doing great, all the better for hearing your voice! And how are you? Good, good! Yes, I am free, actually. You caught me at the right time, I'm at a loose end for the rest of the day. Why don't you come over immediately, if not sooner – I can't wait to see you – take a taxi, my treat – ahaha – what's that – oh, ye-e-es, don't be silly – of course you are, of course I do …'

MR CHARISMA

'Isn't that Rupert Cavendish over there by the travel books?' Fiona Deedle nudged her friend. 'Goodness, Jackie, he is just so damned handsome – no wonder they call him "Mr Charisma"!'

'Oh,' breathed Jackie Clack, open-mouthed, gazing towards the godlike creature who was browsing the shelves just as if he were an ordinary human being. She wriggled in ecstasy inside her quilted anorak. 'He looks somehow different in the flesh, a lot thinner and paler, don't you think, Fiona?'

'You need glasses, Jackie; he's absolutely gorgeous,' Fiona said, transfixed.

'Mm, yes, he certainly is,' Jackie murmured, 'but I wonder if he's as nice as they say.'

Fiona Deedle's mouth set in a grim line. 'I'm going to go over and find out,' she said. 'Can't waste such a fabulous opportunity – we'll never get another chance like this.'

'But are you sure it's him?'

'Of course it's him, Jackie – no-one else has that famous profile, and ooh, can't you just picture yourself being caressed, lying in his arms?'

'Mm, he is beautiful, Fiona, I admit, but, well, he looks so scruffy – that beard!'

'Silly, it isn't a beard – it's what's known as "designer stubble" – all the rage amongst young men these days.'

'And those torn jeans – surely he can afford smarter clothes – he looks as if he's about to do some gardening in that get-up.'

'Honestly, Jackie Clack – that's what's known as "stressed denim" – where have you been hiding for the past few years? In a cave?'

'Oh well, he doesn't look like a Hollywood superstar to me.'

'Oh yes, he does – there's no mistaking that – um – presence!'

'Surely you're not going to ask for his autograph, Fiona! He might not like it, really.'

'Well, let's see how he responds. First of all I'll just say "hello" and take it from there. Are you coming?'

'No, no, not me – I'll wait here, I haven't got your confidence for this type of thing. Off you go then, but don't embarrass yourself.'

Fiona Deedle took a deep breath, fluffed up her hair, and walked across to the travel shelves, stopped, picked out a book whilst taking a sidelong glance at the actor's celebrated profile.

'Hmm, oh, excuse me, I'm so sorry to bother you, but do I have the pleasure of addressing Mr Rupert Cavendish in the flesh, in person?'

The actor turned, raising one eyebrow. Fiona melted under his famously luminous gaze. 'I apologise for interrupting you, but I just wanted to say how much I admire your work,' she said.

'Oh, OK,' he replied, turning away and maintaining a fixed gaze on the book in his hand.

'Yes, I saw you in "The Scent of Rain" and I couldn't get it out of my mind.'

'Is that right?' he said, taking another book from an upper shelf.

'Yes, I was going to send you a fan letter, a thing I have never done before, but I expect you get lorry-loads of them, don't you?'

'Hmm,' he grunted, 'No idea...my secretary does the biz...'

'Oh, I see,' trilled Fiona, 'she manages all that for you, does she? Of course, there must be so much of it – and you're far too busy making movies for that kind of time-consuming thing. I don't blame you at all! And I expect that people must bother you a lot for your autograph, don't they?'

'Gahd – I never do that. Why should I, only to have them sold on eBay.'

'Gosh, I do agree with you there,' his admirer said, nodding her head furiously. 'People should *not* be able to make a profit out of your kindness. But, changing the subject slightly, I wonder whether anyone has ever told you that your acting is on a par with the famous Sir Laurence Olivier's?'

'Sir who?' frowned the star, 'Never heard of him…'

'Oh, probably before your time. Olivier was a famous Shakespearean actor, although he did other parts too, films and stuff, later on in his career.'

'Duh, I can't stand Shakespeare – far too wordy, all that historical drivel, all those long never-ending speeches…' The actor put the two books under his arm and selected another one which he opened and proceeded to peruse with interest.

'Oh, really? But I just wanted to say how I loved you in "The Scent of Rain". I've seen it three times already and will go see it again.'

'Uh huh,' said the actor, scanning his book.

'And that gorgeous co-star of yours, Allegra Dimuantes – what an exquisitely beautiful woman.'

'Huh, that spitting hell-cat,' came the reply.

'Gosh, is that right? Because she comes across as such a sweet person and a really good actress.'

'Nah, she's evil – can't act to save her life.'

'You do surprise me, Mr Cavendish. Well what about the other male lead in "The Scent of Rain", Grabb Muscleman? He's pretty good, isn't he?'

'Nah, can't act to save his life, either.'

'Well, I was just wondering what it must be like to work with people like that?'

'Hmm, dunno.'

'What I mean is, are you all on friendly terms?'

'Nah, we stay well away between takes.'

'And do you all go out together for dinner at the end of a day's filming?'

'No way! I go home.'

'But I believe that you and Allegra Dimuantes are an item (pardon me for being personal).'

'What? Me and that old slapper? Gah, don't make me sick.'

'So it's not true, then?'

'Look, are you from some magazine or other? If you are, you should know I don't give interviews.'

'No, not me, not at all, I'm just a great admirer of your work. You remind me of Marlon Brando to look at – he was always such great actor, wasn't he?'

'Marlon who?'

'You know – Marlon Brando – he did that Method acting stuff.'

'Nah, you've lost me again.'

'He always had to have his motivation for whatever role he was playing.'

'Oh yeah – motivation! I got that – it's the money – laughing all the way to the bank.'

'Oh, ahaha, I love your sense of humour and you're very down-to-earth for a well-known and famous celebrity, in spite of disguising your Bristol accent – oh, what's that book you've got there? All about Tibet?'

'Uh huh.'

'Are you researching for a new role? I'll be able to tell all my friends I saw you reading up on it. They'll be thrilled to bits, I can tell you.'

'Nah, I'm thinking of signing up to become a monk,' he drawled, donning a pair of designer sunglasses. 'I should have worn these before I came in here.' He nodded vaguely at Fiona without making eye-contact and walked away towards the cash desk where he proceeded to blank the sales assistant who immediately recognised him.

Fiona watched him go, her head in a whirl – he had actually spoken to her!

She made her way back to Jackie who had been waiting with barely concealed excitement. 'Come on, what did he say?' her friend asked.

'Well, the first thing he said was how amazing it is to be recognised in such a small place as Quagmire Village where he came to escape from the crowds of fans that follow him everywhere!. Honestly, he is so modest, you wouldn't believe…'

'Oh, what a sweet man! And what was he like to talk to?' Jackie was agog.

'Gosh, he was just as we'd thought he'd be, such a strong character and even more handsome up close. You really should have come over and joined us – we had an in-depth discussion about Larry Olivier and Marlon Brando, all about Shakespeare and acting, and especially about that Method acting thing,' Fiona gushed ecstatically.

'Wow, how absolutely fabulous,' crowed Jackie. 'But did you ask him for his autograph? I didn't see him writing anything down.'

'No, he did offer to give me his autograph as I seemed to know such a lot about his films and that, but I said I wouldn't dream of it – just meeting and talking to him was thrill enough for me. He did appreciate that, of course, because he could tell I was a genuine admirer and not someone just wanting to sell his autograph on eBay, which people do, apparently.'

'Well, that is just awful,' Jackie gasped, 'and I'm glad you refused, but did he mention the other stars in "The Scent of Rain"? I just love that gorgeous Allegra Dimuantes. Aren't they supposed to be engaged or something?'

'No, they're not together any more, he told me strictly in confidence. But between you and me, he says she still loves him and he's going through a very tricky situation, trying to be kind to her whilst getting himself off the hook at the same time without hurting her feelings too much.'

'Wow, he told you all that, did he? How amazing that you actually had a proper conversation with him and he confided in you!'

'Yes, *and* he asked me to go for a coffee with him, he said he wanted a shoulder to cry on, but I told him I couldn't as I was meeting a friend.'

'Well, I never! And you refused because of me? Oh, drat! I wish I'd gone with you now! We could have taken him for coffee at the Pink Teapot Café and I could have asked him about Grabb Muscleman, my hero – I think he's so dishy, so dreamy.'

'Well, Rupert told me *all about* Grabb Muscleman: they're best friends, apparently, and when they're filming they spend all their free time together between takes, and they go on holiday together, too.'

'How marvellous, telling you about his glamorous life – what a sweet man!'

'But listen to this, it's not all good news – he's thinking of signing up to become a monk in Tibet or something: all this Hollywood hoo-ha is getting too much for his delicate sensitivities and he would really like to escape all this fame nonsense because I did get the impression he is a very spiritual person.'

'Oh, no, the poor chap! I *really* wish I'd gone with you to meet him. Now I'll never get to talk to him about Grabb and, oh, I could kick myself…'

'Well, you definitely missed your chance there, Jackie, because, quite honestly, he's *such* a nice man – no wonder they call him Mr Charisma!'

ALL SHE EVER WANTED

Mr Hennessy picked up the telephone and dialled an extension. 'Can you come in, please, Mrs Coalstaythe,' he grated to his secretary who, at the sound of his voice, looked up and met his gaze through the glass partition.

Mrs Jeannette Coalstaythe picked up her notebook, knocked on the plywood door and entered the inner office.

'No, put your book away, missy, I don't want to dictate just now,' Mr Hennessy said, huffily. 'Just sit down for a minute.'

The woman perched on the edge of a straight-backed chair, pushing her spectacles up the bridge of her nose with one finger, and waited. Mr Hennessy slid *his* spectacles down a notch and regarded her over the top.

'Well,' he said, 'what's to do!? I've been watching those two over there chatting non-stop for more than an hour. Yes, the junior, Marlene, erm – *Miss Chatterbox* – and young Neville. What are they up to?'

His secretary blinked, surprised and alarmed. 'Oh, but Mr Hennessy, I gave the two of them the late-payments to deal with. That's what they're sorting out. I thought it was a good idea…'

'Good heavens, Jeannette,' said her boss, frowning, 'it doesn't take an hour to deal with late-payments, or it shouldn't! You ought to have allowed them twenty minutes for the task, no longer.'

'I'm sorry Mr Hennessy, but evidently some of the cases are proving difficult to *reconcile...*' began the woman earnestly.

'Well, it's up to you to keep an eye on them, exercise some control over these young'uns. It looks very much like canoodling to me! And as you are well aware, we at Menston International do *not* allow any kind of fraternisation between the sexes during the working week. We are very strict on that rule, especially where accounts are concerned when, of course, possible collusion could arise. We don't make these regulations for fun, you know.'

'Oh, yes, quite right; sorry, Mr Hennessy – I'll have a word...' The secretary stood up.

'Ask Miss Chatterbox to step in here, please, would you; I have a little job for her to do. And tell Neville he must finish those late-payments on his own – probably get the job done a lot quicker without any distractions from a silly empty-headed girl. And then tell him to bring the reconciliations to me – I'll check them myself this month.'

The girl busy chatting to Neville made a wry face, being taken off a job she was enjoying. Furthermore she liked working with Neville, loved his sense of fun and his kindness. Marlene wouldn't have minded going on a date with Neville, but nothing had been forthcoming from that direction and, naturally, a girl had to wait for the man to make the first move. She liked several other lads, too, but they also remained oblivious to her yearnings.

'All I want is a boyfriend,' Marlene moaned to herself, in a dream of romance as she knocked on the manager's thin partition door. 'Enter,' droned the voice from within.

She stood in front of his large plywood desk, hands folded demurely, feeling increasingly cowed and humbled as Mr Hennessy ignored her presence and continued writing in a ledger. Marlene shuffled her feet. Eventually, the man glanced up, reluctantly it seemed, or as an afterthought. 'Yes?' he barked.

'Erm, did you send for me, Mr Hennessy?' the girl frowned.

'Well now, young woman,' began Mr Hennessy testily, throwing down his pen, 'I'd like you to take these papers across to Mr McCloud-Smythe's office. You'll have to wait while he reads them through and appends his signature here on these pages where I've marked with a cross. Don't come back without them – they're very important! Do you think you can do that, missy?'

Just at that moment, the tea-lady entered the outer office with her large metal urn on a trolley and began dispensing mugs of dark brown brew.

'No, don't wait to have yours, you'll have to miss it for once,' rasped Mr Hennessy. 'Mr McCloud-Smythe is urgently awaiting these papers, so off you go, no dawdling on the way back, either!'

'What a cheek,' thought Marlene, 'making me miss my tea-break. It's just not fair – how I hate being just the office junior!'

And furthermore, she dreaded having to cross the yard to the main office block, having to run the gauntlet of the workmen and apprentices who could see comings and goings through the factory's huge double doors, kept open summer and winter alike.

'I wouldn't mind going on a date with one of the apprentices,' she thought, 'but I'm not keen on all this cat-calling and wolf-whistling, it's too embarrassing!'

She ran across the cobbled yard, fleet of foot, trying to ignore the good-natured whooping sounds issuing from inside the factory doors. Breathlessly gaining the main building, she climbed the grand curving staircase to the penthouse suite of the MD, Mr Bertrand McCloud-Smythe.

The door to the private secretary's outer office was closed. Marlene knocked, waited, and knocked again. Eventually she heard a faint voice call "Enter" and so she opened the door and stepped into an empty room. The door to the MD's office stood ajar. Marlene trod carefully across the deep pile carpet and cautiously peered around it at the two people occupying the inner sanctum, a place rarely visited by a mere worker.

Bertrand McCloud-Smythe, tall, thin and aristocratic, sat behind a huge mahogany desk. Miss

Marina Ash, his personal private secretary, attired in trendy maxi-skirt, strappy sling-back sandals, silk blouse, wide leather belt and gold-hoop earrings, had arranged herself carefully on a low sofa, ankles crossed, skirt meticulously draped, as if posing for a Vogue fashion shoot. She held a shorthand notebook, her sharpened pencil poised.

'Yes, what can we do for you?' she asked in cultured tones, flicking her long hair and inclining her head slightly towards the intruder. Marlene offered the paperwork and timorously explained her errand.

'Mr McCloud-Smythe is busy at the moment. Leave the papers on my desk and come back in half an hour, they *might* be ready by then.' Marina Ash turned her head away, as a sign of dismissal. Mr McCloud-Smythe sat there, grimly immobile.

Marlene nodded nervously, and withdrew. She wended her way back down the curved staircase, fuming and worried. She dared not go back empty-handed to face Mr Hennessy's wrath, and could not contemplate running the gauntlet of the factory yard once more.

Deciding on a whim to wait in the canteen on the ground floor of the main building and at least have the cup of tea she had missed, Marlene sat down at a metal table and began surveying her bleak surroundings.

One of the apprentices had followed her in and took the chair opposite hers.

'Hello, it's Marlene, isn't it?' he said pleasantly. The girl smiled shyly and nodded.

'What's up? Wasting the firm's time, are you?' he laughed, showing nice white teeth. She noticed how his bright green eyes pierced hers. 'Seen you crossing the yard a lot recently,' he said, leaning forward confidentially. 'I've got ten minutes' break, and by the way, the lads call me Sooty.'

The youth had a sense of the ridiculous and made her laugh with his impressions of various colleagues.

The minutes sped by, and as he stood up to go he whispered, 'How about coming for a drink tonight? D'you know the Brookfield pub? I'll meet you outside there at 7 o'clock.'

All she ever wanted was a boyfriend, and now her wish was coming true. Her mother, setting the table that evening, could see how excited the girl was. 'What's he called again? Sooty? Well, what a stupid name! If you're planning on going steady with him, you want to find out what his parents christened him.'

Marlene once more explained this was only a first date and there was no question of "going steady" just yet, but even so the girl's longings took her imagination into the far distant future.

In the Brookfield that evening, Marlene floated in a warm haze, swooning into Sooty's eyes, feeling the chemistry. He leaned across and touched her cheek with his lips, and she was aware of a new sensation, a wave of desire sweeping over her body and into her feet. 'Oh, he's the one,' she thought. 'I've never felt like this before – crikey, what have I been missing!'

At nine o'clock, Sooty glanced at his wristwatch. 'Oh heck, time's moving on, I shall have to be making tracks – so, see you at work.'

The following days floated by on a mist of lustful longing, of hoping to see Sooty in the yard or the canteen. Surely he'd be asking her out again very soon, as she kept telling Jeannette Coalstaythe. She thought she'd spied him inside the factory double doors but couldn't be sure. Perhaps he was off sick, she wondered aloud over and over, although he had seemed perfectly healthy the other evening.

After some days of this, Mrs Coalstaythe, irritated and at the end of her patience, was moved to give the office junior a word of warning. 'Look out, Miss Chatterbox,' she said, 'Mr Hennessy has his eye on you.'

The girl jumped to attention and glanced through the glass partition but, noticing that Mr Hennessy didn't appear to be looking in her direction, carried on moaning and groaning and speculating as to Sooty's intentions and/or whereabouts.

And so Mrs Jeannette Coalstaythe, deciding to let the girl in on the reality of the situation and put a stop to all this nonsense once and for all, said, 'Honestly, Marlene, surely you should have twigged by now, you silly girl – it was a dare, the lad asked you out for a five shilling bet – the other apprentices put him up to it! Now, will you please give it a rest and get on with your work before Mr Hennessy has your guts for garters…'

TIT FOR TAT

Everybody round here knows me! My full name is Margaret McCarty but they all call me Aunt Peg although I haven't any nephews or nieces nearby, nor any close relatives, since you ask. A lot of 'em died in childbirth, if I remember right. Not the men, o' course – but they expired young, an'all, the poor devils, old before their time, mebbe through working so hard down t'pit, breathing in all them deadly underground fumes day in, day out, on and on...

I'm a real character, all the neighbours say so, probably because they're all frightened to death of me, well, apart from that widow-woman down the street, Mrs Rammage, with her second-hand false teeth, wooden nose and purple dog. We'll never go mates!

Because I never pull any punches, that's me! I say what I think – no messin'. And maybe they don't like me flat cap and clay pipe.

I sit here on this scrubbed stone doorstep, repelling all boarders. Can't be doing with callers or any kind of high spirits or jollifications; not even when it was the old Queen's Jubilee – 60 Glorious Years – bah: flags out, parades, street parties – pah, what a load of tripe. I wouldn't join in the shenanigans if you paid me – well, she never did owt for me and mine, that queen – so, san fairy ann, if you'll pardon my language.

But to get back to what I was trying to tell you (and please don't talk when I'm interrupting!) – there is a particular old boy who walks past here every day – he lives in one of them back-to-backs in Gas Street other side of t'railway track.

Well, this old lad, the one I'm telling you about, he always smiles, says "Good morning, Miss McCarty" and looks back over his shoulder at me, but I don't teck on – I just glare at him, blow a smoke-ring in his general direction and pull me cap down over me eyes – aye I do an'all! He doesn't give up though. Mebbe he's a bit soft in the head, being so friendly-like: there's a lot of it round our way; soft heads, I mean.

Anyhow, I know his sort. I know what he's after. Just because I've got me own house, that's what he's after, a woman with her own house.

Yes, as everyone is very well aware, it's a through house with a cellar and an attic, all fully furnished in the latest Edwardian style, and with an embroidered antimacassar on every high-backed chair. He'd like to wheedle his way over my threshold, get his feet under my kitchen table – and the rest. Some hopes! I don't want a chap, any chap, not at my age – nor any age, come to that.

Tell the truth, I never did want one, if I remember that far back. Anyhow, I was always too busy nursing people then laying 'em out and burying 'em to bother about such things: yes, I think you'll find it usually falls on the unmarried daughter to be the carer in most families these days.

Of course, I know when I'm well off. Who would willingly give all this up, the freedom of my own home, just to be a body servant to a man? There's no-one here to tell me not to wear me flat cap, no-one can order me not to smoke this clay pipe and no-one may object to me sitting here on this freshly scrubbed stone doorstep, morning and evening, watching the world go by. Anyway, I don't hold with all that soppy stuff that these empty-headed women gossip about.

And I've never given the old lad any encouragement at all whatsoever, not a jot, although he does have summat about him that strikes a chord wi' me. But thinking about it, he wears a flat cap just like mine *and* smokes a clay pipe, so at least we've got *two* things in common, if nowt else. Anyhow, this chap I'm telling you about – I think he's called Herbert. Hmm? How do I know? Well, I made it my business to find out, if you must be so inquisitive.

And that's not all – happen I know he doesn't work down t'pit, thank the lord – no, he happens to be assistant foreman at Pettigrew's Mill, so he can't be *that* daft, and if I hear anybody saying he's soft in the head, they'll have me to deal with – I can tell you that for nowt!

But ee, poor devil, he's reight thin and scrawny, though his back is as straight as a die, just like a ramrod, so he's no weaklin'. I suppose he's what you'd call wiry rather than thin and scrawny – yes, that's right, we'll settle for wiry.

And that's one thing we *haven't* got in common cos you couldn't call me skinny or wiry – no, not at all: "ee, she's a grand lass, your Margaret" people used to say to me Mam when I was a kiddie growing up. I was allus a big lass for me age!

But this chap I'm telling you about – he needs feeding up, I should imagine. Could do with some good woman to look after him, fill his belly up with Yorkshire pudding, mebbe dumplings and Irish stew, put some meat on his bones – *and* his collar and cuffs look frayed from where I'm sitting: he definitely could do with a few home comforts.

Oh, I should have said – I found out he's not married, but he *was*, for a while at any rate. He's a widower now – his wife died a few years back. Reight poorly, she were, an'all. It were consumption carried her off, evidently. They'd been married less than two years. Poor Herbert, poor old lad!

Anyway, look on the bright side – at least he'll have learnt how to treat a lady! Yes, you heard me, that's what I said – you've talked me into it. When he walks past here in t'morning, happen I'll teck me flat cap off, look him straight in the eye and tip him the wink. And, o'course, it goes both ways – I could do with a handyman about the place – for the odd jobs, y'knaw: tit-for-tat, and it'll save me having to pay some other body!

WHAT A PERFORMANCE

The director provides our refreshments these days, brought his own hostess trolley in from home a couple of weeks ago and loads it with sandwiches and drinks every morning; says he can't afford for any more people to drop out through sheer exhaustion from hunger pangs.

Although between you, me and the gatepost, it wasn't through exhaustion that we lost our Cinderella! No, no – rumour has it that she was – well, shall we say, in an "interesting condition" – if you get my drift.

Anyway, on the Friday in question, she was here all day, rehearsed like mad, seemed happy as Larry, then had her costume fitting, came out looking white as a sheet, went home that evening and never came back! Pooh, she wasn't exhausted at all, more like she couldn't squeeze into the ball-gown which has, actually, a very tiny nipped-in waist.

That's what happened, if you ask me, not that I like guessing and gossiping.

Then, next news, the understudy eloped! Yes, she did; she went off to Gretna Green with one of the stage-hands without a by-your-leave! I think the management might have to sue her, if they can find her!

Of course, the director (Hilary, his name is), had the devil of a job on his hands to find a replacement Cinderella at such short notice, preferably a thinnish one who would more or less fit into the costume to save the hassle and, more importantly, the cost of having it let out, and who, hopefully, had a nodding acquaintance with the script or at least previous knowledge of this particular pantomime.

Hilary got so frustrated he even considered having Prince Charming to play the part (who is after all a woman although she *is* far too tall for a female role, and also she likes to show off her fine pair of legs), and he even considered asking Buttons (who is of course a man) to play the Prince! But the producer argued with him on that point and won the day by declaring that it would go against all that was tradition in the sphere of pantomime, plus a man would not look half as good as a woman dressed up as a man in the short tunic and tights. I hope you're following all this!

So it was back to the drawing board and a desperate search for a new Cinderella. In the end Hilary was tearing his hair out, metaphorically speaking, of course, because he can't really afford to lose any more, poor chap.

But he turned up one morning sporting a velvet beret on his noggin, a very stylish one with a silk tassel, to match his cape with all that frogging down the front.

And this distraction over the missing Cinderella he could well do without, slap bang in the middle of having his apartment redecorated, as he explained it to me one day (quite tearful he was, actually) when, as he said, he should really be helping his partner decide what colour to choose for the new curtains and covers. They're going in for parquet flooring and a grand piano, too, apparently. Hmm, must be costing them a fortune. It's OK if you can afford it, I suppose. Of course, his partner is well known in the world of haute couture, unisex fashion – y'know, clothes for men and women, interchangeable: the firm goes under the name of "Girl-Stroke-Boy" – yes, funny isn't it?! They must be doing well though: you see their adverts everywhere.

But getting back to the question of Cinderella, Hilary auditioned several chorus girls for the role. Well I say "girls" but they are all past their sell-by date, I should have thought. He hoped that at least one of them had been paying attention sufficiently enough to have absorbed, subconsciously, you know, some of the lines. He would have chosen me, but I was too important in my existing role to be sideways shifted.

'Gertie,' he said, confidentially like, 'Gertie, I would have chosen you, but your role is unique – no-one else could do it, not without months of rehearsals.'

But after all that fannying about he had to choose the thinnest girl, for the frock, d'you see, because the costume supervisor had gone home in a huff, (honestly, all these prima donnas with their artistic temperament – it makes you sick). So then he said to her – the new Cinderella female, 'do your best – and if you can't remember the lines, just improvise, if you know what that means. No? Oh, well, you know, make it up as you go along, dearie.'

Then she started playing the prima donna, 'but darling, what drives my character?' – all that psychological rubbish, but Hilary had no truck with it and merely snapped, quick as a flash, 'would a kick up the arse do the trick? Now get on with it, you old tart!'

Yes, we could tell he had run out of patience!

Anyway, we've been rehearsing like mad ever since, hence the hostess trolley – we're not allowed to leave the theatre at all between the hours of 9 a.m. and 6 p.m. We even have to ask Hilary's permission to go to the lav! Whatever next, I wonder? No-one dares complain to Equity!

So, today is the dress rehearsal. Everybody is pushing everyone else, trying to get a look-in, trying to get the best dressing-table, and the mirror with most light-bulbs around it or with light-bulbs that are still working. Most of the company let the make-up girl loose on them. But, not me, oh no, I like to do my own. I won't let the woman near me, she's too rough, so heavy-handed, with arms like a navvy, plastering the Leichner greasepaint on with a trowel if you don't watch out. I always think "less is more" although on the stage I accept that your features have to stand out otherwise your face fades into nothingness.

And also she never does the eye shadow properly, not how I like it anyway, me being something of a perfectionist. I like to use two pairs of false eyelashes on each lid, then I put a drop of wax on the end of each lash, to make them show up better, y'know.

Then I take the mascara and *blend* the lashes together, after which the eyeliner goes on top, curving along the lid, then upwards and outwards in an arc right to the far corners, almost to my temples. It looks gorgeous, very impressive, even if I say so myself, and this extra bit of work makes my eyes look *huge*. And then comes the blusher – I am very particular with the correct use of blusher, about bringing my cheekbones out. Showing them off to their full advantage, y'know.

Then there's the important matter of the hair! I am very painstaking about my crowning glory. After washing it in a special thickening shampoo, I rinse it in sugar-water to stiffen it, and then, after using the hair-drier set to "hot", I backcomb it thoroughly into a sort of beehive before adding a variety of false curls here and there until it looks really impressive. I use a very strong, holding hairspray before placing a huge sequinned hairnet over the whole thing, just as a finishing touch and to keep it tidy.

Oh, but that's enough talking from me, because here comes good old Sybil wearing her half of our costume, with the rest of it draped over one arm. 'Hey, Gertie,' she says, 'get your hind quarters on, quick sharp – I thought we could canter around a bit before curtain up! Oh, and best of luck, luvvie, break a leg!'

DRINKIES

White shirt, multi-coloured tie, smartish suit – Jeremy, the wearer thereof, lounged at the bar twiddling his glass of wine. Then leaning backwards and half-turning to his companion, a young woman in short skirt and killer heels, he began to speak.

'Well, thanks for coming, Florence, especially on a Monday evening. You must have loads of things to do once you get home. Erm, I know you girlies have your hands full of an evening, removing all that mascara and rinsing out your tights, ahaha.'

Florence smiled faintly.

'We,' continued Jeremy, 'and by we, I mean the Litigation lot, usually come here for drinkies on "dress-down" Friday evenings, straight from the office, you know, but I thought as it was your first day at Swansong & Sheldrake – or the House of Horror, as I prefer to call it – you might like to loosen up a bit, gather your thoughts somewhat, before the slog of undertaking your homeward trek.'

'I should be thanking you, Jeremy,' the young woman replied, turning to look at him. 'I've been wanting to speak to you all day.'

'Oh, really?' Jeremy smirked. 'I noticed you kept glancing over, but those lads were like bees around a honey-pot and I couldn't get a look-in.'

Florence made a sympathetic face. 'Well, it was very enterprising of you to catch me outside the ladies' loo and invite me for a drink. The first day in a new job is always difficult, although the time does fly by.'

'Wait until you've been here a week or two – then it'll drag,' the man grimaced. 'But, take no notice of me, Florence, and on a slightly different note, what were your first impressions of the department? Oh, by the way, may I call you Flo?'

'Yes, Flo is fine,' said the woman, taking a sip of her drink.

'That's great, Florrie,' said her companion, 'I can see we're going to get on like a house on fire.'

'No, no, sorry, Jeremy, I do draw the line at Florrie,' said Florence. 'It sounds so common as if I should be wearing a turban over my curlers, with a fag dangling from my mouth. But Flo is OK.'

'Oh, er, yes, I see what you mean – sorry about that. But we are such a friendly bunch in Litigation, in spite of the horrible and tragic cases we have to deal with on a daily basis. Yes, we're all on first name terms in our department, as you've no doubt gathered by now. How did you get on with the others? What do you think of Mr Smartie-pants Leonard?'

'Lenny? Oh, he was very pleasant, very knowledgeable and offered to show me the ins and outs of the computer system – completely different to the one I'm used to.' Florence toyed with her drink.

'Hmm, yes *he* would,' said Jeremy, unsuccessfully attempting to suppress a scowl. 'I shouldn't be taken in by Leonard's party tricks. If you want to know anything, anything at all, come to me, any time, any day!'

'It's very nice to be surrounded by such helpful folk.' Florence replied, picking up her glass. 'The previous office I worked could be really unpleasant at times, full of people who would stab you in the back at the drop of a hat.'

'Not nice, that, Flo, not nice at all! But you won't find that sort of thing at Swansong & Sheldrake, I'm sure. As I said, we're a merry band in Litigation. But I don't think you could say that for Probate! Honestly, they're such a miserable crowd, not that they affect us in any way at all.'

'I'm sure they can't be that bad, Jeremy. My cousin works in Probate and he has only good things to say about the staff.'

'Oh, erm yes, of course. Perhaps I was thinking of Conveyancing – now they're a right bunch of ba... erm – now look here, Flo – are you sure you only want iced water? Can I get you something stronger? A house-wine, perhaps? It's rather good, and would help you to relax, to chill...'

'No, honestly, Jeremy, I'm fine, thank you. I'm feeling quite relaxed.'

'Wait 'til you've been here a while and you'll be climbing the walls like the rest of us – haha – only my little joke, Flo. But some of the folk in Litigation *do* go over the top when they're trying to impress. For instance, how did you get on with Robin?'

'Robin? Oh yes Robbie, he was lovely, so helpful. He showed me all around the department and introduced me to everyone, including yourself.'

'Yes, he did, and all I can say is, *he would*!' Jeremy took a gulp of his wine. 'Some of these chaps are very pushy and you have to take them with a pinch of salt, I regret to say. If you were in trouble they wouldn't give you the time of day. Trust me!'

'Well, it's early days yet. I'll get to know everyone gradually. I did study psychology for a year at college, you know, so I've learned what to look for in body language and all that stuff.'

'Well, Flo, how clever of you, I must say! Such a smart brain in that pretty little head of yours! I hope you're not analysing yours truly!'

'You never know, Jeremy, you never know,' Florence pursed her lips, eyeing him askance.

'Look, let me get you a glass of wine – that water must be tepid by now.'

'No wine, honestly, Jeremy – but I will have another iced water – thanks: I like to keep a clear head.'

'Is that so you can analyse people? I can save you a lot of time by saying that there are several members of staff in Litigation you cannot trust. For instance,

Robin, Leonard, Steven, Michael, Alistair, George and Philip.'

'Well, that's most of the department, Jeremy! It only leaves you!'

'Exactly, Flo. That's what I was hinting at. I'm glad you've seen the light – realised the awful truth at this early stage. You're a new female, the *only* female, in the department and this puts you at great risk. Those lads were buzzing around you like, well, like bees at the honey-pot!'

'So you've already said, Jeremy. Oh, you are funny, quite the comedian. I do like a sense of humour – it brightens the day.'

'But I'm not joking, Flo. You'll see how the land lies. I'm just putting you on your guard, that's all. Watch out when one of them tries to get you on your own!'

'Like you, you mean?' Flo laughed.

'No, no, I'm quite different. I only asked you out for drinkies so's I could warn you about the rest of the gang. But, hmm, on a different tack, erm, are you married at all?'

'No, I'm not, Jeremy – not in the slightest.'

'A boyfriend then?'

'Nope, I'm not shackled at the moment, if it's of any importance.'

'Well, I hope I'm not being too forward, but would you like to come out to dinner one night?'

'*You* are married, though, aren't you Jeremy? I spy a gold ring on your wedding finger.'

'Oh, that!! In name only, dear Flo, name only. This dratted ring won't come off since I put on weight through worry. Iris and I gave up hope years ago, and in fact she should be moving out any time soon.'

'Moving out?'

'Well, if there's any justice she will be. Keeps promising, then changing her mind – but we do have separate rooms so, you see, I can consider myself a free agent. Well? Now will you come out with me?'

'That's very kind of you, Jeremy but, as you must know, that would contravene the company's house rules – I don't believe lowly wage-slaves are allowed to date the partners.'

'Yes, yes, of course I'm well aware of that, Flo, but, if we did start dating, what would be the worst possible scenario?'

'The worst possible scenario, Jeremy? In my capacity as a partner of the firm, I should have to dismiss you on the spot!'

'Oh, we could keep it our little secret, and anyway, why have you been flirting with me all day? I noticed you trying to make eye contact several times.'

'No, actually I wasn't flirting, Jeremy: it was your tie, it was dazzling me – I was intending to ask you not to wear such a jazzy one to the office. A nice dark blue would be more appropriate and less distracting, similar to what the other chaps wear, you know: and, oh, while we're on the subject, I'm banning "dress-down" Fridays, too – a new broom and all that.'

Jeremy sat on his bar-stool, staring, his mouth opening and closing soundlessly, just like a fish.

Florence got up to go, smoothed her skirt, slung her designer bag over one shoulder, and added brightly, 'I am, however, obliged to you for your interesting comments about my staff and bringing me up to speed on their little ways – I'll keep a sharp eye on their activities. Now, I must dash – got to rinse out my tights and get all this girlie mascara off. Bye-bye, Jeremy, oh, and thanks for the drinkies!'

LIES AND ASPIRATIONS

From time to time, Mrs Plunge would pick up the telephone and invite Miss Attercrop to tea. Amelia Plunge and Dolly Attercrop had known each other since nursery-school but had lost contact along the way until they recognised each other one Saturday afternoon in Quorum Thisbé shopping precinct. It quickly became evident that their lives had taken very different paths but they had stayed in touch ever since.

Dolly, who was fairly plain and worked as a lowly-paid library assistant, looked forward to her teatime invitations with keen interest as these were held over in Quagmire Village at her friend's beautifully appointed stone-built house set in its own grounds, complete with outbuildings and stables, which made a change from the cramped flat-share in the unfashionable south side of Quorum Thisbé.

Amelia, on the other hand, was very pretty and also extremely wealthy, with a husband she had married straight from the schoolroom and who indulged her every whim, mainly through fear. It had never been necessary for Amelia Plunge to get a job and she therefore led the life of a lady of leisure.

She greatly enjoyed Dolly's visits, mainly because undisguised envy is very good for the ego, and furthermore she loved to wallow in all the goings-on at Dolly's office, trying to imagine herself in such a situation, getting up early every morning and slaving away at a desk eight hours a day for very little return. She simply could not put herself in Dolly's shoes, and her own materialistic security gave her a warm and cosy feeling. Could Dolly's lot be as humdrum and poor as she described it? Amelia thought some form of help should be offered, but was reluctant to actually press banknotes into her friend's hand. Nevertheless, whenever a boost to the ego was required, an invitation to tea would be proffered – and gladly accepted.

Dolly was ever fulsome in her praise of Amelia's surroundings, her possessions, her position in the local community, the exotic foreign holidays and her indulgent husband. This cloying adoration had resulted in an increasingly-patronising tone creeping into Amelia's utterances over recent weeks but which Dolly had not appeared to have noticed.

The reflected glory accrued by Dolly from these visits was shared with her flat-mate, one Miss Enid Dartle, a likewise drab and unlovely woman. Every detail of Mrs Plunge's house, clothes and jewellery was described in lovingly-embellished detail. Enid Dartle would hang on Dolly's every word, mouth agape, her eyes glazing over as she tried to imagine what it must be like to live such a charmed existence.

On a particular Saturday, as Mrs Plunge and Miss Attercrop sat partaking of tea and tiny cakes from bone china crockery, the gracious hostess put her cup down decisively. 'Dolly, I am so glad you were able to come today – I find myself in a sudden fix!'

'Oh, but darling,' squeaked her friend, sitting to attention, all ears, 'you know I'd do anything to help out: anything, anything at all.'

'Yes, I guessed you would say that. The thing is, I'm having a dinner party tonight…'

'Oh, how lovely – and you want me to make up the numbers? I shall have to go home and change unless you could lend me something to wear…'

'No, no, it's not that, and anyway you'd never fit into any of my dresses…!'

'Oh,' frowned Dolly reddening to her roots, but quickly recovering herself. 'I'm sorry to be so forward, Amelia – do forgive me.'

'No, please don't fret, Dolly dear, don't be embarrassed. The dinner guests are my husband's business associates and their shallow wives, so it will be quite, quite boring, to say the least – I wouldn't want to subject you to that kind of ordeal!'

'Oh, that's kind of you, Amelia. You're so thoughtful. But what is it then – you want me to help you decide which frock to wear?'

'No, it's not that, I'm quite used to dressing appropriately for the occasion, thank you, and I have *almost* decided on the gold lame for tonight, but well, dear, what I am asking of you is this: Dino, my chef, is due to arrive at six o'clock, but, most unfortunately, Luigi, his assistant, cannot get here until ten o'clock at the earliest to do the clearing up, and I was wondering whether you'd oblige me by helping out in the kitchen, peeling vegetables, washing up, that sort of thing – I would pay you so much an hour, and I'm sure you wouldn't refuse a little boost to your purse!' Amelia Plunge felt extremely proud of the way in which she would be able to slip some cash into her friend's hand at the end of the evening, in a non-patronising way.

'Oh, I see,' said Dolly, looking down at her scuffed shoes before recovering herself and lifting her head with a smile. 'Well, yes, of course, dear one, anything at all to help you out. I'd be honoured to be part of your arrangements in whatever way...'

'And as a special treat,' continued Amelia, feeling increasingly benevolent, 'you can help me choose which jewellery to wear tonight. You'd like that, wouldn't you, darling?'

After an hour of watching her friend sorting through sliding cupboards full of dresses and shoes, and chests-of-drawers crammed with necklaces, earrings, brooches and bracelets, Dolly was presented with a large wrap-around apron just as the doorbell rang announcing the arrival of the chef.

The rest of the evening sped by for Dolly, either up to her elbows in soap-suds or at the beck and call of temperamental Dino. By ten o'clock when his assistant arrived ready for the big clear-up operation, Dolly was almost dropping with exhaustion.

Amelia made a point of slipping into the kitchen for a moment. She beckoned Dolly aside and handed her a sparkly hair ornament clipped to a couple of pound notes. 'I saw you admiring this hairclip, Dolly – so I'd like you to have it, as well as the money, just as an extra little thank-you for your hard work tonight.'

Dolly wiped her hands on the apron and pushed back her wispy hair made untidy by the steam. 'Oh, thank you, Amelia,' she said, 'I enjoyed helping out. If you need me again, you know where I am.'

After the last guest and all the helpers had left, Mrs Amelia Plunge sat theatrically fanning herself with a bejewelled hand, and confided in her husband: 'You know, Peregrine, I do envy Dolly – she has her little job, her close friend, no responsibility to speak of, she's grateful for the smallest thing – just leads a placid happy contented life. Quite honestly I'd swap places with her at the drop of a hat!'

Her husband looked askance, whisky glass halfway to his lips!

'No, darling, don't look at me like that – I mean it! I'd exchange with her this very minute, leave all the showy, tiresome nonsense, all the boring guests – what a shallow life this is.'

Her husband gave a wry smile. 'What? You'd prefer to be that drab little nobody – what was her name again? The one you kept hidden in the kitchen all night?'

'Oh, be quiet, Peregrine,' came the sharp reply. 'Granted, Dolly isn't much to look at but she has more humanity and integrity than all our so-called friends put together – I tell you, I'd swap with her any day.'

'Hmm, I believe you, thousands wouldn't,' muttered her husband, swirling and swigging the last drops from his whisky glass.

'Well, cross my heart and may I be struck dead this very minute,' his wife retorted, pausing only to stare up at the ceiling for fully five seconds, before heaving a huge sigh of relief and reaching for her jade cigarette box.

Across town, Miss Dolly Attercrop was confiding in her friend Enid Dartle as they quaffed late night cocoa in front of a popping gas fire.

'Y'know, my rich friend Mrs Amelia Plunge has come to depend upon me to such a degree. She insisted on lending me an evening dress so's I could stay for dinner to help entertain Peregrine's business contacts: that's her husband, you know – Peregrine. I *am* on first-name terms with them all now, of course! I met some really interesting people who seemed to find me, erm, interesting. Peregrine, that's Amelia's husband, you know – he was *very* attentive.'

'Oh, how thrilling,' gasped Enid, 'what did he say to you, what did he say?'

'Well, I can't remember exactly – I spoke to so many people – but he did ask me my name several times. I'm sure to be on their regular guest list after tonight! I may even be moving up in the world shortly, Enid – all I will say for now is "watch this space"! And then, guess what? As a little keepsake, a small thank-you for helping to keep the conversation flowing, Amelia allowed me to keep this – take it, feel it: pretty, isn't it?'

Enid sat with mouth agape, eyes dreamy, tenderly handling the glittering hair-clip, and she had to agree that it was indeed pretty, a fitting souvenir of a splendid evening spent in the upper echelons of society!

Dolly watched her approvingly, nodding blithely, silently promising God that she would definitely attend confession on Sunday.

SAGA

On a whim, I booked a package trip with Saga. I wanted to go alone, and intended to stay aloof, not become over-friendly with anyone else in the group.

The venue I chose was Paris: I had been there in my youth and remembered the unique atmosphere with nostalgia. My single room at the *Pension Victorine* was not exactly the Ritz but it was clean and did have the benefit of a pretty wrought-iron balcony.

That first night, I sat at dinner with two women, Birdie and Helen, and a man named Sid, a self-proclaimed jokester, who welcomed me with "here she comes, here comes trouble". Birdie immediately produced a photograph album of her grandchildren, and Helen began to relate the history of her unfortunate marriage, ending each sad episode with, "yes, the only thing that keeps me from being happily married is my husband". Everyone ignored everyone else. I just sat there in misery, failing to blank out my three companions' ego trips.

The courier arrived, breaking into the three monologues going on around me, and advised there was a conducted tour of the Louvre planned for the following morning. I was pressed to join, but feeling irritated by the relentless chattering, preferred to do my own thing.

The next day, avoiding the dining room and *le petit déjeuner*, I set off for a walk.

Aiming to stick to the main avenues, I proceeded down *Rue de la Victoire* and into the *Boulevard Haussmann*, browsed the boutiques and galleries, and then began to make my way back via a tangle of side alleys where I suddenly found myself seriously disorientated, standing before an attractive garden with little green tables, louvred chairs and a notice proclaiming "*entrée au restaurant*".

Long ago regretting my missed breakfast, I went in and ordered a café crème and croissant. There was only one other customer, a man who stared at me intently. I took a seat at the far end of the room and the man turned towards me.

'May I join you?' he called across the empty space, approaching my table before I had uttered any word of permission. 'I can tell you're an Englishwoman by your accent,' he said, taking the seat opposite mine. 'It's nice to talk to someone in my own language.'

'It must be,' I replied coldly.

'Looking at me as I am today,' he announced, gazing into my eyes, 'you may be surprised to hear I used to own my own factory. Yes, I was a well-to-do factory-owner not too long ago.'

'Oh, really…' I began, devoutly wishing I had not set foot in the damned place.

'But I made the mistake of spoon-feeding my workers,' he continued, 'and the whole business went kaput before I could pull in the reins, financially speaking, as it were.'

I tilted my head and sat there mutely, suddenly losing my appetite for the croissant.

'Yes, I made a silly mistake,' he nodded, 'and I'm glad you agree. You're probably wondering what we produced? Well, we manufactured ice on a commercial scale. I was well-known hereabouts as "the iceman"!'

'Oh,' was all I managed before he launched into further explanations.

'Yes, the factory is now derelict, neglected, empty yet full, of moonbeams, memories and dust, as am I. You see before you a changed man, a shadow of his former self, no longer the "iceman". My name's Jim, by the way – and yours, what's yours? In other words, whom have I the pleasure of addressing? No? No, I quite understand any reluctance to introduce yourself on such short acquaintance – but what was I was saying, oh yes, how the mighty are fallen, which is what you're probably thinking and which is true as far as I am concerned. By the way, dear madame, do you like dinosaurs? Yes? I had a huge mural of such a beast on the factory wall, which everyone admired greatly.'

I shifted uncomfortably in my chair as he went on with his unhappy story. 'The dinosaur mural cost me a small fortune but I never begrudged spending out on little comforts for my workers, such as generous pay, bonuses and holiday leave. Which is why I eventually went bankrupt through sheer reckless kindness and wanting to please anyone and everyone. Of course, my wife left me immediately when she realised I was penniless, and who could blame her? She was a wonderful woman was Lilliana, a very *proud* woman, yes, *excessively* proud, and obviously deserved a man who could take care of her. I could never imagine Lilliana living her life in poverty nor did I expect her to. For example, not being able to afford those little luxuries that make a lady happy would have spelt death to her. Yes, she was absolutely wonderful in every way was dear Lilliana.'

He stopped, took a long shuddering breath, and then continued with his sorry tale: 'The first time I saw her was as a vision of beauty standing on a balcony. I fell in love with her on sight and proposed at the earliest opportunity. We married within two weeks. It was a lavish wedding, all the office personnel were invited and, because I am truly no elitist, the factory workers were not left off the guest list, and I showered them, and her, with extravagant gifts.'

He stopped and sighed, gazing at me, as if expecting some kind of response. When I sat there speechless, he went on, 'However, my dear madame, I heartily regret to say that my Lilliana did have a small affliction, a tiny flaw! That is, she did not like any sort of romance, could not tolerate even the warm, although slight, pressure of my hand on her arm. I hope you, my dear madame, are not likewise afflicted because it does make life very difficult, especially in a marriage or indeed any loving relationship.

'But please, I beg of you, do not think ill of her because I myself want only the best for darling Lilliana. She divorced me very quickly, and I sincerely hope she is happy, wherever she is. I heard on the grapevine that she remarried and had three children on the trot, but this I cannot believe, knowing her frailty, her frigidity at first hand, so to speak.

'I am ashamed to say, dear – erm, what was your name again? No, no, do not worry if you prefer not to tell it. I fear I am being too forward. As I was saying, dear madame, I am embarrassed to say that when the news about Lilliana came to my ears I did contemplate suicide – finishing it all, *kaput*! I sat on a park bench and planned on throwing myself in front of a train, or jumping down a disused mineshaft or even leaping off a wrought-iron balcony. I first saw Lilliana on such a balcony, so that would have some sort of poetic undertones, don't you think?

'Speaking of which, I write poetry. I also paint. Do you like art? I have many portraits and etchings, life studies of Lilliana – she was my muse and I caught her classic beauty a hundred times, but still I could not get close to her, not physically, you understand, although mentally we were on the same wavelength. I sincerely believed that, and still do to this day in spite of the salacious rumours going the rounds.

'I have my own studio, you know – it's in a shed which is now being encroached upon by a considerable growth of ivy. I cut it back regularly but still it grows, keeps out the daylight to some extent. I sleep there, too, in the studio-cum-shed, since I lost my beautiful mansion. It's quite comfortable in spite of the suffocating ivy.

'Actually, I'm looking for a new model, a lady to inspire me, a muse whose image I might capture on canvas or indeed by camera lens. Do you know of anyone who would help me out, might want to see her beauty portrayed by a skilled artist? I can promise she would be treated like a queen! Oh dear, you're not going already are you? But please, I beg you'll allow me to accompany you – I could take your elbow as we walk – you will find I'm the perfect gentleman... We could stroll in the direction of my studio. Oh, I see, you wish to pay a call – in other words, spend a penny. Off you go then, I'll wait here – the powder-room is over there behind the beaded curtain. Don't be long, dear madame – I know what you ladies are like once you start primping and preening.'

I stood up shakily, turned and made for the beaded curtain trying to think of some way of evading Jim's ever-tightening tentacles.

And alleluia, it was my lucky day as I spied an open window leading onto the garden. I ran and ran, never looking back, eventually found the *Boulevard Haussmann* and took it from there.

Arriving safely back at the hotel, the first person I saw in the foyer was Sid who called out "here she is, here comes trouble".

Then a beaming Birdie approached, holding forth her photograph album, closed followed by Helen who linked her arm in mine in friendly fashion.

'I've been telling them the sad tale of my marriage,' she gushed ecstatically, 'but you can hear all about that later – because, first, we'd like to know where *have* you been all morning?'

'Oh,' I sighed, 'it's been a real saga, believe me! But it's *so* good to be back amongst *normal* people.'

SHIPWRECKED!

'Marigold, dear,' gushed Amelia Plunge as she emerged from the crush of bodies and cigarette smoke, dragging a young man by his sunburned hand, 'I'd like you to meet Peter – I know you two will get along famously together!'

Without further ado, the gold lamé-swathed hostess, who set great store by her party-giving talents, swanned off to search out other suitable pairings, leaving the two guests standing by an ornate fireplace, smiling at each other expectantly.

'Well, what have you to say for yourself, young man,' Marigold began, 'for instance, what do you do with yourself all day?'

'I've just spent the past twelve months on a desert island,' offered the youth.

'*Sacré bleue*!   Shipwrecked, were you?' Marigold raised one glittering finger to her mouth in a theatrical gesture.

'No, no, I was employed to go there – to carry out surveys on the....'

'Oh, how *marveillieux* – so fascinating. And such a coincidence, *n'est-ce-pas,* because my husband

Marcus happens to be a surveyor also. He prepares reports for house-buyers, that sort of thing.'

'No,' laughed Peter, 'not that type of surveying. You see, on the island, I had to...'

'Well, just imagine, having to do a survey on an island, especially after being shipwrecked – so fascinating! You see, I happen to love islands, I *am* a seasoned traveller – we went to Guernsey last year and just adored it. Gorgeous flowers, *lovely* people, I could quite easily live on an island...'

'Um,' began the young man, 'there were no people...'

'*Mon Dieu*, no people! Q*uelle domage*; but on Guernsey there are lots of people and they all speak English, you know, and some French, of course, although I do pride myself I can get along with anybody, and it does help being something of a linguist – *oon petty pwah*!' Marigold beamed, helping herself to a cocktail from a passing tray.

'But, as I was saying, there were no other...' continued Peter.

'No, really? Again I say q*uelle domage*! And so very interesting, but I expect you had lots of insects when you were shipwrecked on the desert island – and that's one thing I *cannot abide*, flying insects.'

'Well, actually, I wasn't ship...'

'Especially mosquitoes, I cannot abide them at all, not one teensy, tiny bit.'

'Oh? Well, that's what I had to...'

'*Mais oui*, even ladybirds, ugh, *trés terrible* – some people think they're pretty, but to me they're just horrible, creepy things! And flies, did you get flies? *Mein Gott*, I absolutely *hate* them.'

'Oh, yes,' Peter enthused, perking up, 'there *were* flies, sand flies mostly, but lots of different species, that's what I had to…'

'I remember when we were on Guernsey,' went on Marigold, patting her rigid perm, 'I had to send Marcus out for some insect repellent.'

'Really…?'

'But that wasn't a lot of good – *quelle domage!* – I was bitten to death – so the following morning we went down to the flower market and bought really expensive fly-spray.'

'Oh…?'

'But that made the room stink to high heaven, because we were breathing it in, d'you see! Most unpleasant, *trés terrible*, all very chemical – the fumes, you know. So then we had to leave all the *fenêtres* open, and, of course, more winged creatures swarmed in, great clouds of them.'

'Yes, they would…'

'I'm afraid one simply cannot win, *je regrette* to say. That's the trouble with abroad, the flies and other horrendous animals, like snakes, which I *cannot abide*.'

'There *were* snakes on the…'

'No, no, I shall have to stop you there,' ordered Marigold, holding up one sparkling hand. 'Please *do not* describe those horrible creatures to me, or else I shall have nightmares.'

'Oh, I'm so...'

'I *never* saw *even one* snake on Guernsey, although I once scared myself *rigid* by daring to enter the reptile house at London Zoo. *Mon Dieu*, I ran out screaming! Marcus took me *straight* to the First Aid people who gave me a cup of tea with lots of sugar in it – for shock, you know. *Quelle horreur*! Yes, really – I had bad dreams for weeks.'

'Well, it's best to avoid...'

'Yes, poor Marcus had to shake me awake every night because I was moaning and groaning and waving my arms around in my sleep. "Writhing" as my dear, patient husband described it. No, you see, I simply cannot *abide* the creatures. Not *oon petty pwah*.'

'That must have been...'

'Yes, you're right, it was – it was *absolutely horrendous*! And you must have had a lot of *sand* when you were lost at sea then shipwrecked? Don't tell me about *sand*. I loathe and abhor the stuff! *C'est la vie* - even on *Guernsey* it was hateful. Sand, everywhere: in your shoes, in your hair, in your sandwiches, in your drinks, stuck to your skin!!! Sand, sand, *sand*, _sand_, and yet more **_sand_**!'

Marigold glared, daring Peter to mention anything else that could upset such delicate sensitivities as hers. The young man stood there bleakly and at a loss, as the lady proceeded to speak again.

'Changing the subject slightly,' she said brightly, 'and *pardonnez moi* for speaking out of turn, but I can't help noticing you're very tanned! Did you lie in the sun much when you were lost at sea then shipwrecked on the desert island?'

'No, it was too…' Peter began.

'*Quelle domage*…too hot to lie in, you say…*quelle horreur*!' Marigold warmed to her theme, wriggling inside her beaded top. 'Well, don't tell *me* about sunburn – I am an *ab-so-lute* martyr to it; don't have to lie in it, you know – just walking around in the shade in a sleeveless frock – that will do it and I am *fried* to an ab-so-lute *crisp*! When we were in Guernsey, I had to stay in our hotel room for three whole days and nights with Marcus slathering calamine lotion on my poor *shoulders*, my poor *arms*, my poor *back*! It's these latest fashions, you know: they leave far too much flesh exposed. I blame the designers myself, although I would *never* in a million years describe myself as a slave to fashion.'

'No, no, of course not,' Peter murmured. 'But on the desert island, I wore…'

'*Did you – y*es, how *interesting* – but just imagine poor Marcus having to nurse me! It wasn't very nice for him, *quelle horreur*, spoiling his holiday to a certain extent, although I did insist he went out – sometimes, and then in the evenings he'd go down to the bar for an hour, although between you, me and the gatepost, it was longer than an hour – away half the night on occasion, but I never said anything – well, not much, anyway. Look, there's Marcus, over there by the piano.'

Peter turned and saw a well-groomed man, whisky in hand, surrounded by a bevy of vivacious young women, all evidently competing for his attentions.

'Yoo hoo, Marcus,' screeched Marigold across the room. 'See this young man here? *Quelle horreur* - he was *lost at sea for months then shipwrecked* on a desert island for a whole year!'

Marcus beamed and lifted his glass in a silent toast, swiftly returning to his female admirers.

'No, no, I wasn't actually ship…' Peter began.

'*S'il vous plait*, you must be patient,' interjected Marigold, 'I expect you'll have the opportunity to tell him all about your adventures later on. Now, what do you think of my husband at first glance? Tell the truth now! Handsome, isn't he?'

'Erm, well yes, of course…' came the embarrassed reply.

'He's a lot younger than yours truly, although you'd never know it because I do try to keep myself as attractive as possible for him. Go on, how old am I? Go on, have a guess.'

'Oh, I couldn't possibly,' blushed the young man. 'Now, when I was on the desert island…'

'Yes, I want to hear all about it, every tiny detail. I love islands and, actually, one day we hopped from Guernsey to Jersey (I am a seasoned traveller, you know) but really they looked pretty much the same to me.

And of course I wanted to visit Sark but, *quelle domage*, no cars are allowed on the roads, which is rather silly, don't you think? The woman in charge over there is the Dame of Sark, evidently, and she makes all the laws, and well, rules are rules, *je* suppose. So we didn't actually go, because Marcus does *love* his cars. Yes, *c'est la vie*, I was *trés* disappointed because I am a seasoned traveller, you know, never get airsick or carsick or seasick, always ready to pack my bags and be off at the drop of a sunhat!'

Peter smiled weakly, his eyes darting this way and that. 'Oh, look,' he managed to squeak, 'someone's waving me – see, over there by the door, oops they've just gone into the hall – sorry, must be off – but it was very nice to have met you…'

'Well, *hasta la vista,* young man, the pleasure was all mine,' beamed Marigold, 'and thank you *so much* for telling me *all* about your adventures – I've *never* met *anyone* before who was actually *shipwrecked*…'

SILENT STORM

After my twin sister Jessica died in the convent where she had lived as a member of a silent order for ten years, the Mother Superior, one finger to her lips, handed me a Tesco bag containing the few pitiful possessions my sister had been allowed. In amongst letters from the family, two prayer books, a bible and a rosary, I found a sealed, stamped envelope addressed to a Mr Louis du Creeke, Anchor Antiques, Treepennorth, Cornwall. The words "private and personal" appeared in the top left-hand corner.

The name sounded vaguely familiar to me, and then I remembered with some surprise that when Jessica and I had been on holiday in Treepennorth shortly before she took the veil, we had gone into Anchor Antiques to shelter from the rain. The proprietor had introduced himself as Louis du Creeke and made a point of engaging us in conversation. But, as far as I was aware, that was the only occasion Jessica had had any contact whatsoever with the man.

Naturally I did not open the envelope to read the letter therein as this would have been an invasion of my sister's privacy, but neither did I wish to post it on just in

117

case Mr Louis du Creeke no longer resided at that particular address.

I decided to go to Treepennorth and, if at all possible, deliver the letter myself.

As soon as the sad and pathetic funeral was over, I travelled down to Cornwall and arrived at Treepennorth Village under a torrential downpour.

In spite of this, I made straight for the High Street and stood outside Anchor Antiques sheltering my eyes against the stinging rain, squinting at the sign above the door, which proclaimed "L du Creeke Esquire, Antiquarian".

Ah, but the sign might be out of date and the shop belong to someone else, a son, brother or other male relative of Louis! I had to ensure it was the right person before handing the letter over.

Crossing the narrow cobbled street, I stood outside a newsagent's shop window opposite to reflect on the situation!

In spite of my plastic pixie-hood, mackintosh and galoshes, I was getting very wet, so decided to go inside the shop and gather my thoughts. I made a play of riffling through women's magazines on the rack, vaguely taking in hints on "how to get your man", "how to keep your man" and "why men are all filthy animals" plus an interesting piece on "what jewellery to wear whilst listening to Radio 3".

Intermittently I would look across at the antique shop, hoping to catch a glimpse of the proprietor. I was unsuccessful and as a storm broke overhead, I decided to call it a day. I paid for one of the magazines, by now damply creased, and, braving the wind and rain, reached my hotel and a much-needed dinner.

The next morning dawned bright and beautiful with a deep blue sky reflecting in the calm sea, the early sun warming my skin.

I dressed in white shorts, espadrilles and glazed-cotton top before making for Anchor Antiques. I decided to be more assertive this time, walking straight in through the door with its jingling overhead bell. I began to browse the dark furniture, porcelain vases, candlesticks and other ornate artifacts.

As expected, the proprietor left his desk at the rear and approached me, buttoning-up his green corduroy jacket. 'Good morning, dear lady,' he said. 'May I assist, or is madam just looking?'

The man's appearance did not jog my memory at all, and in fact I was sure I had never set eyes on him before in my life.

'I'm *am* looking,' I replied, 'but not for antiques.'

'Oh, how so?' he queried, pursing his lips.

'No, I am searching for a person, a Mr Louis du Creeke. Do you know his whereabouts?'

'I am Leon du Creeke. Louis was my brother, and I regret to say he died ten years ago almost to the day. Why are you interested in him?'

'I am sorry to hear that,' I frowned, nodding in sympathy. 'I also have been bereaved of a sibling, but more recently. My twin sister Jessica died one month ago. I found a letter addressed to your brother amongst her possessions although I have no idea why she would have written to him.'

'Jessica!' he murmured. 'That is a name from the past. You have my deepest condolences. But, my dear lady, are you saying you never knew what had gone on?'

I was stunned into silence! But my face must have expressed a thousand words because Leon continued, 'Louis pursued Jessica after meeting her in this very shop. How he found her whereabouts remains a mystery but he became obsessed with thoughts of your sister and, I regret to say, actually began stalking her. In the end, she entered a silent order of nuns, as you know. After that he could never get in touch properly. He wrote many times but she never replied, so in the end, in his sadness, he jumped off the East Cliff here in Treepennorth.'

'How dreadful – I never knew any of this,' I said. 'Jessica was the beautiful twin, but she never possessed the personality to cope with the passionate attention she received from men. It troubled her, she saw their admiration as harassment, not as a compliment, and she became more fastidious, more introverted year by year – her dislike of the physical world, her obsessive compulsive disease, hand-washing, extreme tidiness, her growing agoraphobia – made life very difficult. In fact she must have endured more emotional turmoil than anyone realised. Poor girl – she suffered in silence.'

Leon looked at me as two customers entered the shop, and he reluctantly went over to serve them.

'Please meet me tonight for dinner,' he urged over his shoulder. 'Seven o'clock at the Treepennorth Hotel. We can talk about this in private.'

That evening, I wore a sequinned top, long black velvet skirt and suede ankle boots with diamante trim. Leon was waiting at the restaurant, wearing a dinner jacket with satin lapels and a black bow tie. He looked very smart indeed and the sight of him holding my chair for me brought a glow to my cheeks and a nod of appreciation. I do like good manners and appropriate dress, especially in men.

In spite of the sad circumstances, our evening together was most pleasant, and we exchanged memories of our siblings, some of them happy, some not. We discussed what to do about the letter.

'Why don't we meet tomorrow on the East Cliff where Louis died, and read it together?' my companion suggested, and this we agreed would be a fitting tribute.

After coffee and brandy, Leon escorted me back to the hotel through gathering dusk, a heavenly scent of pine and honeysuckle dizzying my senses. He brushed my cheek with moist lips, and my stomach turned over.

The next morning broke misty and damp. Donning a mackintosh, tweed jacket, stout boots and woolly hat, I climbed the flight of steep stone steps of East Cliff and stood at the top in a gathering gloom. Thick fog was rolling in across the bay.

Then I heard Leon's voice in my ear. 'Eileen,' he whispered urgently. I jumped, instinctively turning to him in shock.

'Oh, I'm so sorry,' he laughed. 'Just my little joke! Now, let's get to grips with this letter and then we can go for a coffee.'

'Leon,' I said,' I've decided we should *not* read the letter: it would be an invasion of our siblings' privacy and, in fact, here it is in pieces. I tore it up last night.'

I opened the envelope and threw its contents towards the cliff edge, watching the tiny fragments hovering in the air for a few seconds, wafting in all directions, before floating down towards the misty sea-washed rocks below.

'Oh, why did you do that?' Leon looked distraught and forlorn, standing there in his green corduroy a-sparkle with droplets. 'Now those last words are gone forever – we will never know what Jessica wrote to Louis, about her silence, the storm she was going through: it might have explained things…'

'Leon, it's better to let the matter lie,' I said gently. 'It was their business, not ours. Now shall we go for that coffee, this sea-fret is rather chill.'

'Yes, yes, it certainly is,' Leon said, taking my hand. 'And anyway, I'm sure you're right – I'll go along with anything you say. You and I are the only remaining link with the past. What's your address, your phone number? We must make arrangements for the future. I feel a real connection here, an affinity…'

I snatched my hand away from his and folded my arms tightly across my chest. I shook my head and made a mental note to write to one of my women's magazines about it all, and ask for their take on the matter.

'I'm sorry, Leon,' I said firmly, 'but this is a closed chapter in our lives and we must move on, go our own ways.'

'No, you're wrong there, Eileen,' Leon grimaced, reaching out for me, gripping both my arms, his lips searching for mine. 'Darling, this is the start of a *new* chapter in our lives – and now I've found you, I'll never let you go!'

DECISIONS, DECISIONS

'...and I said to your Auntie Maude, to be perfectly honest Maude, I said, blah, blah, blah...and Maude said, blah, and I said, blah, blah, blahdy, blah...in no uncertain terms.' Velveeta Anstruther illustrated her words with dramatic flourishes of red-tipped, be-ringed fingers, numerous gold slave bangles clanking on her arms.

'That put her in her place, Mummy,' replied Nebula Santiago, pushing a stray wisp of hair under her spotted cotton bandana. 'But then, you're always right, especially where potty Aunt Maude is concerned – taking tango lessons at her age indeed. Now, are you going to just stand there watching or are you going to help me with this sorting out?'

Mrs Anstruther leapt into action and held out the plastic bag in readiness. 'You do have a lot of clothes, I must say, Nebula darling. Far too many, if you want my honest opinion.'

Nebula Santiago made a face. 'Well, let's see what can I spare – it is for charity at the end of the day and I can afford to be slightly ruthless. Now, let me see – oh yes, how about these scruffy old blue dungarees?'

'Darling, they make you look like a frumpy feminist about to burn your bra,' laughed Mrs Anstruther. 'So – into the Oxfam bag they go.'

'Oh? Feminist, eh?' Nebula pursed her lips. 'Well, on second thoughts, they might be useful for pottering in the garden.'

'Please yourself,' her mother sighed. 'You always do. Now, what's next?'

'Let's see, hmm – oh – by the way, Mummy, I should just mention, I saw Mario with a strange girl, they were kissing – in the Oxfam shop doorway of all places. I couldn't help think, here we go again.'

'Oh, Nebula, these hot-blooded Italians can't even keep the eleventh commandment – "thou shalt not be found out". *Into* the Oxfam bag with him, the rat.'

'Oh, don't be too hard on him – he can be very sweet – he sometimes brings me flowers for no reason.'

'Hmm,' her mother snorted. 'When a man brings his wife flowers for no reason, there's a reason.'

'Well, I can't throw him out – he's cost me too many tears, and his company pension will come in handy in my old age.' Nebula continued her sorting...

'Now, take this dress, in black and puce. Ah yes, I bought it for an interview: I didn't get the job, though – no idea why! So, into the Oxfam bag it goes – but no – it cost me two weeks pay and may come back in fashion in a year or two.'

'Oh lord,'Mrs Anstruther sighed, 'we'll be here all day at this rate if you carry on like this.'

'And by the way, Mummy, Mario's new girl is so young, she clung to him like a limpet. He never saw me slink away, crying my eyes out. So, on second thoughts, I think you're right – I should discard him.'

Mrs Anstruther shook the empty Oxfam bag in encouragement. 'I'm afraid you married beneath you, Nebula – but all women do, of course. Now, into the Oxfam bag with him…'

'Oh, Mummy, no – I'll give him one more chance. I can't wipe out ten years of marriage. So, please let's forget Mario for a moment. Now, how about these stiletto heels?'

'Good grief, Nebula, instruments of torture, to be perfectly honest. They made you look like a trollop, wobbling about with your bottom stuck out. Get rid of them immediately, if not sooner.'

Nebula shook her head. 'Oh, I used to be indecisive, but now I'm not so sure. We-e-ell, into the Oxfam bag they go – yes, I used to be so vain but now I'm an old married woman, dressing for comfort. And by the way, Mummy, I heard Mario whispering on the phone to his fancy piece. He never saw me turn and go back to the kitchen table, butter his toast through a mist.'

'Oh, the snake,' gasped Mrs Anstruther, 'tell him to make his own breakfast. Get rid of him – he doesn't deserve your loyalty and affection.'

'You're right, of course. So, I'll take your advice and throw him out – into the Oxfam bag he goes – but, no – I couldn't bear to live all alone, and he'll be there if the plumbing springs a leak or a worn-out light bulb needs changing.'

'So you're keeping him as a glorified handyman, then? Is that what you're saying?'

'Oh, no, Mummy, I still love Mario in spite of everything. Now, back to the sorting – look at this beautiful Boho skirt I used to wear with a pair of big hoop earrings and a lacy shawl. I took Flamenco lessons then, learnt to play three chords on the guitar, had loads of boyfriends.'

'Yes, you had them queueing up for a date,' said Mrs Anstruther drily, 'and any man going on a date wonders if he'll get lucky; the woman knows already.'

'OK, Mummy – enough of the wisecracks. Well, I haven't worn this skirt for twenty years, so, into the Oxfam bag it goes – but no, I saw in this month's Vogue that Indian cotton's all the rage again. And by the way, I heard Mario talking in his sleep, calling out 'Shara, Shara' – that must be his fancy woman's name. He must be stupid not to realise I know about her.'

'But my darling, 'Mrs Anstruther said, 'he's just a man, weak and foolish, and when you were silly enough to wed Mario Santangelo you gave up the *attentions* of many for the *inattention* of one! And as I never ever tire of saying, "Love is Blind, Marriage is the Eye-opener".'

'Mummy, you're a cynical old thing. Mario has a very demanding job – we have to make allowances – corporate banking is a real rat-race.'

'Hmm,' Mrs Anstruther snorted. 'The trouble with the rat-race is even if you win it, you're still a rat. Am I right or am I right? *And* he talks too much.'

'No, Mummy, you're wrong there. Mario and I often have companionable silences; in fact some evenings he hardly speaks to me at all.'

'Ye-es, I know,' Mrs Anstruther said. 'Before marriage a man will lay down his life for you – after marriage he won't even lay down his newspaper. Now, what are you going to do with him?'

'We-e-ell, into the Oxfam bag he goes – but no – I cannot sleep alone – I'd be scared at night without him – he keeps me safe.'

'Honestly – are you really my daughter? I did warn you that marriage is the triumph of imagination over intelligence, but would you listen?'

'Oh, Mummy, you can't teach anyone experience – people have to find out for themselves.'

'What rubbish, Nebula – personal experience is the worst teacher. Think about it! You get the test before the lesson.'

'Yes, well, I only wish I had your insight,' said Nebula affectionately.

'You know, Nebula, what I say is: people always admire what they don't understand.' Mrs Anstruther tapped the side of her nose, jangling her slave bangles.

'Oh, do let's crack on, Mummy, it's nearly tea-time. Now, this pair of jeans I've had for years – they're size 8 and I'm a 14. Straight into the Oxfam bag with them – but no – I'll go on a diet. That new cucumber one works wonders, apparently – I read it in Vogue.'

'You'll never stick to it – trust me! Now, what's next?' Mrs Anstruther shook the plastic bag again.

'Oh, Mummy, by the way, I found a letter in girlish handwriting. The fancy woman says she loves him so and can't understand why he comes back home to me, in spite of his promises. But I know why, it's because he knows which side his toast is buttered. So, into the Oxfam bag with him – but no – I cannot let her win – this tug-of-love will keep me strong – now, where's my glass of gin?'

'We haven't got much in the Oxfam bag yet,' remarked Mrs Anstruther. 'Only a pair of stilettos which might fit me, come to think of it. Now, how about this moth-eaten old grey duffel coat. It should be in a museum, if you want my opinion.'

'I know, Mummy, it has been such a friend. But I can still wrap it all around me when I'm feeling sad – it takes me back to my youth. So, keep it out of the Oxfam bag, there's life in the old coat yet.'

'Right ho, darling, whatever you say,' sighed Mrs Anstruther.

Nebula Santangelo glanced at the clock on the bedroom wall and began clearing up. 'Well, that was a useful exercise – I've managed to sort out a few things,' she said, slipping out of her jeans and jumper and selecting a pretty frock to wear. 'I'm glad I was so firm and single-minded; oh, zip me up, please, Mummy.'

Then, pulling off her bandana, she shook out her long hair. 'Quick, where's that pink lipstick – Mario's coming up the drive. I must run to meet him.'

'Oh, Nebula, just wait 'til I tell Auntie Maude what a silly, blind romantic you are – I can just imagine – blah, blah, blahdy blah, she'll say, blah, blah, blah …in no uncertain terms….'.

GEE, WHAT HAPPENED?

I don't believe any man ever loved me for myself. They were in love with my appearance, my persona, the public image. Not even Jim who actually married me when I was fifteen, but only as a favour to keep me out of foster care when Mamma was taken to the insane asylum. He wasn't too put out when I divorced him to take up that photographic assignment during the war.

It was really funny how I got to be a model! What happened was, Jim had joined the marines and I went to work in a factory. One day these photographers came round and picked me out to pose in front of the machinery as part of the war effort. After that, well – gee, what happened? My life changed, that's what happened – for the better? Maybe not.

Because, these days my career is finished, kaput, and I'm only 36 years old. I'm a has-been, I'm all washed-up at 36! My contract has been cancelled – I guess I've been late on set *once* too often, taken *too* many pills: pills to stay awake, pills to sleep, and no film company, let alone 20th Century Ferret, will offer me work with *my* track record and also I hear they're going to sue me. Well, let 'em! Gee – fame is so-o fickle!

Not that I need to make any more movies for the money, oh no! I've earned millions and millions of dollars with my films.

And I've had some high-profile husbands and lovers, hundreds of lovers, men *and* women, but, as I say, not one of them loved me for myself, the real me. All they saw was a sex-symbol. Huh! And this so-called affaire with the Big Cheese's little brother – well, is it an affaire? He could have married me if only he'd had the guts to divorce that baby-factory he's hitched to, but now he's laying down the law, telling me it's too hot to handle, too close for comfort! Seriously, I laid it on the line – threatened I'd blow the lid off the whole goddam thing. How would you like *them* apples, I said! Huh!

And the Big Cheese is refusing to take my calls, after I wished him Happy Birthday in front of the whole world, an'all. He didn't disown me then, did he? I'm a big star – but they treat me like a hooker to be cast off when they get fed up and wanna move on. I will not stand for it! I will not!! I'll make 'em pay even if it means bringing down the government; you see if I don't.

What is it with these guys? The goddam nerve of that loser Peter inviting me over for dinner tonight, and then he tells me he has a whole bevy of young starlets there who want to meet me – more like as entertainment for his male guests! What is it he's planning – a free-for-all? A gang-bang? Who does he think he's talking to? I'm a big star! I've been done with all that stuff years and years ago when I was just a hungry starlet!

Hmm, I've had to take another sleeping pill – to calm me down, y'know. Just cannot relax, cannot get any rest. I've telephoned a few of my friends but they're all busy and Dr Greenson who talked to me for over an hour did not actually offer to come over. I do depend on him so much and I see him every afternoon – he's already been over once today – he's trying to get me off these sleeping pills but he's flogging a dead horse here. Huh!

Sometimes I think I'm going mad, like Mamma did, and I'm terrified of ending up in the asylum for good – but then, insanity is only a frame of mind!

I've told Eunice to get to bed. She's going on vacation tomorrow and I've told her not to bother coming back, but I expect she will as Dr Greenson wants her to carry on as housekeeper, watching me all the time in case I top myself – *ahaha*. As if!!

But it seems I have no choice in anything any more these days because I'm always so goddam tired. They can do just what they like with me and I have to go along with it.

Well, what shall I do with myself? I could play a Sinatra record, remind me of old times up at Cal Neva. I once had a thing for him but it fizzled out like everything else in my life, and anyhow I didn't fancy hanging around with the heavy gang so much, plus he could be slightly mean, when he was drinking. A good singer though, Frankie boy…

Hmm, shame there's no TV in this room, but anyway I hate watching all those old movies, specially the ones I'm in. I can see so many flaws, so many errors, and I hate the way I look. How can they say I'm beautiful, how can they say I can act? I'm supposed to be a "gifted comedienne" for goodness sakes! My gahd, don't they know a dumb broad when they see one? I'm a complete fraud when it comes to looks, acting *and* everything else. I have such a narrow range – I can't sing, can't dance, can't act. But I always had aspirations and felt the *lack* of a good education.

Arthur used to try and educate me, with books and all, but he couldn't stand my bad spelling. I never could spell, although I do read a lot or at least I used to before I moved here. This house is in such a mess what with all the renovations going on and no closets, clothes and things just left on the floor wherever you look.

Y'know, I once had a burning desire to star in a movie of the Brothers Karamazov but it never came off. No-one would back it – the studio system thought it was too intellectual for the image they were trying to promote for me, so I had to make do with lightweight comedies such as Seven Year Itch, Bus Stop, Gentlemen Prefer Blondes, stereotyped crap like that.

That is why I started my own film company with Lee, to make quality movies, but gee, what happened? That idea fizzled out too, just like everything else! I'm a fraud, a dead loss!

I suppose I could pass the time by reading a little but I would rather get some shut-eye – I've hardly slept a wink lately in spite of the pills.

What is it with sleep? I forgot how to do that, *years* ago. Arthur used to say sleep was my *demon*, and, *golly gee*, he was quite correct for once, although actually I did love him for a time, partly because he looks like Abraham Lincoln but mainly for his intellect, hoping some would rub off on me or at least raise my public profile a little which I believe it did, for a time, especially when it came to working with that awful English snob, Sir Larry.

Anyway, enough of all that – hmm, let's see what selection of goodies I have here on the night-table. It looks like a candy store – pots and pots of bright yellow Nembutals, boxes of chloral hydrates, such a vivid green, plus a few others I'm not keen on.

Eunice tried to get me to take these herbal remedies but they're useless compared with a handful of Nembutals! Huh! That Eunice, she's a spy, that's what she is, keeping her eye on me – in case I try to commit suicide indeed – huh, my gahd – as if!

Now which shall I take – think I'll have just a couple more of these and an extra three or four of those… so, goodnight all, goodnight Norma Jeane – sweet dreams – with a diddly diddly diddly dum – boop boop a doop!

COOL

I have never been married, but I told them all I was divorced so they wouldn't think there was something wrong with me.

I had met the Bellchambers in Italy that summer, having gone on holiday alone as usual, hoping to meet a man, knowing there would be guided tours and suchlike; but Max and Pandora Bellchamber had immediately adopted me and made it their business to take me with them on trips out, insisting I sat at their table for meals, buying my drinks, introducing me to new acquaintances and generally treating me as one of their own.

I was grateful for the company and their evident kindness and generosity, especially as there were no attractive males on the tour apart, that is, from Max Bellchamber himself.

The couple were not obviously pushy, their organisational skills were extremely subtle and done in a bright and breezy way, but it gradually became apparent that I never did have any say in their daily plans.

They told me they ran an hotel in Quagmire Village somewhere in the West Country and asked for my contact details as they would like to keep in touch after the holiday. This I took with a pinch of salt as holiday friendships hardly ever survive, in my experience.

It was towards the end of our stay, one evening on the balcony overlooking the Bay of Naples with David Bowie's "There's a star man waiting in the sky…" playing softly in the background: Max put his arms around me and kissed me full and lingeringly on the lips.

'Vera, I've been wanting to do that all this past fortnight,' he whispered when we came up for air. 'You're adorable and I have plans for you, do you know that, my darling?'

'Oh Max, what about Pandora,' I gasped, nonplussed, but reeling from the effects of his embrace.

'Don't worry about her,' he said nuzzling my neck. 'Pandora is cool.'

After that, I melted in his presence and, looking back over the previous few days, tried to find some hint of his intentions, regretting that I had not made more effort to be alone with him. We never managed to be on our own after that one occasion but I could tell by his body-language that he wanted me.

When the holiday came to an end, I was heartbroken. I felt that our little episode had been all in my imagination and there was really little hope of seeing Max again, although he winked at me when we parted and said he would be in touch.

But the glow stayed with me and I could think of nothing else but Max Bellchamber and longed to be in his arms again, to feel the hardness of his body against my soft flesh, the taste of his mouth on my lips. I thought of writing to him or telephoning the hotel, but did not. I lived in a state of rapturous remembering.

Once, the strains of "There's a star man…" came wafting from a neighbour's open window – and I was right there, back on the balcony over looking the Bay of Naples in Max's arms. He was my star man all right! I'd never felt like this about anyone before.

Then about six weeks later, I received a telephone call from Pandora Bellchamber inviting me to come and stay in their hotel for a weekend house-party. 'We have lots of room, and normally I'd ask you to bring a pal, but we already have equal numbers of chaps and girls coming,' she said, laughing. 'We want to keep things on an equal footing, don't we, Vera darling?'

She sounded very friendly, but surely Max had told her about me, about his affection for me, about his plans for us. Hopefully Max had come clean and asked Pandora for a divorce. Of course, we would still be friends afterwards: Pandora would always be more than welcome to come and stay with Max and me after we were married.

Came the day, I set off early on my two hour train journey, and Max met me at Quorum Thisbé station, as previously arranged.

He greeted me with a bear hug and, picking up my suitcase, propelled me towards his car. 'We have some treats arranged for this weekend,' he explained, grinning sideways at me. 'I hope you're in the mood.'

I began to feel nervous and wondered why he had not mentioned our kiss nor begun to expand on his plans for us, or whether he had told his wife after all.

On our arrival at The Quagmire Inn, I was welcomed by Pandora who introduced me to the other guests. 'Four chaps, four chapesses,' she beamed, 'all divorced at one time or another although some of us have married again – what the cynics would call the triumph of hope over experience!'

Oh dear, I thought – perhaps I shouldn't have lied about being previously married! Perhaps that was the criterion for being a part of their exclusive clique!

The female guests smiled and nodded at me, and then carried on with their chat. They looked very glamorous indeed – one woman wore gold lamé, another one wore black velvet, and I felt like a dowdy frump in my tweed skirt and cashmere jumper.

The male guests were more interested in my arrival and greeted me effusively. 'We like to see a new face at our little gatherings,' they chirruped. One guest, Ralph Grimstone, made a beeline for me. 'Dear lady, allow me to get you a cup of coffee,' he said with a gleaming smile, guiding me towards the buffet, one hand under my elbow.

'Ralph, leave Vera alone, I saw her first,' laughed Max. My goodness, I had never had such attention from the male species before. I began to glow...

Another guest, Edouard Godolphin, joined our little knot by the groaning table. 'You're like a breath of fresh air,' he whispered, his hand on my back. 'How I love the country look in a woman for a change – so sweet, so natural.'

The only male guest who did not make overtures was one Arthur Spume, a severely plain, grey-faced man who merely nodded sternly and offered his stiff hand on being introduced.

The afternoon was spent by the river which ran along the bottom of the garden. Max and Pandora took pains in ensuring all their guests were entertained and tea was served at four o'clock by a very handsome waiter named Luigi who twinkled boyishly as he handed me my cup and plate.

At dinner, I sat between Max and Arthur Spume, a man of very few words and little wit and who, as it turned out, was a lately-retired undertaker with an unfortunate odour of formaldehyde still clinging about his person. I decided to avoid him as much as possible over the weekend.

After dinner, we played cards and Scrabble, neither of which I am any good at. All through the proceedings I kept looking longingly at Max. He returned my gaze with an impish smile and put one finger meaningly to his lips. I took that to mean that our secret would soon be revealed and he would announce to the assembled guests our plans for a future together at the Quagmire Inn without Pandora.

About ten o'clock that evening, Max stood up and tapped the table. 'Attention, please, folks. I have a little surprise for our special guest, Vera. I wonder if anyone can guess her real name? No, no, it's not Veronica. Any more offers?'

I froze in my chair. How embarrassing! How on earth had he found out my full name?

As if he had heard my thoughts, he turned to me and explained, 'I saw your details in the hotel register in Italy. Why do you keep it such a secret, a wonderful name like that?' Then turning to the others, he added, 'Listen folks, I'll let you out of your misery – Vera's real name is Guinevere, and tonight I have invited Arthur to be her partner for the weekend. Please raise your glasses and toast King Arthur and Queen Guinevere!'

A great cheer went up as Arthur reached out for my hand and kissed it with cold, dry lips. 'My queen,' he said, stony-faced. 'Please allow me to escort you up the wooden stairs to Bedfordshire, or should that be Camelot.'

I was horrified and terrified but, not wanting to let Max down, I allowed Arthur Spume to lead me by the hand, meek as a lamb, towards the staircase, accompanied by the sound of Max's voice booming in the background, 'There you are, folks – I told you Vera was one of us – she's cool!'

JOHN, NICK AND LARRY

The first time I saw Nicholas, I knew I should never have been so eager to get engaged to John, but, when John had to go to Australia for a month is when we promised to forsake all others, just to make ourselves feel more sort of secure.

Up to that point, John was the only boy I could ever have imagined actually being married to, and then Nicholas appeared on the scene.

I have been engaged before – about six or seven times I suppose it must be, but of course I never intended to, like, marry any of them, not until I met John, that is.

Those other times, the boys were quite stupid really; they pestered me to death and wouldn't go home until I agreed to say I was forever theirs and admit that we were engaged.

I would hate to be called a flirt, which is why I eventually went along with their wishes. I never had a ring or anything because we were all quite young, about fifteen when it all, like, started.

Now I'm older (I shall be, like, eighteen next birthday), I think it only fair I should make it a stipulation that, in future, any betrothal should involve a diamond solitaire being placed upon my finger – apart from John, that is, because this trip to Australia is costing his parents a fortune and they said they couldn't spare anything extra for trivial fripperies like "mere love tokens".

My mother says I'm boy-crazy, lad-mad, obsessed, and I ought to, like, have my head examined, but what is she on about because I know for a fact she got married at the age of nineteen, although she looks much older in the black and white wedding photographs. She says things were, like, different then, but has never bothered to explain how.

Yes, I was so devastated when John sailed away to Oz that my Auntie Beatrice offered to bring me here to Quagmire Village for three weeks, out of sight of my parents who say I am driving them to, like, distraction. This Quagmire Inn is a nice hotel, but I was so miserable without John: it was almost as bad as having him here, because we do argue quite a lot actually, mostly about silly things, like, for instance, about what we'll call our children when we're married. I want one of each, Joyce and Melvin, but Jack wants four, Charles, Arabella, Kevin and Caroline. Apart from us liking different names, I tell him in no uncertain terms that having babies is not as easy as, like, falling off a log, y'know.

Anyway, at dinner here the first night, there was a table opposite ours with two young men. One of them, Nicholas, kept looking over at me. The other chap, oh, I forget his name; well, *he* was sort of staring at me also –

143

but he wasn't at all handsome, not in the least, so I shall not waste any more words on him, thank you very much.

Well, anyway, the next day, Nicholas was quite bold and asked Auntie Beatrice if he could take me to lunch. Auntie Beatrice shaped her face into an expression of sarcastic relief as if she was actually glad I intended being unfaithful to John! Hmm! Nicholas's friend – umm, I forget his name – tagged along with us at first but Nick had a quiet word in his ear and he sort of disappeared. I was so pleased...

Nick's travel tales were absolutely enthralling that I listened to over lunch and afterwards walking by the river. Apparently he's been sort of all over the world. And also he's full of those "Knock knock, who's there" jokes and had me in stitches most of the time. He said he adored me already and would love to take me with him on his next holiday trip, which will be to the United States of America followed by Brazil and Argentina! Fancy! I didn't bother to bring John into our conversation as I thought it would spoil the loveliness of the moment.

After that wonderful first week when we really got to know each other and never argued about anything, Nick had to go home, back to his parents who live in Kent. He bought me a silver chain necklace and said that, as we are now engaged, he would write to me every day and he really has kept his word. All these passionate letters he sends me are lovely although very badly written – full of punctuation and spelling mistakes. But he must be quite intelligent really because next term he is going to study English at Oxford or somewhere and then be a teacher or something.

During the second week of my stay, when I was feeling more depressed than ever, missing my two fiancés terribly and wondering how I was going to deal with the situation, there was a new boy sitting at an adjacent table with his parents.

I stared at him non-stop until he came over, bowed politely, and asked if he knew me at all, as I looked very familiar to him.

Auntie Beatrice heaved a great sigh and asked him to, like, sit at our table: it turned out that the young man's name was Larry.

Well, the time flew after that as Larry whizzed me around in his sports car. We visited lots of, like, beauty spots and he bought me a gorgeous sparkly bracelet; I'm sure it's real and not fake. He's obviously a very spoilt rich boy, evidently used to getting his own way with his parents who you can tell dote on him excessively. His father owns some factories or something similar in the north although I have only a vague idea where that is. I'm certain that Larry will go far in life and I don't just mean, like, around the world. He is a divine dancer, too – he can do ballroom and jive. I don't think John and Nick can dance, not that I've sort of noticed anyway.

When Larry placed the bracelet around my wrist he said surely I'd guessed we were now engaged as that constituted a betrothal gift because people usually exchanged presents on such occasions. I gave him an almost-clean lace-edged hanky which I happened to have in my handbag at the time. He said the lipstick smudges made it all the more personal as coming from me, his betrothed fiancée.

Then he explained that his parents would be sure to agree that I was the most beautiful girl they'd ever seen, and that a diamond solitaire would soon be placed upon my finger. It was a breathtaking moment!

Well, what's a girl to do? I have been really and truly swept off my feet, but it now appears that I have, like, three fiancés to occupy my mind.

And now, in this, the third week of my holiday, Larry has gone home to his parents' mansion in Surrey. He telephones me each and every evening, declaring his undying love. I have desperate, heart-wrenching telegrams arriving from John all the way from Australia, in addition to the passionate letters arriving every morning from Nick. All three of my fiancés say that my every wish is their command and that they will wait for me forever if necessary, as long as I promise to marry them one day. But I do love them all equally, for very different reasons!!!

So, I've written a list of pros and cons, as follows:

a)   John wants children but can't dance and has no sense of humour;

b)   Nicholas is very witty, loves travelling but probably would never want to settle down;

c)   Larry is not at all witty, and I'm not sure he'd make a good family man as he's too interested in making money, but he is rich, an excellent dancer and a very good kisser.

I've thought and wondered about which one to choose!   And now I've reached some sort of, like, compromise.   I shall invite all three of them to dinner next week when John is back from Oz, and tell them very lovingly that I shall always remain friends with each and every one of them and then announce my decision, which is as follows:

Firstly, get married to Larry: we can go dancing every night and he can buy me jewels and nice clothes etc.   After five years when the thrill has gone, we could get divorced.

Then I'll marry Nick who can keep me in fits of laughter and take me to all the places in the world that he's, like, already visited.   That should last another five years before we outgrow each other (I'll probably be bored stiff with all his "Knock knock" jokes by then, anyway, but sshh, keep that under your hat).

By then I shall still be only 28 years old, young enough to have a family with John but definitely too long in the tooth to go dancing and flitting around the world.

Yes, it is a brilliantly sensible compromise, and I am absolutely certain all three of my fiancés will jump at it rather than, like, lose me forever!

Phew!   Problem solved!

COLD FEET

By some quirk of fate, Jemima and Kenneth were left looking into each other's eyes at the inter-college dance. Immediately smitten, Jemima began to chat charmingly to the youth, and he responded in kind. He liked the comforting feeling of being flattered outrageously and began to think that maybe there was more to the girl than at first met the eye.

Not that Jemima was unattractive; she was perhaps a bit plain, merely lacking a certain something, hadn't found her own style yet at the age of eighteen.

Similarly, and in spite of his apparently relaxed responses, Kenneth felt awkward, but the attentions of this girl boosted his confidence no end and he began to relax into the adulation heaped upon his head, plus he could imagine that this immediate attraction could well end up as his very first love affair.

To these young people, being in love was very important: they were in love with the idea of love, but the fact they were at different colleges meant their meetings were few and far between.

And so they kept in touch by letter, pouring out their passionate feelings to each other on a daily basis. At times, Kenneth convinced himself he was a prince amongst lovers, and the longing to take the girl in his arms was almost a physical affliction.

Jemima, though, was a romantic. She did not require the physical nearness of the beloved in order to be happy. In fact, she preferred the anticipation of dreaming her dreams, inventing outrageous scenarios of an idyllic life together where they lived in a castle with many servants and two perfect children. Her favourite pastime was retiring to bed early "to think" as she described it to Anna, her room-mate, who had already run out of patience.

'I wish I'd never introduced you two,' Anna would groan, watching her friend languishing in a haze of unrealistic castles in the air.

During the holidays, Jemima and Kenneth would meet, at first under the watchful eye of their families, and, after a respectable period of time, allowed to go out unchaperoned to various events. Kenneth, however, preferred walking in the woods and, once out of sight of other people, he would take Jemima in his arms, his body clinging to hers in unconsummated rapture.

Jemima, on the other hand, was never too fond of kissing and she was always the first to break free.

'Look, Jemima, you do realise this is making me crazy, don't you?' Kenneth would moan, time after time. 'Don't you realise that love without possession is love unfulfilled? This is nothing more than a platonic relationship.'

'Oh, don't let's talk about that, Kenneth,' Jemima would reply lightly, offering him a toffee. 'Let's talk about after we're married, where we will live and what children we'll have. What do you think, dearest?'

'What I think is we should go away to a hotel for the night. No-one need know. Our parents trust us now. Wouldn't you like that, Jemima?'

'Oh, don't spoil things with all that stuff, Kenneth. We're still very young, you know, although I feel quite grown-up these days. But I do want to save myself for marriage, don't you? I know – shall we get engaged? I've got this diamond ring my grandmother left me and if you place it on my finger we will actually become legally committed to each other – it's a proper binding contract and everything. If you break it off I can sue you for breach of contract. That should make you feel a whole lot better as you will know I am yours and no-one else's.'

'Oh, OK, let's get engaged then if it'll make you feel more inclined to… I mean, if it makes you feel more secure. But please remember we're not living in the dark ages; after all, it is 1955 and all my friends have, have – well, you know…'

'Well, that's them, this is us – we'll come to each other pure and untouched. It's more romantic that way, like in those Barbara Cartland novels.'

'Barbara who???' Kenneth frowned.

Jemima tutted affectionately at such ignorance!

In the event, they became engaged in secret and, as a plot to keep it from their parents, Jemima wore her grandmother's ring on a chain around her neck during the holidays, only putting it on her finger when she was back at college and could show it off and brag about her fiancé to anyone who would listen.

Kenneth spent hours at the library researching love-making techniques and then practising for long hours on his own.

He began to neglect his studies, was unable to eat or sleep, and recounted endlessly these sad events in ever more passionate terms through his daily letters to Jemima, his beloved.

Then one day in his despair he presented her with a fait accompli.

'I have booked us in at the Royal Pier Hotel in Brighton,' he wrote. 'Just for one night on the 31st July. I hope you won't let me down and I promise you won't regret it, dearest darling. After all, we are engaged to be married.'

At this, Jemima confided in Anna who said, half-jokingly, 'Oh for goodness sake, sleep with him and have done with it – I'm sick of hearing about Kenneth this, Kenneth that, and should we or should we not!'

'Right-ho, I will,' her friend squealed in a state of high excitement and immediately replied to Kenneth agreeing to a night of love at Brighton as long as she could bring Archibald, her teddy bear.

'Anything, anything, dearest darling,' he wrote back. 'Just imagine, soon we will be one.'

Kenneth borrowed a car and they met surreptitiously, having told their parents a tangled web of complicated lies.

As they approached the white buildings of Brighton the chemistry between them was palpable, Jemima suddenly as full of desire as Kenneth. 'Goodbye to my girlhood,' she kept saying.

As soon as they entered their hotel suite Jemima threw herself bodily at Kenneth who held her off gently.

'Not like that, Jemima,' he said. 'I've read up on this, and we have to take it slowly – anticipation is the key to satisfaction.'

'What on earth does that mean?' asked his dearest darling, a bit crossly.

'We'll enjoy it all the more if we take things one at a time – let's savour the moment,' Kenneth soothed. 'Think of our bodies as sacred – we must prepare them, we should go down to the beach – ritually cleanse our bodies, have a leisurely swim before dinner and then we'll have the whole evening to explore each other, only I don't want to rush anything and spoil it.'

'Yes, dearest,' Jemima replied, misty-eyed. 'You're right, of course, and so sweet. Let's put our swimming cozzies on under our clothes – come on then, bags I the bathroom – but first, kiss Archibald bye-bye – he'll have to stay behind because he does so hate getting his little paws wet.'

Kenneth solemnly kissed the teddy bear, and ten minutes later they were on the beach where they flung off their clothes and sandals and ran into the sea.

Both were strong swimmers and raced each other to the buoy and back, then went running back up the beach where they threw themselves onto the damp sand, Jemima gasping and giggling, and Kenneth thinking how lucky he was to have met such a wonderful girl so early on, an enthusiastic, beautiful girl he could spend the rest of his life with.

'Isn't this just heaven, dearest,' moaned Jemima ecstatically, 'I cannot wait to be a real woman. Perhaps we could do it right here on the beach now the sun's going down and then we can do it again after dinner and then all evening and all through the night.'

But Kenneth did not answer.

He was staring at Jemima's bare feet, the first time he had seen them without footwear of any kind. A feeling of icy revulsion swept over him, and he wondered how he had ever persuaded himself he desired her.

Jemima heard the silence and sat up suddenly. 'What on earth's the matter, Kenneth? You look as if you've seen a ghost or something. What is it, what on earth's wrong?'

'Oh, n-nothing,' he stammered. 'Look, it's no good, it was all a mistake, bringing you here. I can't ask you to go through with it.'

'But don't be silly, dearest – I want to go through with it, I really do. Here and now if you like.'

'No,' he said, 'I'm sorry, we'd better go home before things go any further. Let's pack up and get out of here as soon as possible.'

In the midst of his confusion, he was thankful to have instinctively allowed her to believe he had her interests at heart...

God, what a relief, he thought, what an escape – please let her go on believing I'm some sort of hero.

They drove back to the sound of Jemima's suppressed sobs and intermittent half-questions, which hung on the air unanswered.

Never again, thought Kenneth, his face granite-grim as he squinted through the windscreen. In future he would have to insist on seeing a girl stark naked before jumping in at the deep end.

And he saw again in his mind's eye Jemima's feet. For the girl had bony, finger-like toes, toes that were long – too long, it seemed, for love.

BRIDAL VEIL

Just look at this headdress – it keeps slipping down over one eye – any number of pins won't hold it in place. I shouldn't have washed my hair so much – it's limp as an old rag. I'm a stupid girl, a silly Milly. Oh, what a complete nightmare! Aargh!

But I do wish Sandy would turn up and help me. That's her duty – she *is* chief bridesmaid when all's said and done – actually, she's the only bridesmaid, and should really be referred to as the matron of honour out of respect, being a married lady herself, although they don't get on too well at present, Sandy and Stan; he's a rotter to her, apparently, is Stan. Shame because Sandy is a lovely woman. She's a bit scared of what Stan will do next – it's only natural. He cannot be trusted, by all accounts. What a nightmare!

Gosh, how I wish she'd be more punctual, today of all days – it's pushing things a bit, time-wise, particularly as she'll have to get changed into her finery as well. Such a nightmare! I mean, it's not every day her best friend gets married.

No good asking Mum to do anything useful – sitting downstairs, a bag of nerves, just smoking and

fidgeting, picking her nails. Oh, she's as thin as a rail –
got even thinner recently. Well, it isn't every day your
only child ties the knot for the first time, is it? She
thought I was definitely on the shelf at my time of life.
Only natural, I suppose.

Then, six months ago (is it only six months?), I
met my Graham at Sandy's birthday party and things
changed for the better. He was looking a bit bored,
actually, standing by the window drinking beer and
smoking one of those horrible stinky cigarettes, just
watching everyone mingling, with a funny look on his
face actually but, when Sandy did her matchmaking
duties and introduced me as "Milly, her unattached best
friend from work", he looked deep into my eyes, straight
into my soul, he did, and said my name, "Milly" he said,
and I just went – oooh – and my two legs turned to jelly.

He made a joke about such a lovely girl (me)
being single, and we roared, we did. After that, he stayed
by my side all evening – couldn't do enough for me,
keeping my drink topped up (although I only have
orange juice – my poor tummy won't tolerate alcohol,
you see), offering me cigarettes (although I don't smoke,
never have) and even coaxing me to get up and jive, but
I was a lot fatter then and don't dance anyway – terrible
vertigo and no sense of rhythm, me – so we just sat there
chatting.

He was OK about it, didn't mind at all and was
very easy to talk to, wanted to know about my job at the
bank, and all about my flat, how long I'd lived there,

whether I had a mortgage on it, were my parents still alive, did I go abroad for my holidays, stuff that most men would find pretty boring. He was lovely. I fell in love with him right there and then.

I told him the usual background stuff, and added that I *had* been abroad quite a few times. He asked me where I'd been abroad and I said, 'Oh, all over'. And his reply was, 'What? Especially to all over?' Oh, he's so witty. We roared, we did.

But he kidded me on that he didn't like my name – he said it didn't suit me and was far too old fashioned for a trendy bird like me! We roared, we did.

So he started calling me Milly Molly Mandy – it was so funny, an absolute scream. Then as the weeks went on, it gradually got shortened to Mandy, then Mand, then Muh..., although now, I don't think he calls me anything at all. He says he'll soon start referring to me as Mrs Sheepshank, which is, actually, his surname, and which he hates, and so, trying to chivvy him up, I said, 'Cheer up chicken; beauty is in the eye of the beholder.'

That didn't seem to convince him, so maybe I should have said "beauty is in the ear of the listener" but he'd gone quiet again and started doing a roll-up, so I thought it better not to disturb him.

Oh, I've gone off on a tandem now...I've digressed.   But did you know, all the women's magazines I ever read tell you not to talk about yourself – try to draw the other person out, get them chatting. So when I first met Graham at Sandy's party, I made a point of asking what he did, where he lived and that, but he always managed to turn the conversation back to me – only going to show what a considerate man he is, wanting to make me feel the centre of attention. He is quite a bit younger, though – more Sandy's age. My toy boy! It just goes to show. You never can tell. *Un-be-lieve-able!*

'Course, recently he's been a bit, hmm, down in the dumps. No amount of chivvying, tickling, teasing will get him out of it. I suppose he's only worried about the wedding, whether things will go off OK. It's only natural.

I do wish he'd get a job, though. That's the only fly on the horizon, as the saying goes. He has promised to try harder when we're married, and I continue to be supportive, always reminding him, getting him to look through the papers, going down the Job Centre in my lunch-hour to scan the new vacancies in case he forgets to go. His memory is terrible. Such a nightmare it is, at times, trying to get him to remember stuff.

Same as with those awful cigarettes he smokes, they have a very sickly sweet smell. I wish he'd give them up. They make his breath smell terrible. And his clothes, all niffing something shocking. I have mentioned as much, on occasion, but it falls on deaf ears. Honestly, men – who'd have 'em! Hmm!

He does roll his own cigarettes, as I may have already mentioned. Says it's cheaper, but I'm not sure about that. He seems to need more pocket money each week, but I don't begrudge it because he gives so much back to me in other ways. Graham is such a sweetie – most of the time.

Anyway, you have to be pretty quick off the mark, being a jobseeker, as all the best ones go very quickly. I've told him of quite a few new adverts, sometimes calling him on the phone at home to save time and then, when he applies, even the same day, they've already gone. Nightmare, really, trying to get back into the job market when you've been out of work two or three years. The employers simply don't want to know. They always have some excuse for turning him down even on the rare occasions he gets an interview. It doesn't seem very fair when someone is willing to do a good day's work.

He's left his council bedsit now – he moved out months ago and shifted all his stuff into my flat when I added his name to the deeds – well, we are married, or as near as dammit. He always says "why pay the landlord out of my benefit when I can live with you for free and pocket the rent money".

You see, I think he's told the Benefits Agency I'm charging him rent, more than he was paying before, which is a bit naughty of him, especially as he is now joint owner of the flat and isn't actually paying any rent! He thinks it's a bit of a scream, diddling the Benefits people, but I'm not too happy about that. What can I say? It's a bit of a nightmare, really!

I forgot to mention my beautiful cat Heidi. Graham hates Heidi, says he cannot abide domestic pets, even a pedigree Persian like her, but I'm sure he'll learn to love her once we're married. Everyone else adores Heidi. Graham did once threaten to sell her, as she is obviously a very valuable animal, but I'm sure he was only teasing me, the naughty boy.

He did promise to redecorate the flat before the wedding, but started saying things like, "what's the good of going to all that expense and effort just to have the flat smelling of cat again". But you'd think with time on his hands and nothing to do all day he could show willing, but he hasn't even made a start – well, tell a lie – he did call at B & Q for some colour charts, to be fair, but that's as far as it went.

Not that I've stayed at the flat since he moved in. Heidi and I are back home with Mum, pro tem, only five minutes away round the corner. It was my choice to come back home, partly because Mum loves Heidi so much, and having the cat to cuddle is good for her poor nerves, but also because I don't want to tempt Graham's baser instincts by being alone with him before we're married. He is just a man, after all. It's only natural lust, I realise that. I know what men are like – I read women's magazines and watch the soaps! I like my soaps, I do.

Also, and I don't like mentioning this, I did see Graham catching Heidi up the behind with his toe the other week. She maiowed something shocking and shot out of the room, the poor little moggie. I didn't dare say anything to Graham because he most likely caught her up the rear end by accident: yes, I'm pretty sure it was an accident, but, all the same, it did strangely depress me for a couple of days. Then I snapped out of it as I feel confident things will work out once we're married. We'll be just like a little family, the three of us, Graham, Milly and Heidi. I only hope Graham will look after Heidi between jobseeking whilst I'm out at work.

I'm not actually worried unduly about money because I do have a very good position with the bank – been there since I left school thirty years ago. Good pension pot mounting up, too. So, no money worries – for the foreseeable future, anyway. Graham'll probably lose some of his benefits, of course, once we're married, but two can live as cheaply as one, isn't that what they say? I just want to make Graham a good wife, look after him, and that.

Because – well, he had a terrible childhood, poor boy. His father just went out one day, set off for the bookies and never came home. I'm sure Graham won't mind me telling you all this.

It's his mother, really, she's a right slag, dog-rough, always to be found propping the bar up at The Akimbo Arms – goes off with any man (or woman) who'll buy her a Gin and It. She's not fussy. That sort of caper. Nightmare, really! I know Graham is very sensitive about his mother – but he calls her Eva, he won't call her Mum or Mother – Eva, yes Eva. It doesn't seem right somehow, not natural at all…

We saw her once, in The Market Tavern actually – we never go near The Akimbo Arms for obvious reasons – and Graham stood stock still, jaw twitching, gripped my arm so hard it left a bruise, turned me round and marched me straight out again. Bit of a nightmare, really. It took him a couple of hours, three pints of lager and three of those foul roll-ups to calm down again, but then he fell asleep on Mum's settee, so at least he was out of his misery for a while.

Later on, I could hear him throwing up in the downstairs lavvy, poor chap. You can't help feeling sorry for him with such an awful family background and keep on running into Eva.

Yes, as I say, Graham's had a terrible life, which is why I forgave him for going through my handbag that time. He said he was looking for some stamps, but he had my credit card in his hand. He threw it back into the bag but I had actually seen it in his hand. I didn't say anything, just gave him a book of stamps, but that month a cash withdrawal of £250 appeared on my statement, which of course must have ended up in Graham's pocket. I still didn't mention it to him, didn't want to embarrass the poor bloke. After that, I made sure my handbag wasn't left lying around, and changed my pin number the very same day.

I don't think Mum is all that keen on Graham, tell the truth. She hasn't spoken above a dozen words to him in the past three months. Just sits there fidgeting and smoking, picking her nails. You'd think she'd be happy for me, getting off the shelf at last. She's a total nightmare!

It could be that Mum didn't approve of me adding Graham's name to the deeds. But I said to her, *I may as well – we are getting married,* but she wouldn't look at me. Graham didn't force me to change the deeds, it was my idea – yes, I'm quite sure it was.

Gran gets on better with Graham. Forces him to speak to her, she does. Yes, Gran's a game old bird. Such a good sense of humour. We roar, we do.

But I don't think she's too happy about Sandy being a bridesmaid, well, matron of honour, I should say. Gran says Sandy avoids all eye contact. I think she means Sandy can't be trusted, but I said to her, I said "I wouldn't have met Graham if Sandy hadn't been nice enough to introduce us".

And Stan, that's Sandy's husband, he was going to be best man, but ducked out weeks ago. Graham says a part-time barman from The Akimbo Arms will do the honours, but it doesn't seem right to me. A nightmare scenario, and that's the truth! Still, Sandy will be happier without Stan hanging around looking daggers. So it should be a marvellous day, taking it all round. Oh, look at the clock, I just wish she'd turn up.

Oh no, this headdress is slipping again. And these satin high-heeled shoes are killing me – what a pain and a total waste of time – they don't even match my dress even though Frilly Frocks-4-U assured me they would dye to the exact shade – what a load of rubbish – they'll tell you anything to get the business. They're not even an approximation.

Plus, this corset will be the death of me – I can scarcely breathe. Talk about a follower of fashion – that's yours truly to a T. How did they manage in olden times? Beats me. Even skivvies wore corsets below stairs for doing the meanest labouring jobs in the scullery. There was no let-up whatsoever in the corset-wearing department.

And no knickers, apparently – they didn't wear knickers in olden times before the war. I read that in a book.

Well, back to now! I suppose this is it. My big day. A leap into the unknown. Was it, I think, maybe Marty Wilde or some other pop singer who said, erm, "the triumph of hope over inflation" or was it "the unspeakable in pursuit of the uneatable" – anyway, something on those lines, all about marriage, or maybe another subject entirely? I forget. It doesn't matter.

But I've got my Graham to look forward to – a whole lifetime together after we get through this rigmarole. But the family wanted it – all this fuss is for my folks, not us. I'd prefer to slip away, elope – yes – climb down a ladder and run away together. What an adventure that would have been. I say "would have been" because Graham wanted me to elope – he suggested it and was dead keen on the idea, but I rejected it out of hand. I told him straight - *what a thought, no way José* – and he didn't mention it again. Sandy agreed with

Graham though. She said if she loved a man enough and he wanted to elope, she'd go like a shot, no messing. I said *you go then*, and she roared, she did. I told Graham what Sandy had said, and what I'd said, and we roared, we did. Then he got a faraway look in his eyes. *A penny for your thoughts*, I said, but he just glared and went quiet. I must have spoilt his daydream of us going off together without telling anyone.

Oh, bless - he loves me so much, he wanted to hold that image a bit longer. But I always worry when I hear of people eloping – trying to work out how they get the girl's suitcase down the ladder without her falling and breaking a leg or something.

Silly, the things that make you anxious, isn't it? I could worry for England, I could. Anyway, I'd be far too heavy for climbing out of windows, although I have managed to lose some weight to get into this frock. Graham prefers me slimmer, although he liked me fatter as well otherwise we'd never have got engaged.

Yes, I'll have Graham all to myself later on. Although I am a bit nervous over the, you know, erm, physical aspect of things. I'm not really sure what I'm expected to do. Graham will know though. He's a man of the world, so he says, but I'd like to know who he's practised on, because it certainly wasn't me. He won't tell me, even though I've teased him rotten. We roar, we do – he's such a laugh.

He's tried it on a few times, though – well, more than a few, actually, but I've usually been chewing gum or crunching an apple or a sweet. I nearly choked once when he tried to kiss me, and I swallowed a gobstopper whole. I'd only just put it in my mouth a minute or so previous to that, you see, so it was still quite large, and how it went down my food pipe I'll never know. I could easily have died if it had got stuck or gone down the wrong way.

Oh, that was a shock to my system, and I screamed blue murder, I did. Graham was shaken up too. He went very quiet and his jaw started twitching, like it does when he's upset or when I mention the Job Centre or his mother.

But it just goes to show how much he loves me, worrying I might have choked to death before his very eyes.

Now where's that Sandy girl got to? Ah, there she is, I can see her through the window – she's standing by the gate with – oh, it's Graham in his new suit. They're kissing – gosh, I'm glad they're such good friends; and now Graham is giving her the thumbs up and heading towards his van.

Oh, I see – he must have given her a lift – how strange: Sandy lives miles away. I wonder what mischief they're planning for later? They're a real scream, the pair of them! They make me die!

Well, Sandy's frock is hanging in the wardrobe, ready to slip on; I hope it still fits her because she does seem to have put on a little weight lately although I'd never, ever mention it to her.

And here she comes, here comes the girl, pounding up the stairs like a baby elephant – she makes me die, she does!

Hey Sandy, you're late! Mr Pickersgill will be here soon with the taxi! And for goodness sakes, can I have some help with this damned veil?

NEW YEAR'S EVE 2015
(had technological progress not happened)

'Look sharp, darling, Mr & Mrs Cronkinghorn will be here; in fact they're already overdue. I hope they're not waiting at that bus stop – it's so confusing when there's no such thing as a bus.' Mrs Drystone wore her long-suffering face as she crouched over the central fire, stirring a pot of vegetables and lizard-meat with a piece of human thigh-bone.

'Coming, my love – just finishing off this bit of woodwork,' replied Mr Drystone. 'Anyway, the Cronkinghorns are probably coming by dog-sled, although the rough terrain between Quorum Thisbé and here can be quite hazardous. They should never have moved so far away from Quagmire Village – their round-house next-door was quite adequate for a couple with fifteen children. It doesn't do to be so snobbish; people should be content with what they've already got, don't you think, dear?'

'Yes, too true, Desmond,' his wife responded, blowing him a kiss then wiping her nose on a rawhide sleeve. 'Anyway, what is it you're carving day in, day out? I wish you'd go hunting more often instead – I may have to slaughter the pet pig – our measly stock of meat won't last much longer, and it's already crawling with loads of maggots.'

'Oh, just ignore the wriggling creatures, my sweet,' her husband frowned. 'They do augment one's protein intake, and the kids love playing with them – it's an ill-wind and all that.'

Mrs Drystone loped across the earthen floor to her beloved. 'So, what is it you're making out of that fallen tree? It resembles a flat disc. Are you trying to copy the shape of the sun, or maybe the moon? We don't want to incur the gods' anger, you know.'

Mr Drystone ceased in mid-whittle and looked up. 'Melinda my darling, this could revolutionise everyday life. One of these shapes placed under a dog sled would facilitate easier movement over rocky ground – we could call it a "whee" or something; I might make you a spinning whee, as well.'

'Oh, and pray what's that when it's at home, Mr Clever-clogs?'

'It's a device enabling the spinning of wool and cotton – stuff like that. Then of course I'd need to invent a weaving loom to join all the threads together and you could sew garments out of the resultant bolts of material. I can see it all now! And you could knit the wool into items of clothing, sweaters, scarves, bobble hats and suchlike. Knitting needles could be fashioned out of bone. Make your life a lot easier, my dear.' His face glowed beneath a lifetime of ingrained dirt.

'It would be nice not to have to skin all these animals when we have twelve kids to clothe, especially as the flint scraper is usually too blunt to get all the fatty gunk off,' his lady wife said dreamily, casually squashing a mouse with her calloused foot and slinging it into the pot with a satisfying splash. 'But it's all pie in the sky, it'll never catch on. F'rinstance, this shape wouldn't work under the dog-sled on its own; it might require four sun-shapes, one at each corner. I bet you hadn't thought of that design fault, my dearest.'

'Oh, such intelligence is wasted in a lady,' her spouse smiled fondly. 'I shall have to work on that one. Right, I'm downing tools for today, and how is the supper coming along? Do we have enough roots and berries for pudding? Arabella Cronkinghorn is very partial to those, being a bit of a hippie, and I suspect she'd prefer a veggie diet, if truth were told, but of course that would entail starving to death in no time at all. Shall I get the eating utensils out for you, or is it fingers tonight? The kids will be ravenous by now.'

'Well, dearest, you were too engrossed to notice the children have already eaten and gone to bed. It's to be an intimate firelight finger-buffet for four. I've laid out fresh moss to sit on although it's still rather damp and, oops, I hear them coming now! Is my hair tidy; do I need more woad?'

'Oh, vanity, thy name is woman – you look gorgeous, as always,' laughed Desmond Drystone scrabbling towards the entrance where he greeted Mr

Cronkinghorn. 'Tarquin, you old bugger, me old mate, how the devil are you?' he chortled, pretending to box. 'Better late than never.'

'Dammit, yes, I do apologise for my tardiness,' beamed Tarquin, 'I stood at that bus stop for ages before I remembered that buses haven't been invented yet. Silly me, I had to go back home for the dog-sled.'

'We thought as much, you dopey old sod. And where is Mrs Cronkinghorn this New Year's Eve? Isn't she coming?'

Tarquin Cronkinghorn paused, then laughed. 'Oh, you mean Arabella? No – she was injured trying to skin a wild boar – only it wasn't quite dead yet and, to be frank, it was furious – went absolutely berserk. She was a game girl, though, got up and fought back but, naturally, she succumbed to the animal's superior strength – so I had to finish her off, put her out of her misery, so to speak – a form of legal euthanasia, it was. Didn't you get my message? I sent it by cleft stick.'

'No!' chuckled his friend, 'we never received it, perhaps the messenger died on the way – because Life, as we know, is nasty, brutish and short.' Desmond paused, then smiled. 'Drink, Tarquin? What would you like, brackish water or verdigris wine? As you're driving, I can recommend the brackish – an impertinent little beverage with an interesting aftertaste, particularly with a splash of slime juice.'

'Thank you! I'll try the brackish and slime, if I may – it sounds very refreshing, just the job!'

'Do you miss not having Arabella around the house?' twittered Melinda Drystone.

'Nah, not really,' Tarquin replied. 'After all, she'd had a good innings, must have been all of 32 – although it was hard to tell under that mud and woad, all those feathers and furs.'

'Well, it was obvious she was older than you, but who will do all the heavy work now she's gone?' Mrs Drystone enquired, not being a woman who could easily be put off.

'Oh, no worries on that score! I got myself another wife the following day: I went over to Quagville market and caught a youngish one, although, there again, it's hard to tell: she piles on the woad and loves her tattoos and big earrings, that sort of caper, but she's very strong and the kids adore her. She's waiting outside. You can call her Gloop; yes, that's her name – I think – well as far as I can tell.'

'Don't leave her out in the cold,' huffed Melinda, loping out to fetch the girl, graciously leading her in by a mud-caked hand. 'Come along, Mrs Cronkinghorn – I'm Melinda Drystone, this is my husband Desmond Drystone, and what would you like to drink?'

'Urk, glug,' growled Gloop, grimacing into the smoky interior.

'She's rather shy,' offered Tarquin, fondly, 'and, to be honest, she's probably one sandwich short of a picnic, but her heart's in the right place, and that's what counts, especially with the kids. Now, may I propose a toast? Here's to a happy and healthy 2015 and may all our troubles be *more* little ones!'

'Hear, hear,' chirped Melinda and Desmond Drystone, raising their clay bowls.

'Urk, glug,' vouchsafed Gloop, sinking her face into the pig's trough in the corner and guzzling deeply. 'Urk, gurgle, gurgle, urk, glug, glug!'

'Oh, the little imp,' crooned Tarquin Cronkinghorn. 'That is so sweet of her: she's wishing us all a Happy New Year.'

TEN BELOW

So far, I had staunchly declined all recommendations from well-meaning friends but, one day, when I happened to be feeling particularly bored, Persephone telephoned me from the dating agency where she reigns supreme as the Big Boss. 'Geoffrey describes himself as witty, intelligent and artistic,' she drooled, 'and, in return, his only stipulation is for a woman aged 35 and slim which you are – well, your age is right on the button, so one out of two ain't bad, and he won't notice your cute love handles if you wear that body-skimming cardigan I got you for Christmas, so – go along and enjoy yourself.'

Although the cardigan was a size sixteen, mentally I was a size ten and, therefore, just as a favour to Persephone and get her off my back, I went along fairly confidently on my blind date.

Geoffrey and I met at The Akimbo Arms. Taking the pipe out of his mouth, he greeted me with "nice to see you, to see you, nice" – then chirped "walk this way" as he led me with an exaggerated limp to the table, before indicating my chair with a theatrical flourish.

He ordered a bottle of champagne to accompany his T-bone steak and my chargrilled trout. 'One man's meat is another girl's *poisson,'* Geoffrey remarked engagingly, pointing at my fish. I laughed politely whilst deciding the man wasn't at all bad looking although not handsome in the usual way, but he owned an interesting face which was decorated with a well-trimmed vandyke. I like a beard especially on a man who smokes a pipe.

He stared at me a lot, which I took to be complimentary. After the first flurry, the evening cruised along fairly well in spite of a torrent of clichés and catchphrases. I began to long for those shyly petering-out awkward smiles and sentences which usually occur during this type of encounter. I wondered where all his wit and intelligence might be hiding – I could see he was artistic by his facial hair, but still, the relationship should have been over at the end of the meal when he began patting his pockets. 'I didn't get where I am today by carrying money,' he said, before laughingly going on to explain he had left his credit cards and cash in his other jacket and could I please pay for the food and his taxi fare home.

Well, what was a girl do? As I was settling the bill, trying to think of a tactful way to tell him to get out of my life forever and never come back, I thought, oh well, it's probably his artistic temperament making him a bit absent-minded, and seeing as how I'm probably in need of male company after two years in the doldrums, any old port in a storm will suffice.

The lovemaking was better than nothing, I suppose – all twenty seconds of it. His idea of foreplay was reaching for the ashtray on the bedside table to deposit his still-burning pipe. But then, it was comforting to have the physical contact, however swift, and he didn't seem to notice my cute love-handles or my spare tyre at all – which was nice…

Geoffrey worked in journalism and had his own apartment, but he suggested shacking up at my place explaining that "two could live as cheaply as one" and he could rent his flat to some friends who would "pay through the nose" each month, thereby allowing us to lead the "life of Riley" together. Although I had no idea who Riley was, it seemed to make sense and he moved his belongings into my house pretty damn quick!

I wouldn't say he was fight-fisted because occasionally he would throw a few fivers on the bed, remarking "that's for your trouble, my dear" and laughing uproariously at his own distasteful joke.

Of course a few quid now and again wasn't nearly enough to cover his share of the outgoings, not to mention his expensive taste in food. Geoffrey would say "easy come, easy go" before adding that he was having cash flow problems, i.e. extracting the rent from his tenants. He kept promising to go round and "read the riot act" to them and no messing.

I was all my fault really. I should have laid down some ground rules at the outset.

But each time I mentioned the matter of finance all I got by way of reply was "money doesn't grow on trees". Similarly when he came home late, I would quiz him about where he'd been and why on earth hadn't he let me know.

"Oh, I didn't expect the Spanish Inquisition" he would laugh by way of reply, and go on to explain that "hush my mouth, I've been on a top-secret assignment for the paper, so I can't tell you any more than that, unfortunately – you'll just have to trust me". Sometimes he was on a top-secret assignment all night.

I had never met his friends and wondered whether he was ashamed of me. One day I heard him on the telephone mentioning something about "my little lady is a perfect ten". Oh, how sweet, I thought, and I loved him a bit more after that although I couldn't help thinking what an idiot he was not to have noticed my love handles.

Then I had a sudden brainwave and decided to help him out. I called round to his apartment and rang the doorbell.

A very pretty blonde girl, her hair done in corn-rows, answered the door but she looked perplexed when I asked why the rent had not been paid.

'You must have the wrong address,' she said, looking down her aquiline nose. 'This flat isn't rented, it's owned – by me: I'm the owner.'

I knew for sure it was the right place and asked the girl who was living there. 'If you must know,' she sighed, 'I live here alone since I kicked my boyfriend out. I'm sure you've made a mistake. Goodbye.' And she closed the door in my face.

I knocked again and the girl opened the door. 'Is your boyfriend's name Geoffrey by any chance?' I demanded, an idea having sprung fully-formed in my suspicious brain.

'Ex-boyfriend, if you don't mind,' she snapped. 'Anyway, what's it to you?'

I said, 'I suppose he calls you his perfect ten?'

She smirked unpleasantly. 'Yes, when he tries to get me to take him back, which is often. Oh, I see, you must be his "minus ten"! Well, how funny; he's told me all about your love-handles. And now I really have to go. Goodbye.' And she closed the door abruptly.

"Minus Ten" eh? "Love-handles" eh?" The ratbag, the filthy beast!

He'd been using me all along, him and his fur-lined duffel coat, his patchy beard and rancid pipe, and the uncanny ability to remember every imagined wrong I'd ever done, like not pressing his shirts correctly or over-boiling his egg and burning the toast. What a fool I'd been, signing away twelve months of single blessedness to a living hell of clichés!

As I made my way back through a sudden blizzard, I knew what I had to do. By the time I reached home the snow had fallen four inches deep, perfect conditions for my plan.

I locked the front door from the inside, quickly packed up Geoffrey's clothes, then sat and waited.

Pretty soon, he turned up and tried his latchkey in the lock. After a few moments of unsuccessful struggling, he called through the letterbox. 'Hey, babe – the door's locked. Can you let me in, it's snowing out here – I had to leave my car at the station and walk.'

I did not respond but continued to sit and wait, allowing him to suffer as much as possible.

'Hey, baby, can you come and unlock the door – I can see the light on...'

Still I offered no response as I slowly climbed the stairs and approached the bedroom window.

Then he began rattling the letterbox. 'Hey, babe – what's up? Let me in – I know you're in there.'

After a couple more minutes of pleading, he began banging on the door. 'Look, you gotta let me in, it must be ten below out here...'

I opened the bedroom window and leant out over the snowy sill to see his silly hirsute face looking upwards. 'Ten below?' I screeched. 'Don't you mean "minus ten", eh?'

'Well, whatever you want to call it, babe, it's bloody cold out here.'

'Let's call it "minus ten" then, shall we, Geoffrey? Because that sounds a trifle familiar to me! Doesn't it sound familiar to you?'

'Eh? Wha...'? Aw look, babe, let me in and I'll explain everything. I'm freezing to death out here.'

'Freezing, are you?' I squawked in a most unladylike manner.

'Yes, babe, I am! It's brass monkeys out here,' he moaned. 'Please open the door, please let me in and I promise on my mother's dying death bed that I'll make it up to you; it's all been a terrible mistake, honestly, it really has, babe.'

'Well, I'm not totally heartless,' I soothed in a kind and gentle tone, 'so here's your fur-lined duffel coat to keep you warm, but, dear me, what a shame, it seems to have lost its sleeves – oops, dearie me, I remember now – I must have cut them off by sheer accident.'

I slung his tattered duffel coat out of the window and it landed on his head. 'Now, get your ass off my property,' I screamed, 'and go back to your skinny Perfect Ten and perhaps she'll help you find the rest of your clothes – here's a hint, try the charity shops – oh, and for your information, you're the worst lay I've ever had, so put that in your filthy pipe and smoke it!'

I slammed the window shut, plugged into my iPod and settled down in front of the fire with a lovely big box of dark chocolates and a bottle of wine.

Men! Who needs 'em?

SWEET REVENGE

I knew Geraldine Meadowlark only vaguely as a casual acquaintance, occasionally encountered at social events or in the cafeteria at Craker & Frencham's Department Store in Quorum Thisbé High Street. Geraldine worked in "ladies' modes", whereas I was employed in the accounts office, which is where I met my husband Julian who later became Managing Director of the company.

Geraldine and I had never actually spoken before, had never even met over a cup of tea, but still I was not surprised to hear her voice on the telephone inviting me out for a drink at The Quagmire Inn that evening. She sounded excited, unlike the cool, self-controlled woman normally presented to the public. I suspected she was requiring my advice on matters of the heart as I am known at Craker & Frencham for being a fount of knowledge and a pillar of respectability, very often consulted for advice by various employees on an unofficial basis.

It does help that I am in admin, and not on the shop floor, and that I am the MD's wife and also First

Aid Officer, a post which involves attending annual refresher courses on the subject. And, naturally, I often have to bring my innate psychological insight into play when dealing with people's problems.

Of course, I accepted the invitation, more out of curiosity than any great desire to help, if the truth be known, because I had never considered Geraldine Meadowlark to be a likeable woman or someone who would make a loyal friend.

So there I was that evening at a table in the bar of The Quagmire Inn toying with my glass of iced water when Geraldine swished in. She scanned the room, saw me, smiled, and came teetering over on her designer killer heels.

'Oh, Mrs Spreadbury, you should have let me get you your drink,' she said, all concern. 'What is it, a large gin? I know you like a drop or three.'

'Goodness, no – it's not gin, and it didn't cost me a penny – it's tap water,' I replied, forcing a polite smile at what I assumed was an attempt at repartee, albeit a trifle impertinent and misjudged considering we were mere acquaintances and I was the wife of the MD.

Geraldine nodded. 'Aha, yes, I hear you are very economical,' she said.

Very economical! What did she mean by that? Surely colleagues haven't been gossiping that I'm mean, because I'm *not* mean. I give my time and experience freely to people who need advice: but I let it pass, as I am famous for being calm, patient and reasonable.

'Well, Miss Meadowlark, how can I help you?' I said, once she was settled comfortably at the table with her double brandy.

'Oh, please, call me Geraldine,' she began, her face unsmiling, smooth and wrinkle-free.

I left her invitation hanging on the air, and after a pause she continued in an emotionless voice, 'I'm sorry if it comes as a bolt out of the blue, Mrs Spreadbury, but Julian and I are in love.'

My first response was to laugh, thereby disguising mixed feelings of shock and relief. 'What? Is this some kind of joke? If it is, I don't think much to it. You realise that Julian, I mean Mr Spreadbury, is Managing Director, don't you? It won't go down well if I report you to the board of directors.'

'Ah, but it was Julian who suggested I tell you,' she said, smiling sympathetically. 'In fact, he's afraid of your tantrums, of what you'd do to him if he dared to tell you himself.'

Something about the woman's attitude was sincere as if she thought she was telling the truth. I thought for a moment or two before asking her what else he'd told her about me apart from my liking gin, being economical and having fits of temper.

'Oh, I know all about you wanting to carry on working instead of being a housewife and homemaker. Julian thinks every woman should give up work if she's married to a man at the top of his profession. I know you can't have children, but that wouldn't bother me as I can't stand kids either and I'm sure I can persuade Julian to give up *that* idea. He'd do anything to make me happy and it's the only thing we disagree on.'

I was remembering how Julian and I had originally decided not to have children and that recently he'd been moaning on about regretting it. And now I was in my late forties and most likely past my biological limit. Obviously, this Geraldine Meadowlark was still in her early thirties and still viable for a successful pregnancy or two or three!

'What Julian wanted me to say was he needs a divorce so we can get married and I'll give up work to make a proper home for him.'

All I could think to say was 'oh!' but my brain was whirring non-stop in my head.

'Yes,' she continued, fiddling with the diamond ring on her engagement finger, 'he's so generous is Julian, he says you can have the house, and actually when you get home tonight he'll have moved his stuff out, which is why he asked me to get you out of his way and onto neutral ground for a couple of hours. Of course, we'll buy a lovely new penthouse apartment when the dust has settled although Julian says he'd prefer another house but, as I said, he'll do anything to make me happy so I think I've won that battle before it's begun!'

She tilted her head and her heavily madeup face began to crack slightly in an indication of satisfaction.

While the woman was rambling on and on about their plans for an ecstatically rosy future together and how she admired me for being so very reasonable over the whole thing, I was thinking of the times Julian had come home drunk from board meetings or even straight from work if he'd been to a business lunch that had gone on all afternoon.

And I was well aware how tight-fisted he was, too, which is why I continued working so that I could have my own money, because he would never agree to a joint bank account. And how, if I did have to ask for extra housekeeping to pay the bills, he would fly off the handle and rage at me on and on ad infinitum for being such a silly spendthrift: *When will you learn how to manage your finances, you stupid woman – keeping a rein on your household spending can't be that difficult, and where on earth have you put my clean socks?*

My whole life seemed to pass before my eyes as memories flooded in. There were the times Julian complained bitterly because I spent far too much time and effort on colleagues and friends than I did on him.

Then there was the sex, or lack of it. He'd never been a passionate man although he was quick to accuse me of being frigid.

I thought quickly. 'Yes, you're right, Geraldine! Julian never wanted any children and I'm sure he still doesn't. You'll be quite safe on that score. And yes, I'm ashamed to say I've given him a hard time on many an occasion what with my drinking and foul moods.'

'Don't forget your meanness and lack of affection, as well, Mrs Spreadbury! Poor, poor Julian –

he says it's ruined his life. But, oh, my lord, he'll murder me for telling you all this. He insisted that I should be very tactful, gentle and discreet with you, but I never could keep a secret, although he doesn't know that yet. It takes a long time to get to know someone properly.'

'Yes, it does,' I said. 'I think you'll find that love makes fools of us all.'

'Oh, now,' the tart replied, 'you're just fighting to keep your man, trying to put me off, which I can, of course, understand. I'm sorry, Mrs Spreadbury – I do realise I'm taking your husband away but you will get to keep Mandrake Lodge which must be worth nigh on a million – yes, I have seen *all* round your lovely house including the master bedroom, if you know what I mean – Julian took me there several times when you were on various seminars – and, of course, you've still got your interesting career which, I understand, you put before everything else.'

'I cannot deny that,' I said, thinking this woman must be quite mad to be taken in by Julian's twist on the truth and that, in all honesty, they probably deserve each other when all's said and done.

'And Julian says you can keep your present job,' the woman continued. 'Please don't think you have to hand in your notice and move on. He says you are very welcome to keep your job at Craker & Frencham for as long as you wish.'

'Well, that is most generous of him – of you both,' I replied, managing a stiff little smile. 'I would prefer to stay on: that is, if it's not going to embarrass either one of you two lovebirds.'

'Oh, you are such a darling! I really have to congratulate you on your frankness and lack of bitterness,' the woman continued, through ruby red lips. 'I admire you immensely and I hope we can remain friends, maybe meet for a drink when this is all done and dusted and over with.'

'Well, how kind. I'd absolutely love that,' I lied. 'And may I wish you all the best for the future? Please tell Julian there's no need to be afraid of me any more, and tell him I'm sorry for all the hurt I've caused him. If he doesn't want to see me, I quite understand, and we can do everything through our lawyers.'

'My Gahd, I never thought it would be this easy,' the poor, misguided female replied, rambling on and on, while all I could think was, *when a woman steals your husband, there's no sweeter revenge than to let her keep him.*

PLAY-TIME

A ghost of a smile played around Mrs Frobisher's lips: she nodded at the other villagers gathered around a large refectory table in a room off Quagmire Village hall.

'Yes, I'd be delighted to stand aside this time,' she said, straightfaced. 'The stage manager position will be a welcome change for me.'

'I'm glad you've taken it so well, Veronique,' simpered Margery Seligman from the depths of her verger's robes with slung leather belt. 'After all we must be kind and let someone else have a turn at leading lady, mustn't we – ha ha?'

'Of course we must; it's essential we keep our beloved AmDram on a democratic footing,' Veronique Frobisher purred in reply, exercising her cool self-control. 'And I'm so pleased the committee have chosen Zinnia, although I do wonder how she will make time with all her other duties at the surgery.'

'But Mrs Frobisher,' whined Zinnia, 'Freddie, I mean Dr Frobisher, has already given his permission for me to have some evenings off for rehearsals…'

The doctor's wife looked askance at the young upstart stealing the leading role. 'Oh, has he now…?'

'But Veronique,' interjected Margery Seligman hastily, 'we would like you to be understudy, of course, so you're not entirely off the hook. You'll have to attend rehearsals and be au fait with the script and then, as stage manager, you'll shoulder the added responsibility of doing all the sound effects – there seems to be quite a number of them in Ralph's play, bless him – you do like giving us lots to think about, don't you, Ralph? There's a pebbly beach noise during Zinnia's soliloquy when she's harking back to the idyllic holiday in Brighton, there's glaring sunlight going into total darkness for the eclipse scene (a lot of electrical stuff for you to get to grips with there, Veronique, and perhaps dear Max could help you with that) and also the torrentially heavy rain scene when the lovers are trapped inside without so much as a raincoat or umbrella between them. Then there are the props to organise, the tennis racquet, motorbike goggles, bunch of flowers, one cigarette in a case, a box of matches and a jug of water plus two drinking glasses. And also the French windows must open at a touch, no sticking at the crucial moment. Yes, yes, your duties will be quite onerous, I fear, my dear Veronique.'

'Oh, how you people work me,' the doctor's wife simpered indulgently. 'Well, I shall take the manuscript and go on my way rejoicing – I have the Annual Flower Show to organise too, you know. So – let's say I'll do my very best to see you all here on Tuesday evening, 7.30 sharp.' And out swept the doctor's proud wife, trailing an overpowering backdraft of Chanel No. 5.

As soon as the door had closed behind her, the other villagers grimaced and shrugged at each other. 'My God, what an absolute cow – she's livid not being chosen for leading lady,' said Zinnia.

'Serve her right,' screeched Margery, 'she can't have everything her own way all of the time: Dr Frobisher spoils her utterly.'

'Why, what has the dear lady done to offend?' asked Ralph Grimstone, baring his large teeth at the assembled thespians, at a loss to understand all the goings-on. 'She always did a very good job at playing the leading lady.'

'Ah, but your play is rather special, Ralph,' rejoined Eve Wildgoose, 'and I'm afraid hoity toity Veronique Frobisher is getting rather too rich in years to play the romantic lead especially opposite Sebastian who is young enough to be her son, so san fairy ann to her.'

'Oh, Eve,' said Jackie Clack admiringly, 'I didn't know you could speak French – is there no end to your talents? Go on, say something else in French…'

And so the rehearsals began, at first fitfully and then, after two or three weeks, in earnest.

Those Quagmire stalwarts, Dorcas Gorringe, Jocasta Fontenoy, Max and Pandora Bellchamber of The Quagmire Inn, Dorothea Loomis, and even Dorinda and Percival Catchpole, the fairly vulgar landlord and landlady of The Akimbo Arms, gave their all to Ralph Grimstone's script. Abigail Drysdale, the local soothsayer, would be providing a short guitar accompaniment to a romantic interlude in Act II, just before the total eclipse scene.

Mrs Frobisher drove herself harder than the others. She learned the script by heart, organised Max's help with the electrics and even gave advice on the costumes, much to Jackie Clack's annoyance.

'*I've* been designated Wardrobe Mistress,' the young woman complained to Margery Seligman. 'Can't she keep her nose out of my pie; she always has to be involved in everything.'

'Well, in spite of your mixed metaphor, I have to agree with you, my dear,' remarked the lady verger, smoothing her long robe and adjusting her slung leather belt. 'But just use your tact, nod your head and smile at La Frobisher, and then do your own thing.'

The said La Frobisher worked especially hard on her own costumes as understudy. Her dresses were far more elaborate than those created for the leading lady, but nobody said anything as no-one wished to rock the boat at this stage of the proceedings.

Ralph Grimstone's play, entitled "Total Eclipse of the Heart" was a 1920s drawing-room comedy murder mystery in two acts with many a twist and turn, resolving, fairly unsatisfactorily, by the curtain. As the playwright was fond of proclaiming "comedy is normality gone askew".

The dress rehearsal went smoothly and was a great success. The French windows opened beautifully as Sebastian entered with his racquet, crying "anyone for tennis?"; the heroine's cigarette was lit perfectly on cue; a bunch of flowers rested in the right place, ready to be presented with a flourish by the hero; and a jug of water stood on the table ready to be decanted into one of the glasses. The sound and lighting effects went like a perfect dream.

The whole cast and production team were ecstatic in their praise for the doctor's lady and her stage management skills.

'Oh, think nothing of it,' she purred, delicately shimmying her understudy flapper dress and patting her neatly shingled wig. 'It comes easily to a person of my organisational abilities – let us hope it goes as well on the first night.'

As reported by Desmond Bullivant in the arts section of the weekend Quorum Thisbé Times, Mayor Coldspring and his lady wife, town councillors and other dignitaries attended the first night of Ralph Grimstone's play, taking their seats amidst a hushed expectancy before witnessing the collapse of the leading lady onstage after one puff of her cigarette only ten minutes into Act One.

At first the audience believed it was part of the plot and began to applaud but, when the curtain was hastily rung down, Margery Seligman appeared onstage to explain that, as Zinnia Peterkin had unfortunately been taken ill, unused as she was to inhaling tobacco smoke, the show would continue in five minutes' time with the company's understudy Mrs Frobisher in the leading role.

Desmond Bullivant went on to sing the praises of Mrs Frobisher, how wonderfully well she played the ingénue in spite of her more mature years, with clever comedic timing followed by such depths of feeling and sincerity that the audience were moved from uproarious laughter to heartbroken sobs in the blink of an eye. "Bathos" was mentioned several times. He did wonder whether the leading lady was improvising her own lines as the rest of the cast seemed at a loss most of the time but it could, of course, have merely been astonishment at Mrs Frobisher's artistic aplomb in the main female role.

In any event, he suggested that Veronique Frobisher's name should be credited alongside that of the playwright, and further expanded that the lady could easily have had success on the West End stage as an actress or writer if she had not decided to dedicate her life to assisting her doctor husband in administering to the sick, the old and the infirm in Quagmire Village. "Full many a flower is born to blush unseen…" was quoted as an allegory.

After the successful four-night run, Veronique Frobisher announced during the after-show party that she had already begun writing next year's play with herself in the main role as a twenty-two year old scientist who saves the world from certain oblivion, and she thanked Zinnia for her brave effort in getting up off her sickbed in order to watch the final performance and attend the onstage party, with a severe warning for her never ever to take up smoking as a pastime.

Later that evening when Dr and Mrs Frobisher were at last in their own home enjoying a nightcap, the lady, still sporting her jewel-encrusted flapper dress and sequinned skullcap, looked over at her husband and said simply, 'Thank you, darling.'

Freddie Frobisher gazed lovingly at his wife. 'Oh, it was nothing!' he murmured. 'It's an easy matter to incapacitate a person for a few days without doing them lasting damage! And if the girl hadn't inhaled that cigarette, there was always the drugged glass of water that would have put her out for the count.'

'You're so clever, darling Freddie,' the lady smiled. 'But just one thing more: we must invite Desmond Bullivant to dinner again, he'll be useful for next year's production, although I disliked being described as "mature"! Methinks you should have a word with him on that particular point.'

'I'd do anything to keep you happy, my dearest darling, you know that – now, put that martini down, come over here and thank me properly!'

STAIRCASE TO PARADISE

Reuben had the lean and hungry look of a Victorian parson, with his square-cut beard, black suit and preacher's hat, shiny with age. But he was in fact a poet, a self-proclaimed one, as only rarely did he ever sell any poems, and then only to those obscure literary journals with very small circulations. Even so, he seemed reluctant to part with his work, believing that earning money from his writing was immoral and amounted to commercialism.

He also deemed it immoral to accept any paid work nor would he sign on at the labour exchange for unemployment benefit. 'Money should be abolished and everyone survive by bartering,' he often pronounced.

His home was a shabby one-room flat over the Green Dolphin Antiquarian Bookshop in Soho where he occasionally helped out the owner, Mr Fish, in lieu of paying any rent.

I first caught sight of Reuben there as I searched for a first edition in connection with my work, and was immediately enthralled by this cadaverous, dark figure wrapped in an aura of spiritual intensity.

He looked up and saw me staring and, upon his command "come with me", I found myself climbing the three flights of bare wooden stairs to his flat under the eaves, drinking tap water and listening as he accompanied himself on the Spanish guitar whilst reciting a passionate love poem.

Yes, I really truly believed I had died and gone straight to Paradise.

He prevailed upon me to move in with him, which I did with all speed, against my parents' wishes. He also insisted I left my job at the library. 'All ownership is theft, Thelma,' he warned,' and that includes payment for work; oh, and by the way, I can't keep calling you Thelma – from now on, thou shalt be known as Mary.'

My family believed we had a relationship based on lust, but the truth was I remained his chaste mistress.

'We're above all that, Mary,' he would intone, holding me off if ever I approached him. 'We have a meeting of minds, our relationship is on a higher plane based on mutual respect.'

My parents, on being assured of this, were nonplussed, remarking he was even stranger than they had at first imagined!

Embracing wholeheartedly the bohemian life, I took to wearing threadbare plum velvet and left my long hair unwashed. I looked up to Reuben and hung on his every word like the rest of his followers. I felt honoured and blessed at having been singled out to share his life.

It was so romantic, starving in a garret – during the summer months at least, but in the depths of winter we were cold and hungry and really *would* have starved had it not been for the Berwick Street Market costers anxious to off-load unsold stock as they dismantled their striped awnings at the end of the day's trading.

'We're doing them a favour, taking it off their hands,' Reuben would say, carrying armfuls of rotting fruit and vegetables back to our attic.

'I'll get a little job,' I said tentatively as the prospect of yet another winter fast approached. 'The money will buy us some luxuries, like proper food and heating, for instance'.

'You're my luxury, you're my muse,' he moaned. 'I cannot write without you by my side. But I do not like to see those generous hips and rosy cheeks disappearing, so yes, you may do a few hours a week if you can find a suitable position – but only on one condition.'

'I'm glad you're not angry, Reuben,' I replied, 'because I acted without your permission. I've already been offered a job at Il Latino Coffee Bar, just washing up, clearing tables, that kind of thing, you know. Erm, what was the one condition?'

Reuben smiled that secret smile, his eyes brilliant in their deep dark sockets. 'I knew about your job-offer – you cannot keep secrets from me. And the condition is that you don't accept any cash, only food. Tell Guido what I said. He'd be mad not to agree. And as for winter heating, we have our inner warmth – it's mind over matter, my dear Mary.'

And so I went to work for three hours each evening for Guido at Il Latino Coffee Bar.

It was pleasant to have a change of scene, somewhere warm, new people to engage with.

But each night I would rush home to Reuben, up the three flights of dusty stairs to Paradise, where my beloved would be waiting, with a new poem to make my heart sing as I sat at his feet adoring him before emptying out my raffia bag full of bread, cheese, ends of salami, ripe tomatoes, lettuce and even the occasional tin of coffee powder which kind Guido had provided, all in lieu of payment.

Life was free from care, on an even keel, and Reuben and I were very happy together for quite a long while until the day a bombshell dropped out of the blue to spoil our bliss.

Mr Fish, our landlord, ruefully shaking his head under thinning grey hair, broke the news that he would soon be retiring and had already sold the premises to a property company who would charge us a nominal rent plus electricity from the following month: a tenancy agreement had already been prepared.

I wondered aloud to Reuben how we would meet the monthly rental of £10, but all he said was that God would provide.

As time went on, it became quite obvious to me that he had never given a thought to paying any rent, the electricity bill was ignored, and we were reduced to living by candlelight when darkness fell.

After several months of written warnings, we received a Notice to Quit advising us the date on which to expect eviction unless the sum of £60 was forthcoming. Reuben gravely announced he could not expect me to suffer for his art, to continue sharing his poverty, and we would have to part for the time being. He said I should return to my parents' home and hope they would keep me, at least on a temporary basis.

In my despair I confided my sad tale to Guido who immediately produced the sum of £200 which comprised unpaid earnings he had saved on my behalf. *'Assumere questo* – take thees, *cara mia,*' he said. *'Quell'uomo,* he loco, eh? that crazy guy – *niente, finito* – I give you job, eh? *Si,* waitress, and more! *Capisco?*'

'No, Guido, it's you who doesn't capisco, I mean, understand,' I sobbed, 'Reuben isn't loco, he's a genius, he needs me, I'm his muse.'

And it was very reluctantly, in equal measures of gratitude, sadness and relief, that I took the proffered cash from Guido's warm hands.

Then, because I knew Reuben would never accept my earnings, I handed the whole £200 to the new landlords, thus clearing the arrears and settling in advance any charges for the foreseeable future.

I obtained a receipt in Reuben's name and placed it in an envelope with a note written in a disguised hand saying "from a disciple". I left the envelope in Reuben's locked wire letterbox on the top landing and, later on, I saw it had gone.

I looked for some sign, some change in his manner now that we were saved from eviction and need not part after all, but he remained the same intense poet, agonising over his writing and bemoaning the fact that we would be forced to go our separate ways in just a very few days' time.

He helped me pack my few belongings and still no mention was made of the receipt.

He said he'd pawned his guitar to pay for my ticket home, whilst he himself intended to hitch-hike to Cornwall to stay with some literary friends. But I knew this was his little game.

Of course, I realised he was keeping his news about the receipt until the very last moment, when, believing me to be anxiously anticipating the bailiffs' imminent arrival, he would laughingly announce his surprise, i.e. the arrears had been paid off a week ago and we could stay together after all!

So, the day of eviction dawned and he insisted I should leave before the unpleasantness began.

He carried my luggage down the three flights of stairs from Paradise and escorted me to the nearby taxi rank on Shaftesbury Avenue.

'Victoria Station, please, cabbie,' he said, and then turning to me, murmured, 'I won't come with you – prolonged goodbyes are too painful, but I'll write very soon.' He kissed me on the cheek...

Then it was I inwardly acknowledged the true state of affairs, I knew my moment of revelation had come, but I hesitated and let it go. I could not embarrass him to such a degree; I could not ruin his life by revealing I was the anonymous donor fully aware of his actions (or that I knew his real name was Melvin Sludge). For people will readily accept lies – but honesty shocks!

Reuben waved as the taxicab drew away from the kerb, and the driver half-turned, growling over his shoulder, 'Victoria! That right, Miss?'

'No, not Victoria,' I replied, leaning forward urgently. 'I've changed my mind. Just take me round the corner, to Old Compton Street – to Il Latino.'

SUCH A GOOD GIRL

I was born lucky. Lucky Lucia, that's me! My parents are doting and indulgent, and all through life I've wanted for nothing. School blouses had monogrammed lapels, and the name-tapes sewn inside my clothes were embroidered at Harrods. I had my very own hockey stick and tennis racquet in spite of being useless at games but my parents said it was good to be bad at sports as it proved I was ladylike and not ill-bred like the other girls.

We were not rich by any means and we lived in an ordinary house in an ordinary street. But my parents wanted the best for me. They scrimped and saved, and every summer holiday we went abroad, and in the Christmas break they took me to Switzerland. None of my classmates had such mind-broadening experiences as seeing the Matterhorn up close or marvelling at the wonders of Herculaneum or The Alhambra at Granada.

But being the object of others' envy did not worry me unduly as I was secure in the love of my parents. 'Just ignore them, Lucia, they're only jealous,' they would say, lovingly.

I was also fortunate in being born beautiful. My hair is blonde, thick and lustrous, my eyes glow like luminous sapphires and I am tall and slim, a perfect 10. People used to say I should be a model but Mummy and Daddy had other ideas and insisted I stay on at school and study hard for university.

But I was never the academic type. When I failed to achieve even one O-level my resourceful parents said it was good to be bad at exams as it proved I was honest and anyone could pass if they crammed or cheated.

They immediately paid for me to attend Pitman's Secretarial College where I managed to stay the course in spite of being terrible at spelling and punctuation. My parents said it was good to be bad at written English as it proved I was too high-minded to worry about unimportant technicalities.

And all this time I had never had much contact with the opposite sex. My all-girls' school and then secretarial college had Christmas parties and dances where boys were invited but on those occasions my parents invariably arranged to take me to the theatre or the opera. By the way, I was named for Donizetti's Lucia di Lammermoor, and I loved the mad scene at the end where she comes on with her bloody nightdress: it was my favourite bit; it always made me laugh!

As I said, I was discouraged from meeting boys. 'It's best to stay away from young chaps – they're rough creatures,' explained Daddy, who should know, as I believe he was a boy himself once.

'You'll have plenty of time for that kind of thing later,' Mummy said, before going on to say I should avoid being unduly influenced by my classmates who appeared very common.

'Vulgar trollops, the lot of them, plastered with lipstick and mascara,' she would say in disgust. 'You're such a beautiful girl, Lucia, precious baby – just be your own person.'

And of course I never did need makeup to enhance nature: my eyes are naturally lilac-lidded, with eyebrows well-marked and very dark in contrast to my luxuriant golden hair.

When the time came to leave college with minimum qualifications, my parents helped me to fill in countless job application forms.

Sometimes I was asked to attend for interview, but was always disappointed at the outcome, and for a long time all I received were rejection letters.

'Oh, don't worry, my precious,' Mummy would say. 'I didn't like them either, and we wouldn't want you to take just anything.'

Then, came the day when I was offered an interview at Bleasdale & Associates. I begged to be allowed to attend alone – just this once. My parents reluctantly agreed although they still insisted on waiting outside in the car.

This particular company appeared to be a one-man insurance agency and the eponymous Mr Bleasdale with his rosy, kind, middle-aged face sat behind a large mahogany desk, peering over his half-moon spectacles and swinging from side to side in his director's chair.

'Oh, a Pitman's girl, I see! I take it you can type?' he beamed, peering over his half-moon spectacles at me. Before I could reply, he added, 'When can you start? Next Monday OK?'

My parents were very pleased I'd landed a job all on my own, and on such a short interview too! They praised me to the skies for my interpersonal skills, and the three of us went out to dinner that evening.

'Well, our precious baby is turning into a career woman,' my mother crowed, beaming proudly. 'Such a good girl deserves an extra special treat, so tomorrow we're going to town, buy you some new outfits for the office – skirts and tops and jackets, mix and match, you know – we can't have people saying you ever wear the same thing two days running.'

My first week at work went by in a whirl with Mr Bleasdale overlooking my many mistakes and, in fact, praising me to the skies and generally being like a second father towards me, making the coffee, buying cakes and even retyping my work.

I was so lucky! He obviously believed it was good to be bad at things, too.

As time went on, he took an interest in my welfare. 'And what were you up to with your boyfriend last night? I hope you didn't do anything I wouldn't do,' he'd say as we sorted the morning post together. 'No boyfriend yet? Oh, don't give me that – a lovely girl like you must be spoilt for choice – they must be queuing in the aisles to take you out.'

I laughed this off with a shake of my head and got on with my stamping, feeling shy and uncomfortable. I had no interest in having a boyfriend and eventually told him so. 'Huh, you're not one of those, are you?' he said. 'One of what?' I replied, flummoxed. 'God, you really are an innocent, aren't you, Lucia?' he said, with a strange look on his face that I could not fathom.

Eventually, I began to dread our daily sorting sessions but Mr Bleasdale never seemed to pick up on my discomfiture and insisted upon quizzing me about my personal life, as he called it. It did occur to me to tell my parents about this daily torture but I wanted to see if I could deal with it myself instead of relying on them to sort out my problems because, at the end of the day, I was secure in the knowledge that anything I did would be all right by them.

I concocted a little plan in an attempt to appeal to Mr Bleasdale's better nature and hopefully call a halt to his disgusting and impertinent remarks, and so, the very next morning, as he was giving me the third-degree on the colour of my underwear, I pretended to break down in tears. I'd felt sure this would put a stop to his tiresome teasing, because I do know that any man, my Daddy for instance, hates to see a girl crying.

As I bowed my head and continued ripping envelopes, stamping the correspondence and sorting them into piles: letters on the left, statements on the right and receipts on the spike, he moved swiftly to my side of the desk and put his arm around my shoulders. *Oh, this isn't what I wanted,* I remember thinking, recoiling as his garlic breath warmed my cheek and a waft of his overpowering aftershave drifted up my nostrils.

'Come, come, young lady,' he crooned, 'I'm so sorry, I didn't mean to...' But his eyes began to bulge, and blood trickled from his nose and lips as I drove the spike further into his chest where it remained as he tottered over backwards and fell heavily to the floor, where he lay gasping and staring up at me in stunned incomprehension. His expression struck me as so comical that I threw my head back and laughed – I laughed and laughed...I laughed until he died.

*   *   *   *

Nowadays, I'm quite content, happy even: it was too gloomy in the first place they put me and I couldn't even reach the window bars to look out.

And then, after what seemed like a long time in the dark, I was moved here where it's much brighter: the staff are quite different, they're highly trained and very kind...

Also, for the first time in my life, I've made some loyal friends who, amazingly, don't seem jealous of me at all – in fact, they seem to really like me, for some reason that I haven't worked out yet...

Mummy says they perhaps look a bit common and I shouldn't be tempted to go in for tattoos and piercings – "you're a beautiful girl, Lucia, just be your own person" – but, at the same time, she's obviously mighty relieved there are no members of the male sex in here to harass or torment me.

I do look forward immensely to visiting times, though, and when my parents come to see me they bring lots of presents – they praise me up to the skies and insist that sometimes it's good to be bad.

'Our precious baby,' they say, 'you did the right thing and we're so proud of you, we love you – you're such a good girl'.

NIGHT WRITER

In the small village of Quagmire there lived a schoolteacher, probably in her mid-thirties although she looked much older.

Miss Jocasta Fontenoy, a plain woman, had but one redeeming feature which was her glossy brown hair but which she chose to wear scraped back in a bun. To embellish her schoolmarmish appearance, a pair of wire-framed spectacles perched on her nose-end in spite of the fact that the wearer was only slightly short-sighted.

The eight-year olds under her care at Quagmire Junior School lived in awe of their teacher: she ruled with an iron fist in a velvet glove but was, all the same, totally devoted to her young charges. She was well respected amongst her many friends and neighbours in the village, and engaged wholeheartedly in the many local activities.

Jocasta Fontenoy lived all alone in a cottage surrounded by a pretty garden crammed full of hollyhocks, lupins, red hot pokers and other tall flowers.

Her cosy home stood a few yards away from Quagmire Junior School and she appeared happy and contented with her lot.

But people did, of course, gossip about the schoolteacher's single state, wondering whether she had ever had a relationship with a man, and, if not, was it by choice or simply Providence?

So it was a surprise to the many villagers of her acquaintance when she returned from an Education & Health seminar in the nearby town of Quorum Thisbé, entirely transformed in appearance and personality. Miss Fontenoy had discarded her spectacles, let down her abundant hair, enhanced her lips with a touch of pink, and had acquired a sparkle in her eye.

'It must be a man's influence,' everyone said, and indeed, Miss Fontenoy quickly put the word about that she had, in fact, met someone at the seminar, a Professor Harrison Shrubsole, who had made a beeline for her: they had quickly become friends, finding many interests in common.   Evidently, they had spent all their time between lectures in each other's company, and upon parting, exchanged demure kisses plus telephone numbers and addresses.

'I had another letter from the professor today,' sighed Miss Fontenoy to her friend Percina Mellowe, a teacher in the senior school over in Quorum Thisbé. 'He writes to me each and every evening, however late it is, and he sometimes burns the midnight oil well into the early hours.'

'He is very enamoured of you,' said Percina Mellowe, who was an avid fan of astrology and fancied herself as a clairvoyant. 'I feel it in my water.'

'Yes,' beamed Miss Fontenoy, 'he calls himself the Night Writer – in fun, you know, and so thoughtful that he's enclosed a five pound note for stamps and telephone calls so I can write to him and ring him.'

'I see,' said her friend. 'That is certainly very generous of the professor, and I predict this relationship will blossom and bear fruit. But why on earth cannot *he* telephone *you*?'

'Well, he could, of course, but he's funny that way – he likes me to ring him late in the evening, just as he's writing his letters to me; he says it gives him inspiration just to hear the telephone bell and know it's sure to be my voice on the other end.'

'Are you going to see each other soon?' Miss Mellowe wanted to know. 'Long-distance relationships are all very well, and I daresay it seems quite romantic, but surely you yearn for each other's company in the flesh – if you'll pardon the expression! Where abouts did you say he lives?'

'Oh, in Scotland, I'm afraid,' simpered Miss Fontenoy. 'Although he isn't Scottish by birth, and I can assure you he doesn't wear the kilt! No, the professor has a very cultured, very English voice, and appearance, of course, *and* he always wears a spotted bow-tie: very dapper indeed. I shall buy him a bow-tie and send it to Scotland. He will be very delighted, I'm sure.'

Miss Fontenoy gradually collected quite a stack of letters of several pages each, which she took delight in brandishing under the noses of her friends, colleagues and acquaintances. 'We're longing to see this professor of yours,' they would say. 'When is he going to come and see you? Surely he doesn't expect you to travel all the way to Scotland on your own!'

Very soon, the schoolteacher had a letter to show them, a letter containing the desired information: Professor Shrubsole had arranged a free week in order to visit his beloved, and had instructed the lady to book a room for his use at The Quagmire Inn. This she did with all speed, and from then on Miss Fontenoy, and everyone of her acquaintance, lived on tenterhooks of excited anticipation.

Came the day, came the bad news.

It was a Saturday morning and Jocasta Fontenoy hastened to telephone Percina Mellowe, imparting the information that the professor had been obliged to cancel his visit after an unexpected development at the university. It was well known that Miss Mellowe's tongue was akin to jungle drums and the knowledge, therefore, was spread far and wide.

Of course, The Quagmire Inn booking had to be cancelled, and the landlady Mrs Pandora Bellchamber, extremely disappointed about the whole situation, agreed to waive the deposit which was duly refunded to the sad-faced schoolteacher.

'We were really looking forward to making your friend very comfortable here,' said Mrs Bellchamber, ruefully. 'Please send our very best regards to Professor Shrubsole and let him know there will always be the best room in the house available for him whenever he wants to visit us here in Quagmire Village.'

A few days later, coming up to the school holidays, the villagers were not surprised to hear that Miss Fontenoy had decided to visit Scotland and had actually bought her train ticket, the professor having forwarded several five pound notes to cover the cost of travel together with a promise to meet her at the end of her long journey.

Came the day, and Miss Fontenoy set out for Scotland on her mission to visit the professor, several of her friends excitedly turning up at Quorum Thisbé station to wave her off. For the next few days, villagers had nothing else on their lips but Miss Fontenoy's love affair. 'How exciting,' they said. 'Perhaps she'll come back with an engagement ring on her finger.' Friends and colleagues began to cogitate on what to purchase for a wedding present.

After nine days, Percina Mellowe received a brief telephone call from Miss Fontenoy, announcing her proposed return to Quagmire Village the following day. 'Shall the professor be coming with you, Jocasta?' asked her friend, but further information Miss Fontenoy would not impart.

Upon the schoolteacher's homecoming, villagers were clamouring for news of any developments in the romance, and a sad but nobly-resigned Miss Fontenoy would say only that the whole thing had been called off for the simple reason that, after much heart-searching and many tears, she had decided to put her responsibility towards Quagmire Village School before her personal happiness. In other words, she could not bring herself to leave Quagmire and take up residence in Scotland.

The schoolteacher's friends and acquaintances were shocked, but also full of admiration for so dedicated and altruistic a lady in their midst. Any thoughts of wedding presents were put on the back burner where they stayed in the event of a change of heart between the two erstwhile lovers.

In spite of more letters from the professor begging her to go to him, Miss Fontemoy remained resolute, and gradually all talk of the schoolmarm's romance dwindled into legend.

Some years later, Percina Mellowe, now headmistress at Quorum Thisbé Senior School, travelled to Leicester for a seminar and saw on the list of presentations that a certain Professor Harrison Shrubsole was to give a lecture on "Health in Education".

Miss Mellowe made it her business to approach the professor and make his acquaintance. After the usual introductions and niceties, the headmistress decided to take the bull by the horns, and began, 'You may be wondering how Jocasta Fontenoy is faring these days.'

'Jocasta? Jocasta, erm, who?' was the frowned response. 'Sorry, I don't think I've…,' the professor straightened his yellow spotted bow-tie which was wobbling on his laryngeal prominence.

'Yes, you must remember her – the schoolteacher from Quagmire Village?' pursued Miss Mellowe. 'She travelled up to Scotland to see you.'

'Did she, by Jove? Scotland, you say? A long way away – I'm based here in Leicester. And anyway, dear lady, the name doesn't ring a bell – you must have the wrong chap.'

'Are you sure, Professor? She seemed to think she knew you quite well.'

'I do meet a lot of people on these blessed seminars,' replied the academic. 'I shake hundreds of hands when folk express their appreciation of my lectures, y'know.'

'Yes, I see what you mean, and you're probably right,' frowned his inquisitor, more than a trifle nonplussed. 'Yes, probably just a handshake.'

Which left Percina Mellowe wondering whether her friend had really received those love letters through the post or, in thrall to her obsessive fantasies, had Jocasta Fontenoy herself been the Night Writer?

CARDS ON THE TABLE

They say that marriage is a lottery where men stake their liberty and women their happiness, but still the majority of people rush headlong into it without a backward glance. In other words, marry in haste, repent at leisure! But I had really loved my wife Brenda, and I believe she loved me – in fact, our marriage *was* happy: it was living together afterwards that was the problem.

During the first year or so, as we furnished our new house, I'd assumed that what we had might well be described as happiness. I looked forward to evenings and weekends when I escaped my responsible office job. Dressed in jeans and wielding a paintbrush, I would busy myself decorating each room in turn while Brenda consulted colour charts and swatches of curtain samples between concocting experimental meals she had seen on the TV cookery programmes to which she was addicted.

Then Brenda began watching gardening programmes and made plans for a really extravagant water feature which would take up half the garden.

In between times, Brenda took it upon herself to supervise and criticise my efforts: "Look, Reggie, you've missed a bit – *no*, not *there* – yes, right up in the corner! You'll have to get up the stepladder again and do it properly" and "I don't like seeing brush marks – you'll have to go over that door-frame again".

The emotional side of our marriage gradually became a routine event and something of a chore on Brenda's part, mainly for the reason she didn't like the bedclothes being rumpled or seeing my rapidly-thinning hair coming out on the pillow. In fact, after initially being rather proud of my wife's love of detail, it gradually dawned upon me that Brenda was meticulous and fastidious, a perfectionist to a fault. She was compulsive about tidiness, cleanliness and the normal functions of everyday life.

At first my philosophy had been "look around and you'll find someone worse off" but the day Brenda began correcting my vocabulary in public – *for goodness sakes, Reggie, it's not "you was", it's "you were"* – I was stung enough to add "pedantic", "insensitive" and "rude" to the previous list of her faults, whilst it came home to me how much power women have over men – and the basic control is nagging.

So, when my marriage began to go pear-shaped and then finally went belly-up, I knew it was time to start thinking about living instead of merely existing although I had no idea at the time what I could do.

We divorced by mutual consent, and Brenda was allowed to keep the house in lieu of any of my pension rights: I could not help but think of the old adage which goes, "a man is not complete until he's married, and then he's finished".

And now I was a single man, flat broke, lonely and living back with my middle-aged parents; lonely, that is, until one of my office colleagues remarked that action is the antidote to despair and advised me to join one of those chat-rooms on the internet instead of spending my evenings at the pub crying into my beer.

I could not wait to find out about this cyber world, and soon logged on to the Make Friends web-site. I clicked on the photograph of "Amber", a woman with long auburn hair. I messaged her and we began chatting in cyberspace. 'Let's put our cards on the table,' she wrote, 'let there be no secrets between us. I'll get the ball rolling by describing myself as a forty-two-year-old widow, no ties, a good pension from the Manhattan Bank (courtesy of my ex-husband) and I own my own town-house in New York City, not far from Ground Zero.'

I laid my cards on the table, too, all about my broken marriage and how Brenda had tried to take over every aspect of my life. Amber replied, quoting "no-one worth possessing can ever be quite possessed" which I thought was a brilliant summing-up of my situation.

I could hardly believe I'd found such an understanding woman, a woman of the world, one of superior intelligence and attractive appearance to boot, albeit twelve years my senior!

We communicated daily, and eventually she telephoned me. I was overjoyed to hear her voice; it was well modulated and silken, unlike those women on TV with their squawking nasal utterances.

'Are you as muscular as your photo, Reggie?' she purred, seductively.

'Yes, I am, actually,' I replied, overcome by her sincere flattery. 'I used to go to the gym before I was married, then other things got in the way.'

'I need a strong man,' she said, sounding a trifle sadly I thought.

'Oh, why so?' I asked, a little bemused, wondering if it was leading to the telephone sex I had vaguely heard about.

'You know, for work around the house, yard work,' she laughed. 'I'm only a weak woman, absolutely useless with a power drill or snow shovel.'

'I'll come over and help you,' I said, jokingly. 'I like decorating and gardening.'

'Mmm,' she replied, dreamily, 'artistic flair is good but I do need a really physical man around here for…erm, various reasons.'

'Wow, this gets better and better,' I smirked to myself, more than a little excited.

Then, just as I was feeling more confident, another bombshell fell into my life: after I had worked for them since the age of twenty-one, my firm suddenly went into liquidation and I joined the ranks of the unemployed. My parents were supportive but I plumbed the depths of despair once again and resorted more and more to the all-engrossing chat room.

But Amber immediately sensed something was wrong. 'Reggie,' she wrote, 'cards on the table - remember that one can lie with words and also silence, and if one cannot invent a totally convincing lie, it's better to tell the truth.'

And so, with her loving encouragement, I confessed that not only did I have no house and no money, but now I was unemployed. 'It's a global recession,' I moaned. 'I'm on the scrap-heap at the age of thirty! Last week I was just poor, but now I'm in debt.'

'If you can't change your fate,' Amber said, 'change your thinking.'

'But I don't know what to think,' I replied.

'Reggie, loneliness is the worst kind of poverty – come to New York and live with me. I'll buy you a one-way ticket and settle your debts.'

'But we've never actually met; we don't really know each other...'

'I know you enough by now, Reggie – you're a lovely, genuine person. I need a man of integrity – I cannot abide home-grown Americans, they're too brash. You're more my type. *I* need *you, you* need *me*. We could have a wonderful life together – I'll take good care of you, and in return you can do all the heavy work around the house for me, and build a beautiful water-feature in the back yard.'

Obviously, I couldn't believe my luck! Sweet Amber! Such a generous proposal was a very attractive way out of my financial and emotional troubles.

Pretty soon, I waved my confused parents goodbye, and flew to a new life in America where Amber was waiting for me at JFK. I saw at once she was even more beautiful than her photograph. She kissed me passionately and ushered me to her car.

The Manhattan town house was more than I could have expected in my wildest dreams, and Amber gave me a conducted tour around all four floors including the basement.

After dinner that evening, we went to bed and it was the most wonderful experience, nothing like the hurried scuffling I'd endured with Brenda. What had I been missing all these years? I fell heavily in love with Amber and she with me.

We went sightseeing around Manhattan or simply stayed home when, between compulsive love-making sessions, Amber cooked marvellous meals whilst I did various jobs around the house and yard.

One day, in the midst of my happiness, Amber's lovely face took on a serious expression. 'Reggie,' she said. 'You remember we said cards on the table?'

'Yes, of course,' I replied, bemused. 'Why? What's up? You suddenly look very worried'

'Well, I'd like you to build a water-feature very soon, before winter comes.'

What is it with women and their water-features? I wondered to myself.

'That's no problem,' I said staunchly. 'Is tomorrow soon enough?'

'Yes,' she said, 'that'll be perfect, but first – there's something… it's the only secret I have actually kept from you…'

She led me down steep wooden steps into the basement and approached a large chest freezer against the far wall. She unlocked and lifted the lid, looking quizzically at me as I recoiled in horror at the sight of an old man's corpse curled up in the foetal position, frozen stiff, eyes wide open, staring straight at me!

Amber touched my arm. 'It's like this, Reggie. I'm still drawing his pension, and I needed a guy I could trust, a strong man like you, my darling, someone who would love me enough to help. I'm only a weak woman, I couldn't possibly manage the job alone'.

'Wha…what is this, what's going on?' I stammered, my knees beginning to wobble.

'Let me explain! I'd like you to chop him up and bury him under the water-feature, please, Reggie,' she said, smiling and nodding encouragingly, handing me a meat cleaver…

A SLIGHT CHILL

That particular morning there was a slight chill in the air but, warmed by a secret inner glow, she left the window wide open as she dressed and carefully applied lipstick and face powder – "war-paint", as Donald fondly termed it. 'It's gilding the lily, Phyllis, you don't need any enhancements whatsoever,' he would often say.

Gazing into the mirror, she moved this way and that, admiring her slightly mousy hair in its new short cut, swooning at thoughts of Donald, her husband of one year, due to return that very afternoon after a business trip to the United Stated of America.

Six weeks without her beloved Donald: it seemed more like six years. How she had tolerated the separation she would never know: the tears, the frequent spasms of abject longing, the emptiness, the elation when he telephoned – his voice, travelling all the way across the Atlantic sounding as if he were speaking inside an echo-chamber – and the fall back to the hard, unforgiving earth when the call ended.

But today, D-Day, Donald Day had arrived at last and downstairs in the kitchen she was too excited to eat breakfast, managing only several cups of strong coffee.

She tied a floral apron around her waist and flicked around the spotless G-Plan furnishings with a feather duster, humming sentimental love songs, before tuning into the Light Programme for a selection of music played on the Hammond Organ followed by fifteen minutes of Mrs Dale's Diary.

As time moved on she began to think of preparing luncheon in time for her husband's expected arrival at 1.30 and stood in the kitchen for a while, unable to concentrate, in a blissful dream of love.

Eventually, she shook herself into the present moment, got to grips with the situation in hand and decided on a suitable menu.

Taking a half-chicken from the meat safe, she washed it under the cold tap before rubbing it with oil, salt and pepper.

Then she chose the vegetables: *let's see, roast potatoes, boiled parsnips and cauliflower would be nice.* For pudding, it would be Donald's favourite, tinned rice, served with preserved plums.

Phyllis put pans of water on to boil and placed the chicken and potatoes in a slow oven. Then she was at a loss. The only thing now was to watch and wait.

She stood gazing out of the kitchen window until the meal was ready, but far too early it seemed as there was no sign of Donald. She left the food in a low oven to keep warm.

By three o'clock Phyllis was feeling bedraggled and disappointed. Even the careful flower arrangements were beginning to wilt in their vases. She ran upstairs to comb her hair and apply more lipstick and powder.

Taking a comfortable position by the open sitting room window she fell into a light doze. The sound of the front door opening awoke her with a shock. *Oh, he's here, but just look at the time, it's gone five – I shan't mention that though; Donald doesn't like being reminded of his shortcomings, even obliquely…*

'Oh Donald, where on earth have you been, I've been panic-stricken, you could have phoned me…' she moaned, unable to stop herself, her face a picture of abject misery.

'Sorry, darling,' he grimaced, holding her away and brushing her cheek with his lips, 'you simply cannot depend on the trains these days – autumn leaves on the bloody line – what a country, what a shambles; it wouldn't happen in the States.'

'Is that all I get, a peck? Aren't you pleased to see me after all these weeks away?'

'Of course I am, silly girl, I'm absolutely exhausted, that's all. I never got so tired in the States, it's full of civilised people there, not like here, dammit! Heathrow is peopled by slobs and zombie. I can hardly believe I'm back in this God-forsaken country.'

She thought Donald looked thinner, his features more finely drawn, and his tanned skin suited him. Even more attractive than ever, she thought, a warmth sweeping over her body and into her loins as she anticipated what was to come.

'Shall I help you with your luggage?' she suggested, ignoring his irritation, hoping to get him up the stairs when she would make everything right.

'No, leave it where it is, I'll take it up later – I have to make an important telephone call before I do anything else.'

'Oh, you've only just got back – can't it wait? Look, talk to me for a minute, don't you notice anything different about me?'

'Hmm? Is that a different apron you're wearing?' he asked, scrutinising her for the first time.

'No, it's my hair – I've had it cut short just for you. The hairdresser said…'

'Well, my God – what on earth made you do that?' he scowled. 'I prefer long hair, as you very well know, and anyway it looks more mousy short; you ought to have it bleached like they do over in the States.'

'Oh Donald, you never said you liked it long,' she said, choking back her disappointment. 'Well, never mind, it'll soon grow again.'

'Let's hope so,' was his acid rejoinder.

'Now, Donald,' she said, pulling him towards the settee, 'come and sit down beside me, tell me all about your trip.'

'I'll have to make that telephone call,' he said, jangling his keys impatiently, 'but I will just say that life is damned different over there – the weather is so much better, more sun, less rain, every home has a television set and what they call an ice-box.'

'Ice-box – what on earth is that?' she said, screwing her face in puzzlement.

'It's where the Americans keep meat and milk – things that go off in the hot weather,' he replied impatiently. 'They're so far ahead of us in every way.'

'Well, what's so new about that? We have our meat safe. It's been quite sufficient for our needs up to now, hasn't it?'

'No, I don't mean those tiny box things you have to keep outside – what I mean is proper refrigerators with freezers, they run on electricity – you can make your own ice-cubes, even ice-lollies if you freeze some fruit juice – popsicles, the Yanks call them. Oh, life is so much better there, very sophisticated, more civilised. And the people – ha! I met this couple, the Stottlemeyers, Bobbie-Jeane and Chuck, ex-American Air Force. They're the *best*. I know Bobbie-Jeane won't mind if I tell you she's had silicone injections in her, you know, chest, as well as sun-streaked hair extensions, all done at the Manhattan Beauty Clinic.'

'Really – I've never heard of…'

'And Bobbie-Jeane is only 32 but she's already had an eye-lift. Chuck has had a hair weave – I wouldn't mind one of those myself. People are more image-conscious in the States. Oh, I tell you, their quality of life is damned superior to this dead-and-alive hole'.

'But Donald, you've always loved England, and anyway you always tell me not to improve on Nature.'

'Oh that!' he said. 'I've changed my mind, OK?'

'But Donald…' she repeated, at a loss.

'Now I must make that call, the Stottlemeyers will want to know I'm home safe,' Donald said, and then, warming to his theme, he continued, 'do you know, they employ a maid, so I did have to modify my accent quite a bit to get through to her.'

'I thought you sounded a bit, erm, different…' Phyllis began.

'Oh yeah, six weeks across the pond and I already sound like a native-born New Yorker. It's easily picked up. Anyway, this maid of theirs, she's what they refer to as "the help", like in the films, or, as they say over there, "on the movies". And the Stottlemeyers, they're what's known as "swingers". I went to one of their club parties, and, ahem, well, it was a real eye-opener.'

'Oh, are they music-lovers? Do you mean a dance band type of thing?'

'No-o, it's nothing to do with Glenn Miller, Phyllis, more like "dangerous pleasures"! You should "get with it" as they say. Anyway, to cut to the chase, the Stottlemeyers are coming to England next week! Yup, Chuck wants me to go into business with him which will mean more trips Stateside, or we might even have to move there which would be fantastic.'

'Move? What about my mother?'

'Oh, your mother'll be all right. She can come and visit, maybe once every couple of years or so. But just think, we could afford to have our own maid.'

'Maid? What would I want with a maid…?'

'*Yup*, you'll get on like a house on fire with the Stottlemeyers, especially Bobbie-Jeane – she's *very* friendly with everybody and, I must say, has a very sharp wit, especially for a woman. So, I've got my work cut out now. First thing is to book them into a nice local hotel. You'll have to start doing your homework, like, for instance, what food to give them – they'll probably be eating here most days.'

'Eating here?'

'And not just a measly chicken dinner either – Americans have a *whole* chicken *each* when they feel like a *snack*.'

'Oh, do they really?' Phyllis frowned, mindful of the miserable offering drying up in the oven. 'Erm, shall I get you a cheese sandwich – you must be starving.'

'No, never mind that, I had something on the plane; just pour me a Southern Comfort, will you? And make it a large one – there's a bottle in my airline bag – I must go ring Bobbie-Jeane, she'll be getting worried. And for goodness sake, Phyllis, take off that damned frumpy apron – there's a frilly one in my bag – you know, like the American hostesses wear when it's the maid's day off! Put that on instead.'

Phyllis moved quickly, instinctively, ready to obey, but first she crossed to the window and closed it against the slight evening chill.

WHAT SAY YOU?

Keeping watch, she felt the familiar surge of anticipation as the postman approached the house, weaving his way down the pathway leading to the front door. She ran into the hallway and waited until the longed-for letter fell with a satisfying plop onto the doormat.

What philosophical conundrum does my friend James have for me today?

She made towards her tidy desk before neatly ripping open the envelope and commencing to decipher the copperplate handwriting:

"Dear Dorcas, I think we have thrashed out fairly satisfactorily Einstein's assertion of imagination being more important than knowledge. What say you? Before setting out a new poser for us to discuss, I have some welcome news – or what I hope will be welcome news! I shall be flying down from the frozen north for a seminar next week and thought it would be ludicrous not to meet after corresponding with each other for however many years. What say you...?"

This turn of events was something the woman had half longed-for, half dreaded for the past ten years or so, and the rest of the letter she scanned in an uncomprehending haze, her mood quickly changing from joy to anxiety.

Dorcas Gorringe had long ago fallen in love with James, with the idea of James, and immediately saw that this physical encounter could spoil their meeting of minds, the regular correspondence between them being the abiding passion in her otherwise humdrum life: what else did she have as a distraction from her part-time job at Quagmire Library and caring for her increasingly crotchety mother?

Her thoughts began to run amok: *Will he expect to come here? Heavens above, I'd have to cook for him! What a nightmare, and I can't rely on Mother to be polite either, and anyway the house needs a lick of paint – perhaps it might be better to meet in a restaurant, somewhere neutral.*

Feverishly she sorted out a photograph James had sent to her when they first became pen-friends via the library in-house magazine. This snapshot, most likely out of date even then, showed a handsome young man with a beard, but it was easy enough to calculate that, by now, James must be in his mid-fifties as she was in her late forties. And, of course, the fuzzy photo she had sent in return had been taken in her twenties when her hair was long and thick, her face full and dimpled with the freshness of youth. *What will he think of me? Will he be disappointed in me? I'd be heartbroken if he didn't reciprocate my feelings.*

Having never even spoken to each other on the telephone, they arranged by hastily-scribbled notes to meet for lunch at the hotel where he would be staying and, came the day, she dressed carefully in a new tweed suit bought especially for the occasion.

She tried wearing some lipstick and powder for a change, and fluffed out her short hair in an attempt to soften her angular face.

'Where are you going dressed up like a dog's dinner,' her mother demanded. 'You're always gallivanting off, leaving me on my own.'

'Mummy, how can you say that – I hardly ever go out, apart from work.'

'Well, don't be long, that's all – I might want you to call Dr Frobisher later on to see to my leg – I've been awake half the night with it!'

James had not yet arrived when she entered the Quorum Thisbé Hotel restaurant. She could feel her heart hammering, as her cheeks flushed with two points of colour. Never in all her life had she felt so agitated.

She ordered a glass of iced water and pressed the blessed coldness to her forehead.

Suddenly James was there, standing beside her chair and leaning forward to brush her cheek with sticky lips, a recently-smoked cigar obvious on his breath.

'Dr Livingstone, I presume,' he said, laughing. 'Dorcas Gorringe – I'd have known you anywhere.'

'Hello, James, how lovely to see you,' she managed, with a shy little smile.

He sat down opposite and looked at her. She shrank under his level gaze. 'This is great,' he said, unconvincingly. 'Well, at least it's a nice day for it.'

'Yes, it's unseasonably warm, isn't it?'

'It is, but we shall have rain before nightfall.'

There was an uneasy silence, each casting about for fresh conversation matter.

'And how's your mother? I was hoping to meet her. From what little you say, she's quite a character.'

'Mother isn't up to having visitors,' Dorcas said, glad of something to discuss. 'Some days she needs gagging and tying down.'

'Ah, there it is, a spark of your humour coming through,' he smiled. 'I hope you're not nervous of me – I do look forward to your letters, you know.'

'Yes, I know, and so do I – look forward to yours, I mean,' she said, noting his combed-over hair, untidy beard and beetle brows.

Strange how she'd had an entirely different mental picture of him all these years.

'Sorry, what was that? Oh, yes, I'll have the cheese salad, please. Just melon for starter. No wine – I'll stick to water, thank you.' *Oh what a trial this is! I shall have to think of something witty or at least interesting to say – he'll be thinking I'm some sort of dumb cluck. I really cannot abide it. I wish I'd never agreed to meet him…*

'Before we tuck in, Dorcas, may I propose a toast,' James said, raising his glass. 'Here's to our continued correspondence, and to scratching the itch with our pens, so to speak.' They clinked glasses, red wine and iced water.

She managed to take down some of the melon as her companion noisily consumed a bowl of tomato soup. She tried not to recoil from the smell of the soup which always put her in mind of stale body-odour.

When the main course was served, Dorcas picked at her salad whilst James tucked into a huge steak with all the trimmings.

'You won't grow fat on that, Dorcas – you're eating like a bird,' he said with his mouth full.

'I'm sorry, James, I'm not very hungry and, as you know, I am a vegetarian.'

'Oh dear, I hope this sirloin isn't offending you at all, Dorcas, but, like most red-blooded men, I love my meat,' he grinned, licking his knife.

Mentally squirming at his bad table manners, Dorcas shook her head. *Really, they didn't know anything much about each other at all, only their respective opinions on matters philosophical.*

'Did I mention that I am now a divorced man, footloose and fancy-free?' he said, the spinach in his teeth and gravy in his beard a real distraction as she tried to maintain eye contact without looking at his lower face.

'Erm, no, you didn't,' she stammered. *Dear Lord, which way was the conversation going now?*

'And the boys, as I'm sure I've mentioned, are away at university, off my hands, thank goodness – oh yes, I'm a free man, I can do whatever I like now,' he smirked, draining his wineglass and simultaneously reaching for the bottle.

'I should have mentioned, James,' she said, abruptly changing the subject, 'I have to be home for Mother fairly shortly; she can't be left for very long at present. I said I'd be back by 3 o'clock as she wants me to call the doctor to come and see her again, so I shall have to get the 2.30 bus, if that's all right with you.'

'Dear me, how disappointing; I was hoping you would show me the local nightlife, if you know what I mean! You could freshen up in my room – no? Oh well, I can't offer you a lift, I flew down here, but I can get you a taxi, maybe come back home with you and meet your dear mother.'

'Erm, no! As I explained, Mother isn't too well at present,' she said, wild panic gripping her. 'It's best if I catch the bus.'

'Oh, well,' he grimaced, 'perhaps next time.'

She refused dessert and coffee and continued to sip her iced water.

James finished his spotted dick, drained his cappuccino, and replaced the cup with a clatter that startled her. *I'm a bag of nerves – when will this ordeal come to an end?*

James was speaking, some vestiges of froth clinging to his moustache. 'Well, thank you for today – I'll be able to picture you as I devour your letters over the next however many years.'

Dorcas nodded mutely. *Oh, never again, never again - it's all been spoilt.*

James helped her into her coat as she wriggled into it, trying to avoid any contact with his mottled hands. 'Oh, wait one moment,' he said,' I must just go water the horses – ha ha, I hope you don't mind my little euphemism there!'

High colour rushed to her cheeks. How horrible, how embarrassing, so impolite! Such language when they had only just met. Had he no sensitivity?

As they walked towards the bus-stop, James whistled "The Bluebells of Scotland", piercing her eardrums: *was there no end to his offences?*

Enduring another touch of his wet lips on her cheek, she stepped onto the bus and, with enormous relief, waved goodbye through the window. 'Write soon,' he mouthed, miming.

All that afternoon Dorcas felt bereft and bereaved, her thoughts in a turmoil of revulsion, sorrow and indecision: what else in her life could ever be as compulsive and inspiring as exchanging ideas with James's disembodied brain? Could she ever overlook his physicality and bad manners? Eventually, she sat down at her desk. Pulling the writing pad towards her and taking up her pen, she wrote:

"Dear James, Is it possible to love someone for their mind alone? What say you?"

LOCKED IN

I never knew that the Queen Mother's television was rented! I could hardly believe my eyes when I read it in the newspaper today. That was while we were waiting for Dr Frobisher to call later on in the afternoon.

Dorcas had called out the doctor because I'd been kept awake by a pain in my back, but that awful locum came instead, nose dripping, sneezing all over the place. I laughed and said something like "physician heal thyself" but he just ignored me, gabbling a load of nonsense about Dr Frobisher being out on an urgent matter. Honestly, some people have no sense of humour!

He's very nice is Dr Frobisher, such a kind man – everyone loves him but I'm sure that Dorcas and I are his favourites. Dorcas goes to see him regularly about some trivial complaint or another. Such a patient man, he ought to kick her out for wasting his time, but he's not that sort of chap.

On the other hand, I never call him out unless there's really something drastically wrong with me although I am 91 years 6 months old. I'd hate to "cry wolf" and then be ignored when it was actually serious.

So this morning, as I say, we called the doctor out but that Nurse Wildgoose creature turned up instead. It was my back, you see – such a terrible pain especially when I tried to stand up. The Wildgoose woman just dug about a bit, and then all she said was I should get out of my chair and move about more often. I tried to tell her about the Queen Mother's rented television but she said there was no time to stop for any chit-chat, so she wasn't here more than two or three minutes. I think I heard something muttered between sneezes that Dorcas was possibly being a little over-protective...

Anyway, I was glad the useless creature had gone but I was still in a lot of pain, and in fact I felt worse, what with all the unnecessary prodding and poking about. Dorcas said she would write a letter of complaint to the practice manager but I told her it wouldn't be any use as they're all hand-in-glove there. We only like Dr Frobisher: we don't like anyone else at the surgery.

Later on in the day I felt my head was fit to burst. Dorcas rang the surgery and spoke to the receptionist, telling her what had gone on and insisting that Dr Frobisher call and see me.

I shouted to Dorcas to tell her about the Queen Mother's rented television, but she didn't seem to hear me. Evidently the receptionist said she would call an ambulance as the doctor was out at the moment.

So, that is how I came to be in Quagmire Cottage Hospital, lying here on this hard bed, listening to everything that's going on around me, although it's slightly difficult to hear as it does sound as if people are talking far away.

Actually, I get the feeling they think I'm almost dead – but I'm not! I can hear, as I say, although I can't see very well, only through a tiny chink in my left eyelid; however, I don't seem able to move my body or head at all and of course I can't speak otherwise I would tell them about the Queen Mother's rented television and also give them a piece of my mind for bringing me in here. I want to be at home; I haven't quite finished reading this morning's newspaper.

But I hope I don't die because that would mean Dorcas being left all alone. She has her job at Quagmire Library but apart from that she only has me. I hope she remembers to tell them all about the Queen Mother renting her television – I think that is truly incredible.

I also hope this hospital room doesn't have a walk-in cupboard, I can't quite tell from this blasted reduced vision. I was once trapped inside the walk-in stationery cupboard at school. The other kids locked me in as a lark but I was terrified and screamed the place down. I've had claustrophobia ever since.

My bedroom at home has a large walk-in wardrobe and I'm sure it's haunted. I've told Dorcas but she just tells me not to be so silly even though I've described the ghost that lives in there. It's a lady in a white hooded gown who appears sometimes and beckons me to go inside the cupboard with her. I know if I did, I'd never get out again, I'd be trapped, locked in. I've asked Dorcas to take all my clothes out of there and have the doors nailed up, but she just laughs and pats my arm and tells me I am quite safe in my own home.

She is a good daughter, though, is Dorcas. She works hard and still does everything for me. I hope I don't die because then she'll find out that I never married her father, only changed my name to his by deed poll. No, I didn't know him very well or for very long, only for about a week or so.

The fact is, Dorcas was conceived in a walk-in linen cupboard in the hotel where I worked at the time. Her father was a travelling salesman, Hubert Gorringe. He locked me in the cupboard, went on his way and I never heard from him again. I used to think Hubert would come back for me but he didn't. I never forgot him but, even so, I never tried to trace him: you didn't do such things in those days. I just got on with life, moved to Quagmire Village where no-one knew my story, and did my best for the baby.

Oh dear, I wish I could speak and then I could tell this latest doctor standing beside my bed all about the Queen Mother renting her television. It's so incredible, I can't get over it! The doctor is saying something to Dorcas now about "locked-in syndrome". What does he mean by that? I can recall being locked in the stationery cupboard at school. Surely they don't know about that or about Dorcas being conceived in a linen cupboard at the hotel or about the ghost in my wardrobe? Are they reading my mind? If they *were* reading my mind, at least they'd know all about the Queen Mother's rented television. It's an ill wind, as they say!

If I could get the Queen Mother's rented television out of my head for a moment, I'd be able to concentrate on what they're saying, the people around my bed. I can't hear as well now, because their voices are a bit bubbly, a bit like being under water.

Apparently the doctor is describing to Dorcas an operation they plan for me. But now he's asking her permission! What a nerve! Well, all I can say is I hope she agrees because I am only 91 years 6 months, a mere stripling these days. I don't want to die just yet – I still have music inside, and I do want to tell everyone about the Queen Mother's rented television set.

I'm trying to speak but I can't even move my lips, can only manage a grimace. 'Oh, do look, doctor!' Dorcas is saying. 'Mother is smiling, she's trying to speak. It's all right, Mummy darling, you're in good hands, just relax and don't worry about anything…' And then she turns to the doctor and says, 'No, I don't think an operation is the right way to go for my mother, not if there's the danger she's going to end up with that locked-in syndrome thing. It sounds horrendous and I think she's suffered enough – just let her go – after all she's had a good innings, she *is* 92.'

Ninety-two? What is she talking about – I'm only 91 years 6 months, a mere stripling! Ninety is the new seventy – hasn't she heard of that? What a betrayal – by my own damned daughter!

But now, I can just make out a large walk-in cupboard opposite the foot of my bed, and there! – there's the lady in white coming out of it towards me, beckoning. It can't be a nurse because she's wearing a hood – I think it might be my usual lady in white from the walk-in wardrobe at home. She's followed me here, she must really want me to go with her. Shall I go or shall I stay? Oh, the thing is I do feel quite comfortable now, drifting off, no pain to speak of, so I might as well go with the flow!

My only regret is that I never managed to tell Dorcas to let them all know about the Queen Mother's rented television set! It's absolutely incredible – I just can't get over it...

WAITING ROOM

It was a nightmare plodding along the train track in these winklepicker shoes. But it was never predicted how fierce the storm would be, and I only hope Frank is keeping his eye on the animals, making sure they're not buried in the snow which is probably even deeper at Quagmire Valley Farm. Of course my fun fur coat is a big help in this freezing weather and I imagine the sparkling snowdrops on these false eyelashes must look quite fetching.

It was a ridiculous idea deciding to travel back from London on Christmas Eve. I should really have gone home two or three days ago but I just couldn't tear myself away from those bright lights, the shops, Oxford Street; Soho; Benjamin!

I was quite happy to leave the festive preparations to Frank and the others but who knows what they get up to when I'm away, and Frank will never let on. They'll be wondering where I've got to. The phone lines are down so we are quite marooned here. It would all be rather exciting, really, if it weren't for this slight whiplash injury I suffered when the train came to a halt with such a thump against the snowbank.

And now, looking around this dusty old waiting room, which hasn't seen a lick of paint since the 1930s, I see the rest of the stranded passengers milling about, trying to make the best of it, unpacking bits and bobs from their luggage. There's a young mother with her baby and people are being really kind to her. I'm keeping my distance though as I can't bear to see breast feeding which is rather odd, seeing as how I'm married to a farmer and used to seeing all that biological stuff on a regular basis, but it seems different with animals, more natural and not so disgusting.

The stationmaster is an absolute angel and has boiled some water in the urn to make us a hot cup of tea but, for some reason, I'm not thirsty. He also invited us to partake of some dusty cakes which reside under a glass dome on the counter but I won't take up the offer as I don't seem to be very hungry either – too much adrenaline, I suppose.

Oh, well, at least I'll lose some weight – this is all quite an adventure, although I was chilled to the bone at first when I heard the grim-faced guard telling a stupid story about a ghost train, something about claiming the soul of a sinner on Christmas Eve. What superstitious rubbish and what a Job's comforter. I shall put in an official complaint about that guard once I get home. He should be trying to calm people down, not putting the fear of God into them.

There's a vicar here who seems to be doing his best. He's trying to do his pastoral bit, but I shrugged and turned away when he approached me. He probably has a Christmas service in the morning and maybe Midnight Mass tonight – well, he's bound to miss both of them now. Good – the sanctimonious fool!

Some people are lying on the threadbare carpet covered by railway greatcoats. The poor devils must have been knocked out cold when the train came to a halt. I wonder who they are. I'm trying not to look over in that direction, to be brutally honest.

I saw a uniformed nurse amongst the passengers and I did try to explain to her about my whiplash but she was so busy with the mother and baby that I might as well have saved my breath and, anyway, I'm well aware there are other walking wounded apart from me. She can't attend to all of us, I suppose.

A female who continually scribbles in a notebook has a gash on her leg. A very tarty trollop is holding her wrist and whimpering, and even the vicar has a black eye. So much for the Lord's protection!

This salesman sitting next to me is an absolute pest. There's some blood trickling from his nose but, even so, he never stops talking. What's he saying now? Oh, yes, he's trying to sell me some lingerie – my God, he's a traveller in ladies' underwear! How funny! I must remember to tell Frank when I get home.

And I shall also have to tell him about Benjamin! But I intend to wait until after Christmas or maybe until the New Year. It would serve no purpose upsetting Frank and the others over the festive season.

Yes, Frank is a dear man but I just don't love him in the same way any more: I've fallen out of lust. This kind of thing happens every day all over the world so I'm not going to waste my time feeling too sorry for him, otherwise I might change my mind and live the rest of my life with a man I do not fancy.

Because, after all, I'm not much use to him. In reality, the only contribution I make to his life is of an ornamental nature. And of course Frank has several people to help him at Quagmire Valley Farm including Mrs Mendoza for the cooking, Miss Springett who does the housework, Gordon and Mike with the animals, and Graziella the au pair/dogsbody. I'm sure he wouldn't miss me – except – I'm lying: of course he would miss me – he loves me; I'm his trophy wife.

I've tried to put him off by being horrible to him, bitchy to the womenfolk, haughty to the farmhands and patronising to the au pair, but it doesn't seem to have affected his devotion to me in the slightest. He just goes on loving me...

Of course, I could lay it on the line and tell him that he'd be better off without me, but is that true? Would it be better to remove myself from his life altogether? Who knows? Oh, I wish I weren't so irresistible to the male sex.

In fact, I now seem to be surrounded by adoring men in this very unlikely setting of an ancient railway station waiting room. There's a dodgy-looking soldier, a dapper chap in a red bow-tie, a student type in a college scarf, a spotty teenager, the engine driver, and even the vicar and grumpy guard have joined the travelling salesman in vying for my attention.

It's such pathetic behaviour and I do not feel at all flattered for a change. They've all got an eye on the main chance, even under these adverse conditions.

Oh I just wish they would go away and leave me alone as I do feel rather sleepy now. I could drift off into such a pleasant reverie...

But, goodness, I'm suddenly wide awake – what's that noise? My God, it sounds like a train hooting, getting nearer, approaching; but how is that possible when the snow lies two feet thick on the track? Oh, no, no, no!

I push my way through the sycophants crowding round me, and my feet seem to have wings, flying over the threadbare carpet towards the people lying on the ground. They look so comfortable that I want to lie down with them and have a nap.

So I kneel and lift a corner of a coat – and there's my own face gazing back at me. My God, they didn't even have the presence of mind to close my eyes. I pull the coats off altogether and, just as I thought, the salesman, the red bow-tie, the vicar, the teenager, the engine driver, the student, the grumpy guard and the soldier are lying there beside me, pale as ghosts, eyes wide open – sinners all, losers all: my admirers and companions in death.

SNOWBOUND

Clouds heralding snow were gathering above the valley, but this, I knew, was to be expected out in the wilds of the Yorkshire Dales in the foothills of the Pennines. I had jumped at the chance of six months' solitude knowing the cabin had no telephone but was otherwise self-sufficient with its own generator, and so I did not fear being cut off from the nearest neighbour almost five miles away over rough terrain.

I planned to use the self-imposed exile to write my Magnum Opus and, apart from a transistor radio and my old Imperial typewriter, was back to nature, living a rustic existence.

Then the snow kept its promise, and a blizzard blew incessantly for three days. Would it never end? Local radio bulletins gave bad news with much relish: this was the heaviest snowfall in living memory, bringing down telephone and power lines for miles around and "worse was to come", as they predicted in their usual gleeful manner.

On the evening of the third day, unable to connect with my muse, I was sitting on the window seat watching a snow flurry, just a few flakes now, when, by the light

248

of the full moon I saw footprints outside, glittering on the frosted surface and, with one bound, I had opened the heavy wooden door.

In the porch stood a young woman, shivering, black hair sparkling with snowdust, white fur coat wrapped tightly around her slight body. 'How did you get here?' I gasped. 'Come in, quickly.' Bringing her inside the cabin, I gently helped her out of her sodden garments and into spare clothes of mine which, of course, looked huge on her slender frame. Once she was settled by the ingle nook, I brought a hot drink to kindle some warmth to those colourless cheeks.

'I was blinded by the blizzard and lost my way. Can I stay tonight?' she asked. 'My name is Bianca.'

'You poor thing, of course, but I'm afraid we'll be snowed in for longer than one night. It's a wonder you weren't frozen to death. How far have you come – where did you leave your car?'

My impassioned queries went unanswered, as she shook her head, shrugged her shoulders and rubbed her hands, warming them at the pot-bellied stove. I did not wish to add to her obvious distress, and felt I could not press the point at this stage.

That night, heavy snow fell afresh and, realising we would be marooned for quite some time, I thought to make the best of things, being secretly glad of the company in spite of my original reclusive intentions. The Magnum Opus could wait a few more days, and, after all, nothing is wasted on a writer and this was a perfect opportunity of making the most of an unforeseen experience. I had every intention, of course, to keep my diary updated.

I made up a trestle bed by the far wall for Bianca, but in the night I lay on my side, watching her sleeping. 'I hope this bad weather goes on for weeks,' I prayed.

The next day dawned and, with it, fresh hope for me as the snow was still falling from a lowering grey sky.

My unexpected guest and I began to relax in each other's company, we enjoyed cooking together, laughing at the same silly jokes, doing jigsaws, drinking mulled wine by the ingle-nook, dancing to romantic music on the radio and, very soon, I fell in love with this slip of a girl with her sapphire eyes and long black hair: Bianca, a woman without a flaw, wearing my nightshirt. She did her best to please me, hung on my every word, limpid eyes deep with love. 'I don't want this to end,' she said. I asked no questions but felt a strange tugging at my heartstrings.

I made two or three faint-hearted attempts to make a start on my writing project but, each time, Bianca very easily seduced me away from the typewriter and I melted thankfully into her slender body. Even trying to write my diary was impossible with such a sensuous distraction hovering by my side, watching my every move, nibbling my ear, stroking my hair.

When April came, the snow began to thaw, eaves and trees dripping water, all thoughts of the Magnum Opus had long fled my mind as I watched Bianca growing ever more pale and thin, almost transparent: she hardly ate and did not respond to my banter, my words of affection, yet I could see mute love still glowing in those eyes, enormous now, in her translucent face.

'Don't leave me now, please don't go,' I begged.

'It can't be helped,' came her sad reply.

I was holding back the days now, trying to deny all signs of the end of winter.

One morning, in my anguish, I reached out to caress her, but my hand clutched at thin air. Helpless, I saw Bianca slowly fading from sight, blowing me a kiss as she vanished. I heard her name being called – "Bianca…" – and realised the voice, hanging crystalline on the air, was my own.

I reached up and touched my face: her farewell kiss had left drops of saltwater on my cheeks…

SHED

Cathy turned from the washing-up and saw Matthew standing in the kitchen doorway, his eyes enormous dark pools in his freckled face.

'What's up, Matt – seen a ghost?'

Matthew shook his head slightly and continued staring at his mother.

'Cheer up, duckie, I've got some good news – you'll never guess!   When I told Oliver about you coming top in Chemistry, he suggested a trip to the zoo this afternoon as a reward. It's going to be a nice day and we can watch the lions feeding – you'll like that!'

Still gazing at her young son in the doorway, Cathy began to dry her hands on one of the new tea-towels bought in honour of her new boyfriend's visit.

Matthew looked down at the gleaming floor-tiles and growled, 'Who's paying?'

Cathy threw the tea-towel onto the draining board and sighed impatiently.

'Well, what a thing to say, Matt!   Don't look a gift horse in the mouth! Oliver's treating us, of course. You'll have to watch your manners and say "thank you" nicely. I don't want to see any more of your sulks and silences. It's not very polite, is it?'

The boy gasped and ran to his mother, hugging her tightly around the waist and burying his head in her comforting bosom.

'Oh, come on Matt, what on earth is the matter – tell me, please!'

'No, no, mum, I can't,' the boy mumbled, his cheek pressing against the diamante and glass buttons on Cathy's green satin blouse. How could he tell her that Oliver had just this minute taken a ten-pound note from her purse on the dresser? How could he ruin her new-found joy? She had certainly seemed brighter, happier, since Oliver had entered their lives. Anyway, would she believe him if he told her? His thoughts were interrupted by the sound of Oliver whistling in the hallway. Matthew quickly detached himself and ran out of the back door into the garden and down to the shed where he kept his pet rabbits.

Cathy turned from the window and saw Oliver standing in the kitchen doorway.

'I'm afraid Matthew has one of his moods today,' she said. 'What can we do with the child? He's not the same boy two days running.'

'He's been spoilt rotten, the brat,' Oliver said and came over to kiss Cathy on the lips.

She nestled into his shoulder. 'Oh, don't say that, Oliver. How can he be spoilt in a one-parent family: no designer trainers for him, you know.'

'Yes, but he's not as badly-off as some – he has a comfortable home, nice clothes, more than enough food, even a computer,' Oliver said. 'He needs to learn some manners.'

Cathy busied herself with the dishes, thinking that the least said the better.

Meanwhile, Matthew was feeding his rabbits in the shed, desperate thoughts tumbling through his young head. As he poked a cabbage leaf through the bars of Smokey's cage, his eye strayed to a container on the topmost shelf. *He knew what that was…*

Later that day, Cathy could hardly believe that Matthew had pulled himself together and was being polite, even quite friendly, towards Oliver as they drove to the local zoo.

They had a relaxed and jolly afternoon watching the animals, followed by tea in the cafeteria and, as it was such a hot day, Matthew asked for some bottles of lemonade to take home although Cathy could have sworn there were two or three left in the fridge.

As soon as they reached the house, Matthew ran to the shed to see his rabbits. Cathy and Oliver sat in the kitchen deciding what to cook for dinner, congratulating themselves that the day had gone so well, when they heard Matthew calling from the garden, 'Oliver, Oliver, come and see this.'

'There you are,' Cathy smiled as Oliver rose to go. 'A boy needs a man in his life – I told you things would settle down if we were patient.'

Oliver couldn't believe his luck. An affectionate and pretty woman with a good job and her own house – these could all be his if things continued well, and now the only fly in the ointment, the brat, had decided to accept the situation.

'What is it, Matt, what do you want to show me?' Oliver opened the shed door and peered into the murky interior. 'You need a light in here – I'll fix you one the next time I come.'

'Over here, Oliver – it's Smokey – I think he might have a sore nose. Can you see it? You'll have to kneel down here to get a good look.'

'Blimey, it's a bit dark to see a rabbit's nose!' Oliver said, 'And it's very warm in here, too – we're in for a heavy thunderstorm tonight, I think. Not good driving conditions…'

'Well, if you can't quite see the rabbit's nose, how would you like me to show you around the shed? It's quite an interesting shed. Lots to see in my shed.' Matthew was unusually animated. 'Look, here's my bike, and this is my spade. Here is last year's calendar on the wall. I know – we could have a little drinks party right now. Would you like some lemonade? I'd forgotten all about this bottle in the cool-box. It's nice and cold. Mum lets me keep it down here to save me trailing back to the house every time I feel thirsty.'

How could a man refuse? 'Erm, well, OK, Matt.' Oliver was bowled over by this show of friendliness. The boy was being effusive in his attentions. What a change! Of course it must be my innate charm, Oliver thought, smirking into the dusty dusk of the shed.

'Cheers!' Matthew handed a paper cup to Oliver, raising his own to his lips. Oliver took a gulp, coughed and said, 'God, that's strong, it's burned my throat. What a kick. Are you sure it's only lemonade?'

Matthew stared at Oliver through the gloom, 'Mine seems to be OK,' he said, swigging his paper cup of lemonade to the dregs.

'Oh well, 'Oliver laughed, taking another sip, 'It must be all the fags I smoke – maybe I should cut down.'

Strangely, Oliver did not feel he could stay for the dinner Cathy was preparing and said he would drive straight back home to avoid the looming stormclouds. Cathy helped Oliver pack his things and he left for his flat in the Midlands, with a promise to email or telephone her in a day or two.

After no word from Oliver for three days, a nonplussed and lovelorn Cathy tried his mobile phone at regular intervals over the next week but there was no response to the ringing tone. They'd originally met online, and she really didn't know much about him at all.

But he had said he was self-employed and worked from home and so, the following weekend, Cathy took a train up to Wolverhampton.

She knocked on Oliver's door, although she could tell the property was probably unoccupied simply by peering through the letter-box at a mound of unopened post lying in the hallway.

At a loss, Cathy called at the next-door neighbour's house and rang the doorbell.

The frizzy-haired, pierced and tattooed woman cautiously opened the door on the chain and replied in response to Cathy's enquiry that people kept themselves to themselves around these parts, and she was no gossip, but all she *would* say was that if it was the same bloke, he had committed suicide.

'Suicide?' echoed Cathy, stunned.

'Yeh suicide! Paraquat, it was – they found a lemonade bottle of it in his car. It took eight days for him to die – in agony, so I'm told. Very sad it was, I must say. Evidently, he had a mountain of debts, owed child support to several different women, and he was about to file for bankruptcy – he must have been desperate! Apart from that, I didn't know him at all.' The woman sniffed, nodded in sympathy and went back inside her house, slamming the door.

It was a painful few months for Cathy, trying to come to terms with the situation: let down once again by a man – a girl simply could not even trust them to stay alive, evidently!

But it had been a lucky escape for her and Matt. Twice bitten, three times shy, that would be her watchword, her maxim for the future, once she had gathered the ravelled ends of her life back together again.

And Matthew was her rock, she saw that now, and, from here on in, it would be just the two of them, all the way down the line.

Turning from the sink, Cathy smiled as she saw Matthew standing in the kitchen doorway.

The boy grinned and rushed across the scuffed floor-tiles, hugging Cathy round the waist, burying his head in her comforting bosom. His cheek lay pressed against his mother's frayed grey sweater for several moments, then, raising his head, he saw sunbeams sparkling on the washing-up bubbles, and the faded old tea-towel, looking more like a dish-cloth, hanging on its accustomed peg by the sink.

All was well!

ERIC'S CHOICE

Eric Bintworthy was a leading light in the annual Quagmire Maytime village fete and had, for the past however-many years, walked off with first prize for his chrysanthemums and had lately begun to develop a new strain of fuchsias.

The envious but increasingly resigned villagers had begun to dread the approaching competition although it made a few of them strive harder in attempting to topple Eric from his throne as the Flower King and, in fact, they had on occasion pulled a dirty trick or two although their attempts at sabotage had never stopped him walking off with first prize.

Horticulture was Eric's abiding interest, in addition, that is, to his three chaste mistresses, April, Julia and Georgina, who happened to be best friends and whom he loved equally for their differing attributes. He had never indicated which one he intended to marry but, for the moment, they were all happy just being in each other's company. "My harem" he would say to them, cooing and fondling affectionately.

One evening as he supped a beer with his three girls in The Akimbo Arms, he suddenly put down his pint glass and announced, 'I'm getting bored with all this success, all these flowers – I feel it's a foregone conclusion that my new fuchsias will get first prize this year – it's not stretching me any more.'

The girls were aghast. 'But you can't give up,' they said, as one voice. 'You can't let all this jealousy and bad feeling put you off.'

'Oh, I don't give a fig for that,' said Eric stroking April's arm, pinching Julia's cheek and patting Georgina's shoulder in one smooth and practised movement. 'I feel that my talents are wasted just concentrating on growing the best flowers. I'd like to try something else as well – baking, for instance.'

'But you don't bake, you can't even cook,' they replied, looking at each other, smiling and tutting, aware of how they did his household chores between them in order to leave him free to concentrate on his important horticultural activities.

'I can but try,' he said, beaming. 'Come round tomorrow, say about 11 o'clock, and you may be surprised at what I can achieve.'

The next morning, on the dot, April, Julia and Georgina turned up at Eric's house and made for the kitchen through a pall of acrid smoke. Their beloved was crouching by the oven, peering anxiously inside at a lemon meringue pie which was burned black and as flat as the proverbial pancake.

'Is this what you call an achievement?' April smirked. 'I think it's **back to the fuchsias** for you!'

'Oh, blast it,' Eric said, flouncing out to the garden. 'I haven't actually given up yet, you know. I'll try it again later.'

'Well,' said Georgina, 'what a mess! Let's clear up this chaos and then make him a nice lunch to cheer him up, poor lad.'

'Yes,' nodded Julia. 'I think we all agree that **an Eric and pie** just don't go.'

Later that day, the girls came up with a dirty trick idea of their own. They decided to create an original dessert, and enter it into the Quagmire Maytime competition under Eric's name.

They announced their suggestion to their beloved who was overcome with emotion. *Those girls must really love me to break the rules, cheat for me, come up with **May tricks** of their own*, he thought fondly.

Of course, Eric won not only the horticultural section for his new fuchsias but also the baking section for his innovative American Pie (consisting of equal parts of pumpkin, blueberries and apple topped by shop-bought filo pastry). He was ecstatic to win both sections.

After the event, wearing two rosettes and carrying two silver cups, he took the girls out for a celebratory meal at The Quagmire Inn.

'When are you going to marry one of us?' they asked over the starter of prawn cocktail followed by steak and chips followed by Black Forest Gateau, cheese and biscuits, and coffee and liqueur. 'You've kept us hanging on for long enough.'

'How can I decide?' he replied. 'I love you equally, you're all amazing in your different ways.'

'You'll have to think of a way,' they chorused.

'OK, you win,' he agreed, reluctantly, ' I'll give it some thought.'

A couple of days later, they were all sitting at Eric's kitchen table when he announced his plan: 'I shall give each one of you £1,000 and you must do your best to buy me a wonderful present with it.'

The girls agreed it was a fabulous idea. They took the cash and began to make their respective arrangements.

April was a methodical and knowledgable girl who never took risks. She had great fun searching the antique shops and found an oil painting costing £1,000 which was valued for auction at Christie's for in excess of £10,000.

Julia was a reckless type of person and she put the whole £1,000 on a horse, which happened to come in at odds of 10:1.

Georgina had a different attitude to life. She splashed her cash on a designer bag, and shoes.

Came the day of reckoning some weeks later, the girls sat around Eric's kitchen table once more.

'I'm ready,' he announced gravely.

April handed the valuable painting to her beloved together with the auction house valuation.

Naturally, Eric was bowled over by the intelligence and foresight that had gone into his gift and he kissed April tenderly by way of thanks.

He looked over at Julia who triumphantly handed over a briefcase containing the £10,000 plus the £1,000 stake, all in banknotes.

Eric was, of course, moved to tears by the bravery the lady had shown in risking so much money on an outsider. He kissed Julia tenderly by way of thanks.

Georgina was next, and she stood up, did a twirl and announced, 'Darling Eric, this is my present to you, seeing me so happy with my Gucci bag and Manolo Blahnik killer heels. Don't you think I look gorgeous?'

Eric was stunned by the thoughtful and inventive way Georgina had used the money. 'You look fantastic, darling,' he said, kissing her tenderly by way of thanks. 'How clever of you to come up with such a creative way of pleasing me.'

Georgina sat down again, and three pairs of eyes gazed expectantly towards Eric who gravely announced, 'I appreciate more than words can say the way each of you has shown her devotion and loyalty to me. I am overcome with love. But please, I beg of you, let me go through my thoughts in private for a couple of days. Come round on Saturday, as usual. I shall announce my decision and then we can all go out for a nice lunch.'

Eric burned the midnight oil pondering on his dilemma, his impending decision. He realised he had to make that choice and he could no longer put things off.

He did not wish to lose his three girls entirely and realised it would be impossible to keep them on a string for very much longer.

He knew that with canny April as his wife he would feel safe and secure for the rest of his days.

On the other hand, Julia was more devil-may-care and life with her would be an exciting roller-coaster.

As for Georgina, sweet Georgina, with her girlish ways and love of fripperies, what could be more endearing?

In the end, it was no contest, the choice was very easy for Eric to make and so he proposed, was accepted and got wed as soon as possible.

But, "hold on", I hear you cry! 'Don't go, don't finish there! Who did he end up with? Which girl did he choose?'

Oh, come on; surely you've worked it out?

No?

Well, you know what men are like ..... >>>>>>

Can't you guess?

OK, OK, I'll tell you......>>>>>>>>>>>>

Eric

chose

the

girl

with

the

biggest

breasts!!!

UP IN SMOKE

Eventually, I managed to whimper, 'So the old harridan is coming to stay!'

'Yes,' he replied smoothly, 'she is, but please do not be so derogatory about Mummy, if you don't mind. The old girl tries to please.'

'The thing is,' I huffed, 'I cannot understand why you still call her Mummy – good grief, you'll be forty years old next birthday.'

'Mummy is what the Prince of Wales calls the Queen! If it's good enough for Royalty, well, who am I to argue?' Monty shook his crumpled newspaper and folded it back.

'Oh, you're so gullible; it's all spin,' I snapped, and yes, I admit we were being irrelevant, but in spite of talking ourselves up a blind alley, Monty and I were well aware that Nina was a disruptive influence whenever she came to stay.

Plus, oh lord, it meant dragging out, once again, the gruesome ornaments and pictures she had bought us on every conceivable occasion and having to display them around our tastefully minimalist abode. And then we would have to listen to endless reminiscences of how Monty's dad proposed to her on the pier, interspersed with very stern lectures on healthy living.

'But Pamela, you knew she'd want to see us now we're pregnant – it *is* her first grandchild.' Monty put down his newspaper and smiled across at me. 'Be fair, she has waited a long time and so have we.'

'I know, but Nina is so controlling – every morning will be taken up walking on the pier with her, and she's bound to give me her advice on breast-feeding: she'll insist we call the baby some outlandish name, the poor little unborn thing. Just think of the handle she saddled you with – Montgomery Alamein Micklethwaite!' I laughed bitterly.

'Oh, yes,' Monty looked thoughtful, 'that's another thing – don't call me Monty once she arrives; please always remember to give me the full Montgomery – Mummy is very patriotic and in fact she had quite a crush on the Field Marshall during the war.'

Well, I did know, Lord help me: I'd heard it ad nauseam from Nina's own lips on many occasions and I didn't need her only-begotten son trotting it out again.

Very soon, Monty and I started preparing for Nina's fast-approaching visit: we hauled out the horrendous dung-coloured vase with the green dragons and perched it on the hall table, hung the three-dimensional picture of a ship in full sail on the landing, displayed various ugly ornaments and hastily polished brassware, retrieved Nina's choice of bed-linen and towels, and put every last item on show somewhere in the house. Oh yes, we also remembered to bring out the kitchenware, glassware, floral dinner service and matching tea-set in readiness.

'There,' Monty said, looking around with a satisfied smirk on the morning of Nina's visit. 'That should keep the old girl happy.'

'It's more than I am,' I replied sulkily. 'It doesn't look like our home any more.'

Nina arrived decked out in diamonds, just in time for dinner, and we were soon caught up in her chatter and swathed in her smoke.

As she lit a pink Balkan Sobranie cocktail cigarette after the main course, she coughed deeply and said, 'Pamela darling, the broccoli was delicious if a mite too salty, and talking of salty, did I ever tell you I met naughty Lord Montgomery of Alamein during the war? He was only a Field Marshall then, and of course was elevated to the nobility later on. He was utterly charming, a bit of a flirt, but at the same time a real gentleman, and he actually said to me...'

'Yes, Nina, you've told me before,' I interrupted her, a bit abruptly I thought, before I could stop myself.

'Oh, really I...' Nina's voice trailed off for a moment before rallying. 'Well, anyway, Pamela dear, we simply must go for our constitutional on the pier tomorrow. I can show you the very spot where my darling spouse proposed to me – he was such a good husband and father – I miss him to this day, and by the way, dear, please don't put too much sugar in the custard, I'm sweet enough, haha, and, oh yes, what are we planning on calling our new baby, the precious child?'

I had the wicked idea of winding her up, so I said straight-faced, 'I like Septimus for a boy, and Ermintrude if it's a girl.'

'Oh!' Nina's eyes flickered: my sarcasm was obviously not lost on her. She looked at me quizzically but, lighting a blue Balkan Sobranie cocktail cigarette, began a fresh onslaught. 'Whatever you say, dear, although I had thought traditional family names would be nice, but never mind. Now then, about breast-feeding, you'll need to drink Guinness and persevere during the first few weeks, you know…'

Oh Lord, she's expecting me to call the poor kid Montgomery or Nina, I thought, and after a few more minutes of torment, I made the excuse that I was feeling nauseous. So, giving Nina a quick peck on her parchment cheek, I kissed a bemused Monty goodnight and took myself off to bed – it was only 8.p.m. and we hadn't quite finished eating. Well, I hope she gets the message, I thought, rather cruelly. Why was I always the one who had to compromise? Why couldn't other people take their turn? I have my pregnancy to deal with, for goodness sake!

Come to think of it, I was feeling quite sick, probably through breathing in that foul smoke! How could Nina lecture me on wholesome living when she was polluting the air in our home? Oh well, the old trout was getting on in years, so I ought really to make allowances and look forward to the day when we waved her goodbye.

I believe I'm a good person really, and my inner soul realised that Nina was only trying to help, but her idea of maternity wear and baby clothes did not match mine in the slightest. She insisted on taking me to Debenham's over in Quorum Thisbé and, flashing her credit card, encouraged me to try on the most garish garments festooned with flounces. 'They'll hide the bump,' Nina announced loudly with a wink to everyone in earshot.

I protested at her generosity but she ignored me and bought the lot, plus three dozen nappies and a whole layette in white and yellow, together with cot, highchair and baby buggy.

'Debenham's are just terrific – they'll deliver all this stuff by tomorrow morning in good time for us to go for our walk on the pier,' she smiled, patting my arm with her bejewelled hand.

That flaming pier again – God, how can I bear it, I wept inwardly. And Lord help me, she has such awful taste – apart from her diamonds, that is. I'll strangle her if she doesn't stop buying me things.

'Pamela,' Nina said, puffing on a green Balkan Sobranie cocktail cigarette the following Sunday as we strolled along the pier for the umpteenth time that week, 'are you looking after yourself? Eating for two, I hope, although I haven't noticed you increasing your calorie intake? Oh, look, dear, here's the very spot where my darling proposed to me – I miss him to this day…but I must say you look dreadful with those dark circles under your eyes and that greasy hair hanging in tendrils.'

'Nina,' I said through gritted teeth, 'I am perfectly fine. Remarks like that are not designed to make me feel a million dollars, are they?'

Nina stopped in her tracks and stubbed out her cigarette. She coughed and stared at me, her eyes watering a little, maybe from the smoke, maybe not. 'I think it's time Nanna Nina went home,' she croaked, 'I'm rather frail these days, and I miss my own bed.'

As good as her word, she packed and left that very evening, Thursday, the 29th July.

Hmm, Nanna Nina, indeed! We waved her off although I couldn't raise a smile. When we came back inside, Monty said, 'Mummy shouldn't be driving at her age, you know. I worry about the old gal – mightn't we encourage her to move down here, closer to us? She could be a great help with the baby.' He had a strange look on his face.

What a thought – having the old frump living in close proximity! 'Monty,' I said through stiff lips, 'the day that Quagmire Pier vanishes in a puff of smoke is the day I shall invite Nina down here to live. *Comprenez*?'

Well, dear reader, if you have been following the national news with the very modicum of attention, you'll now have an idea of how things are turning out, considering the pier burned down that very night! I shall begin the outcome by stating that although I am not at all superstitious or religious, such a sign cannot be viewed as mere coincidence.

At my insistence, a surprised and overjoyed Monty began building a granny annexe.

I feel certain dear Nina will be of great assistance with our twins Septimus Montgomery and Ermintrude Nina when they arrive early next year, and the granny-to-be is already doing her bit by trying her damndest to give up smoking.

And as the phoenix rises from the ashes of Quagmire Pier and those Balkan Sobranie cocktail cigarettes, so shall my dutiful relationship with Nanna Nina blossom and grow: I hope – but don't hold your breath!

DAFT AS A BRUSH

Hello! My name is Harold – Harold Hairbrush. That's what my lady calls me anyway – she likes to think of herself as something of an intellectual and probably stole the name from that spoof history book "1066 and All That" by Sellars and Yeatman, if she ever actually got around to reading it.

Not that I've read it myself, as I'm only a tortoiseshell brush after all is said and done, but I do like to keep up to speed on things, make sure I'm *au fait* with the world at large.

I do find that difficult, though, lying here on my front most of the time, on my lady's dressing table. Sometimes she will take me into the bathroom and give me a wash and scrub with that thing she uses on her nails. I won't deign to give it the name "brush", a little piddling thing like that.

And it's a bright shade of vomit green, the horrible article. I refuse to communicate with it, even when it's rubbing away at my bristles. I blank it out, I have to think of something else entirely, like, how wonderful it would be if my lady had really long hair.

My one desire in life is to run my bristles through waist-length tresses. Hmm, lovely! Anyway, back to earth – my lady soon puts me back on the dressing table after giving me a good shake under the hairdryer.

I'm not on the dressing table alone – oh, no! My lady is not at all tidy! There's a plastic tube of hand cream; a growing pile of used tissues; a cigarette lighter (yes, my lady is a dedicated smoker and stinks of stale fags); three pound coins gathering dust; a food-encrusted fork (which she uses for eating takeaways in bed and, my goodness, that fork really needs a good soak); a whistle key-chain with 12 keys, each one belonging to past and/or present boyfriends – a sort of tally, like notches on the bedpost, if you like, of her sexual conquests; and a dog-eared book of poetry bought long ago from a charity shop – never even been opened, let alone read, because she is a right poseur, my lady is, and as I previously mentioned, a wannabe intellectual – hah!

But sorry, I digress – and also on the dressing table are three ball-point pens, two of which have long since dried out, and a small china dog also from the charity shop. The china dog and I are quite entertained by my lady and her questionable activities.

Of course, the china dog and I know everything that goes on in the bedroom! But we're loyal and have agreed that our lips shall remain sealed, and, speaking personally, you'll never get any secrets whatsoever out of me – we-e-ell, except for the time my lady threw me at her boyfriend, screaming "Take that, you beast" – nearly broke me, it did, and my bristles really found their mark – they left a red mark on his head. Served him right too, accusing her of having an affair – how dare he suggest such a thing?

Then she broke down in floods of tears, shrieking, 'Oh, look what you've made me do, you nearly broke Harold, and see, he's lost three bristles because of your hard skull – oh, you're so lazy and slow – why couldn't you have dodged out of the way?' And she threw herself on the bed sobbing as if her heart would break.

He then rushed off and stormed out, slamming the front door. *She* instantly stopped crying, leapt off the bed and rang a man named Roger who seemed to calm her down quite a bit. Roger came over very soon and they closed the bedroom curtains, so I'm afraid I can't tell you what went on then because it was somewhat dark but they were making quite a lot of noise, not actually speaking, but making a lot of other types of noise. The china dog and I just tutted to each other…*Oho, here we go again...!*

My lady seemed to like Roger very much, but when the other chap didn't come back and Roger moved in, things began to go pear-shaped pretty quickly – (by the way, I don't really know what pear-shaped means but I've heard my lady say it such a lot of times recently, so hopefully you'll get my drift).

I felt so sorry for Roger, or in fact any man, and there were many, at least 12 going by the key-ring, ensnared by my lady's charms. I do like to remain loyal to my lady, but the china dog and I agree that she is a right vamp, if you want our honest opinion, and she does treat men very badly, the poor devils – even I realise that and I'm only a hairbrush.

Anyway, what happened next was both wonderful and terrible – and this is me speaking now, from personal experience at a ringside seat. It happened while my lady was out one afternoon, and Roger was in.

He telephoned a woman named Gloria who very soon arrived at our house. Sunbeams were streaming in through the bedroom window, so I saw straightaway through the dancing dust particles that Gloria had absolutely gorgeous, beautifully thick, long blonde hair almost to her waist. My bristles were – well – bristling with anticipation. Would she? Or would she not? I held my breath...

Well, first of all the curtains were pulled across to shut out the sunlight and then, as thirty-something people seem to do, Roger and Gloria made lots of noise at the other side of the room.

And – alleluia – when they'd quietened down, Gloria *did* pick me up, carried me into the bathroom, and brushed me again and again through her lovely tresses. I was in ecstasy; I freely admit it. I was orgasmic! This was what a brush was for – I wasn't meant to merely scrape through a feathery minimalist style like the one my lady affected. I liked getting my teeth, or my bristles, into some real meat – i.e. a proper head of hair. How I wished that Gloria would take me with her, but, no, after pulling out a few stray strands and giving me a cursory shake, she put me back on my lady's dressing table: I, however, somehow managed to hold onto one hair!

When my lady came home exhausted, the poor dear – and we have to hand it to her, dedicated shopping is her forte and, apart from sexual conquest, her main interest in life – she threw herself as per usual on the bed for a while, then got up and approached the cluttered dressing table.

Well, you've guessed it! She picked me up and absent-mindedly began to yank me through her sparse string, examining me worriedly for any excess hair-loss, when she suddenly shrieked and, holding me at arm's length, began pulling one very long blonde hair from between my bristles.

Of course, when Roger returned, my lady was lying in wait and he wondered what had hit him – well, it was me, actually, right between the eyes. A couple more precious bristles fell to the carpet.

But old Roger was a hero – he picked me up, put me in his pocket as Exhibit A, packed his bag and took me with him to glorious Gloria, who was awaiting him with open arms across town in a concrete tower block apartment rented from the Council.

But although Roger won his ABH case, he was ordered to hand me back to my lady, together with some silly bits of jewellery and a couple of manky fur coats that he'd borrowed from her, after she'd spitefully counter-accused him of theft!

So, here I lie once more, on my front on the dressing table, still loyal to my lady.

Well, that's what she thinks! However, I'm not that daft – vindictive yes, but not daft, and the small china dog has enjoyed every minute of it!

IN/OUT

My hero is Mr Darcy from Pride and Prejudice. I love that story so much, it's my favourite of all time, and I've seen it on TV and at the Odeon. I also saw a film called Bridget Jones's Diary which didn't seem to have much to do with the Pride and Prejudice storyline, well hardly anything at all really, and apart from him being called Mr Darcy it was actually unrecognisable, if you want my honest opinion.

Yes, Mr Darcy is my ideal man, so much so that I even tried reading the book a few years back but never got very far (it was hard going, all those words!) – my mind kept wandering to that image of him in his wet shirt after he swims across the lake, and I was so impatient to read that bit that I dipped in and out of the book but couldn't find it at all, no matter how I tried, so I gave up and watched the video again instead.

Anyway, when I saw a dating advert about someone called Mark describing himself as a Mr Darcy lookalike searching for his very own Elizabeth Bennett, my heart nearly bounded out of my chest and I just had to jot down his details. Later on, I told Rosie about it.

'Get in!' she screamed and so, together, we composed a nice letter of introduction that very evening.

We decided to put that my name was Elizabeth, a Personal Assistant in communications, with big baby blue eyes and blonde hair, medium build, and liked cinema, TV soaps, theatre, Hello magazine, and nights in/out.

Not that I go to the theatre very much, in fact I've been about twice in my whole life and then only to the local pantomime, but it looked good on paper, made me sound like a woman of the world, all sophisticated and glamorous, the sort that appears in Hello. I posted my letter to a box number at the local newspaper office.

I didn't think I'd get a reply but, at Rosie's suggestion, I went on a crash diet and dyed my hair blonde, only it turned out a sort of burnt straw colour. Well at least it wasn't boring old brown any more – but I was starving hungry all the time.

The day I received Mark's reply via the box number, sheer panic took over. His letter, which was written in a beautiful round hand, suggested that I telephone him to make an appointment to meet. I was at my wits' end! Rosie was sympathetic.

'Look Patsy,' she said, 'all you have to do is pick up the telephone.'

'But I can't,' I said, 'my voice gets higher and higher when I'm nervous.'

'Well, I'll ring him and pretend to be you,' she said. 'Come on now, are you in or out?'

'In,' I squeaked.

What a good friend I have in Rosie! She telephoned Mark and made a date for 8 o'clock the following night in the beer garden at The Akimbo Arms.

'He sounds lovely,' she told me, 'so educated and sexy, a real-life Mr Darcy, but don't forget to answer to Elizabeth because he thinks that's your name and he loves it a lot.'

I suddenly got cold feet. 'Oh, there's so much to remember,' I moaned. 'Why did I start all this?'

'Come on, Patsy,' Rosie huffed, 'you can do it; don't let me down after all my efforts on your behalf.'

'Well, as long as he's not proud or prejudiced like the real Mr Darcy,' I said, 'I cannot abide moody men.'

'Now, this is no time to change your taste in the opposite sex,' she said, 'I'll go with you. Don't worry your pretty little blonde (*ahem*) head, I shall stand a respectable distance away. I want to make sure he's not an axe murderer or something, and then if you decide he's not your type, I can come over in response to a pre-arranged signal – like a wave or something.'

'You are so clever, Rosie,' I said, 'What would I do without you?'

'The Lord knows and he won't split,' she replied.

Rosie had told Mark to look out for a blonde-haired girl in a cotton dress and matching jacket in turquoise blue with white piping, white handbag, white stiletto heels, little white cotton gloves, a shell necklace and earrings (clips, not pierced), purple lipstick and lashings of mascara. He'd said he hadn't yet decided what to wear for the occasion but would certainly recognise me from the description.

My heart sank – Rosie had obviously forgotten to check what I'd planned on wearing and now I would be obliged to get dolled up like a retro dog's dinner – why not a revolving bow-tie and floor-length kilt while I'm at it, I thought rather cattily.

However, these negative ideas were kept to myself: Rosie doesn't like criticism when she's organising people's affairs, and I try not to upset her because I depend so much on her opinion and guidance.

When we arrived at The Akimbo Arms beer garden the following evening, the word had obviously got around – there were four more of our workmates from the Quorum Thisbé call centre already there, Samantha, Latoyah, Aleesha and Kylie, dressed to the nines and giggling like silly schoolgirls.

'Never mind them, Patsy,' Rosie said, 'there's strength in numbers – at least you're not going to be dragged away and strangled, not while we're here to chaperone you. Now relax and enjoy the evening.'

A stag party of some kind appeared to be under way at one of the long trestle tables: a number of young men were drinking, indulging in high jinks and making a lot of good-humoured noise.

One of their party cocked his head and looked long and hard at me, and Rosie whispered, 'Oh blimey,

Patsy, *get in* – you've clicked,' and she laughed like a hyena on speed.

'No, I'll wait for Mark – you lot had better get lost – he'll be looking for a girl on her own,' I said, going to sit down at one of the small tables by myself.

'Yes, you're right,' squawked a mirthful Rosie. 'We'll go park ourselves near the lads – may as well enjoy ourselves while we're keeping an eye on you,' and so she and the girls moved towards the stag party's table in what they obviously believed was a seductive manner, swaying their shapely bodies and pouting their glossy plumped-up lips.

I felt really conspicuous, like a clown sitting there in that ridiculous get-up, and got through three glasses of wine pretty quickly. I had to buy them myself, of course. My chaperones appeared to be having the time of their lives soaking up double vodkas, courtesy of the stag party.

After half-an-hour of raucous jollifications, they all trooped off together to "Chop Sticks" for a Chinese meal as Rosie kindly advised me with a shriek, arm in arm with one of the lads.

'Oi, Mark, you wicked boy,' I heard her chortle as he patted her rear end. Yes, I do realise Mark is quite a common name but it still gave me a jolt to hear her say it and made me wonder sadly where *my* Mark had got to!

I sat there, trying to decide how much longer I should wait in the gathering dusk when Rosie popped back and asked if was OK on my own.

I nodded miserably and she said that, um, really, they were all quite worried about me and would I please promise that if my date hadn't turned up in another fifteen minutes to admit he was a no-show, put it down to experience, and go home for an early night, adding that she'd see me tomorrow at work to supervise my mountain of photocopying.

And so, although a murky drizzle had begun to fall, I waited for exactly another quarter of an hour as instructed (after all, Rosie is my line manager and I have follow her orders), then I took myself off home to my warm bed.

Honestly, I don't know how I'd go on without Rosie's good sense: she always knows the right thing to do. Really and truly, I am so lucky to have her as my best friend as well as my boss.

YELLOW

It was dusk on a late autumn afternoon when Simon left the office, kicking through fallen leaves on the pavement, towards the bus stop. He had been able to escape on time just now using some false pretext but, if the truth were told, he was feeling too fatigued and depressed to work late this evening.   Even so, he was dreading the tiresome journey home, but tonight he was in luck, and the bus arrived early.

As Simon edged along in the queue, a sixth sense made him glance round, and he caught his breath at the sight of a girl in a bright yellow coat.

Tall and tanned and young and lovely!

'Sounds like a cue for a song,' he thought.   And he hummed the tune silently.

Simon was carried along by the crush and found a seat at the back.   As usual, the bus was full of flinty-faced, sombre-clad commuters reading the evening paper or staring into space.

Simon could never feel any affinity with these people. *I'll never be like them – no hope, no spark of joy in their dreary little lives.   This time next year, I could be out of the rat-race and backpacking around the world.*

He watched the girl in the yellow coat pay her fare, saw that her smile was wasted on the world-weary driver only intent on giving correct change.

She moved down the aisle of the bus, her body swaying, a sunbeam shimmering amongst the drabness. Simon was mesmerised by her approaching presence, recognising what he truly believed was a kindred spirit.

Through the mist of his thrall, he suddenly realised there was only one spare seat and it was next to him. Oh what luck! He shifted along exaggeratedly, allowing her to sit.

She sat, offering thanks with an enigmatic tilt of the head, her mind probably far away, maybe somewhere warm, perhaps the place where she had acquired that smooth, golden skin-tone and sun-streaks in her long blonde hair.

By way of reply, Simon pressed his lips together, gave a brief nod – the best he could manage under her bright spell. If only he had the nerve to speak to her, ask her to go for a drink, even!

Such overwhelming nearness caused a hammering in Simon's chest – *Don't let her hear it,* he prayed and, gazing straight ahead, his face was like granite, the shade of his suit and prematurely-greying hair.

ELOPEMENT

Without a backward glance at Mangrove Lodge, her father's residence, Frederika dodged deftly into the taxi and sat staring at the cabbie's frayed shirt collar and lank tendrils of hair.

'Mummy and Daddy trust me, they won't think to check the school, which gives me enough time to make a clean getaway,' she had decided, her head a maelstrom of confusion and guilt. She had thought this thing out and meant to go through with it: nothing should stand in the way of her heart's desire.

At Heathrow Airport, instead of making for the Swissair desk, Frederika joined the queue checking in for the flight to Boston, Massachusetts, and was soon on the plane seated next to a middle-aged man in Business Class awaiting take-off.

'Are you going across the pond on business or pleasure?' The white-haired, dark-suited chap was scrutinising her in a friendly manner: after all, they had seven hours to kill in each other's company.

'Well, both, really,' Frederika replied, wondering how much to tell, how much to keep back. But she was very excited and wanted to externalise her thoughts, to crystallise them so they could be better examined. 'I'm actually going to Boston to get married.'

'But how wonderful,' the elderly man smiled. 'Only, I was wondering why you keep looking towards the door, as if half expecting someone to join you.'

'Oh, I see – do I appear so nervous then?' the girl laughed uneasily, thinking why not tell this kind man all about it? I'll never see him again, he can be my confidant, something on the lines of the Ancient Mariner and the Wedding Guest, and maybe he will have some good advice to give.

'Brides are usually nervous, but I am wondering why you're travelling alone. Are your family not going to your wedding?' Her companion looked puzzled.

'I may as well tell you – I have to ease my burden. I'm eloping! My family think I'm going back to that stupid finishing school in Switzerland – so now you know the truth.'

'But won't they worry about you? Surely the school will check when you don't turn up?'

'No, I've got a few days' grace in that regard. I lied about the new term, which doesn't start until next week. I know it's a sin to tell a lie, but desperation made me do it. I can let them all know once this business is done and dusted, then it'll be a very neat *fait accompli*.'

'You must be very much in love to go to these lengths,' remarked the man dreamily. Then he turned to Frederika with a serious expression and remarked, 'I'm assuming your family disapprove!'

'Ahem, well it's a different religion for a start, you see!' Frederika suddenly wanted to put the record straight, even with a stranger. 'I've been taking instruction in the true faith, but in secret, as my parents, particularly my mother, who is such a snob, would never countenance such a thing. I did broach the subject almost two years ago, begged them, in fact, more than a few times, but they were dead set against it, so I've arranged matters on my own. They thought I'd just forget it in due course, but my love grew stronger over time. My new family are ready to welcome me with open arms.'

'Hmm, let's see, I can tell that you come from a privileged background. I hope you don't think me impertinent, but I recognise the name on your hand luggage. Aren't you connected with Dr Frobisher of Quagmire Village? No, please don't feel nervous – I don't know him personally, only from reading his referrals: I happen to be a surgeon at Quorum Thisbé General Hospital.'

'Well, you've guessed straight off. Yes, I am his daughter. Sad isn't it? You see, he's Church of England and I wish to marry into the Roman Catholic faith.'

'Well, these things happen in life. He'll come round eventually. But how about your fiancé and his family, can they provide for you?' The man felt he was being rather too personal now.

Frederika didn't seem to notice, and replied, 'They're poor but self-sufficient and happy, and I know it's not my father's money they're interested in. I have very few possessions with me. I was told just to bring myself. They'll be meeting me off the plane in Boston.'

'I guess they're in farming, from what you say,' suggested her inquisitor.

Frederika laughed joyfully. 'Well, yes, you could say that, amongst other things – my fiancé is rather good with sheep.'

'Nothing wrong with that, my dear, and all I can say is you seem very content about your decision, but don't be hasty, don't cut yourself off entirely from your parents, and – good luck in your new life.' Her companion had, naturally, many reservations about the whole matter.

The remainder of their journey across the Atlantic passed very pleasantly, and eventually they were touching down at Boston's Logan International Airport where they bade a friendly farewell, feeling as if they had known each other for years.

Goodness, how remiss of me, I didn't even ask his name, Frederika realised as she strode towards the Arrivals lounge carrying only one small suitcase.

Her erstwhile companion watched her walk away as he struggled with his many pieces of luggage, until she was swallowed up in the throng. He shrugged, feeling bemused, uneasy, as if he had been an unwilling party to a deception.

The girl was not worried: she was thrilled to have arrived at last after all these many months of planning.

A middle-aged woman approached and gathered Frederika into her arms in a warm embrace.

'Welcome, my child, my daughter, how lovely to see you, come along, let us get you home.'

'Hello mother,' Frederika whispered, safe in the circle of plump comforting arms, before being led towards a dark blue people-carrier in the car park.

After a short drive, they arrived at an old house set in gardens screened by high trees, the rooks cawing a welcome. The newcomer was taken to a small neat bedroom where she unpacked and changed for supper.

Her rosy-cheeked new family were around the table and they excitedly told her that all the arrangements had been made and tomorrow she would be married in the church . 'Oh, so soon; but I am sure this is the right thing to do,' she thought.

Early next morning, after a cramped night in the hard narrow bed, Frederika was helped to get ready for the wedding ceremony. They dressed her in a long white gown with a diaphanous veil covering head and shoulders. 'Oh, you look so beautiful, my child, my daughter,' they said.

She was led into the stone chapel, strewn with fresh flowers, where she prostrated herself wholeheartedly before the altar, full of joy, arms spread wide, wearing her new gold wedding ring as a bride of Christ.

A BRIEF CASE

'…and there's just time to grab a coffee before I get all this photocopying done,' mused Helena Goodbody patting her fair hair; this was a reflex action employed whilst thinking, as her shoulder-length curls were naturally tousled.

Helena's patchwork skirt swung as she strode in tasselled calfskin boots towards Quorum Thisbé College cafeteria. The day outside looked quite breezy, befitting a seaside location, although the spring sun streaming through long windows was warm.

But Helena's thoughts were not on the weather, nor indeed her paperwork: she was ruminating on ex-husband Theo and his latest attempts at persuading her into a long weekend away. These days Helena preferred life as a singleton even though she still regarded Theo as her anchor, her mainstay. After all, they'd had twenty-five years together, albeit childless – old habits die hard.

She turned through double doors into the cafeteria and was almost knocked over by a young English tutor, Isabelle Deakin, whose glazed eyes gazed at Helena in shock.

'Hold on, Isabelle – what on earth's the matter? You look as if you've seen a ghost!' Helena gripped the woman's arm and sat her down at a table by the door. 'Now then; tell me what's wrong.'

Isabelle looked around wildly and gasped, 'It's my briefcase – it's been stolen – it's gone, disappeared. It has all the poetry competition results, the winning entries and certificates! Oh, what can I do?'

Helena tried to soothe. 'It's not your fault it was pinched. Crime is all around us – it could happen to anyone. Why don't we simply report it to the principal?'

Isabelle groaned. 'No, no, not just yet. I'll tell Mike, erm, Mr Kindersley, later on after classes. He might be very angry about it, about my being careless, I mean. Honestly, I feel such a fool for not taking more care with important documents. Perhaps you could help me look for it, Helena? The Poetry Prizegiving isn't until the 22nd, which gives us just over a week to do something about it.'

'Well, I don't know,' Helena said. 'It could be very difficult. Where exactly were you when you realised it was gone?'

'In here, of course. I was just having a coffee at this very table, reading the college newsletter, and I'm sure the briefcase was on the floor by my chair. When I got up to leave, it had gone. Then I thought I'd retrace my steps back to the Staff Room, just in case, but there was no sign of the briefcase, so I came back here to have another look, see if I'd overlooked it.'

Isabelle sniffed and looked close to tears.

'Yes, I see. There's no-one in here now. Who else was around when you were having coffee? Did you notice anyone nearby?'

'No, I was too preoccupied reading the newsletter.' Isabelle was looking very nervous.

'And where is the newsletter you were reading? I don't see it anywhere,' Helena was puzzled.

'Oh, I must have – oh, I don't know. Perhaps Katie took it when she cleared the table.'

'But the table hasn't been cleared – look at all this dirty crockery. Are you sure you sat here?'

'No, perhaps I didn't sit at this table. I can't be certain now. Please don't confuse me any more than I am already.' Isabelle covered her eyes with both hands.

'But how can I help if you won't try to remember exactly what happened?' Helena asked. 'Look here, go to your next class and I'll see what can be unearthed. The rest of my afternoon is clear, except for some copying.'

Isabelle Deakin was full of thanks and made a speedy exit. Helena decided that a few questions at the crime scene could throw some light on recent events.

A young woman serving behind the counter smiled from under her canteen forage cap as Helena approached. 'Hello, Katie. I wonder if you can help me. I'm trying to locate someone who was in here, say, ten minutes ago, at or near the table by the double doors.'

'It's been fairly busy this afternoon, but it did thin out about fifteen minutes ago. Then there were three people, the Comstock twins and a new girl, sitting over there by the window. Can't say I noticed anyone at the table by the double doors. It's draughty there, so people avoid it.' Katie was holding back a sneeze.

'Did you remove a college newsletter from that or any other table?' asked Helena.

'No. Why? Who says I did?' asked the girl, swiping her top lip with her sleeve.

'No-one said anything – I was just wondering!' Helena was trying to sound encouraging. 'And when you say there was nobody at the table by the double doors, didn't you see Isabelle Deakin sitting there a few minutes before I came in?'

'Miss Deakin? No, she wasn't sitting at any table. I saw her come in by the far door, rush straight across and nearly knock you over,' sniffled the young woman, searching for a tissue in her commodious pockets. 'Does that help?'

'Thank you, yes it does, it helps a great deal,' Helena could smell a rat now as well as a little fishiness, and she left the cafeteria more puzzled than before. Someone's lying, she thought, and I mean to find out what's going on.

Helena knew the Comstock twins, Keith and Kenneth, and she finally tracked them down in the gymnasium. They were two peas in a pod, and invariably closed ranks in the face of authority.

'Hello, lads, I'd like to ask you some questions,' she said in a friendly fashion.

'Hi, Mrs Goodbody. But don't come too near, we've both got colds.' They began to towel the sweat off their brawny shoulders.

'There's a lot of it about. Thanks for the warning. Maybe you caught it in the cafeteria. Erm, when you were in there this afternoon, did you happen to see Isabelle Deakin at the table near the double doors?'

They raised their eyebrows at each other. 'Why, what's she done now?' Keith's grinning face was shiny with perspiration.

Helena ignored the insinuation. 'Well, let me come at it by the soft underbelly. Who was the girl sitting at the table with you? Is she perhaps a student at this college?'

'No, not a student. That would be Shirley Beasley. She's fairly new; just started in the office; admin, that sort of thing,' Kenneth said. 'But now you mention it, Shirley *was* asking about Isabelle Deakin, wanting to know how long she's worked here and stuff.'

'Hmm, interesting. And to repeat my first question, did either of you see Isabelle Deakin in the cafeteria this afternoon?'

The Comstock twins regarded her archly. 'Couldn't say we did, Mrs Goodbody. Sorry we can't be of any help there.'

Right, thought Helena, next stop the office, do my photocopying and see this Shirley person. She strode off determinedly, patchwork skirt flaring, to the first floor suite of offices.

She immediately knew who Shirley Beasley was, simply because hers was the only unfamiliar face.

Helena began shuffling her papers, glancing sideways to get a good look at the new girl, who was attractive in a hard way, with sleek black hair, red lipstick, long painted fingernails and gold hoop earrings.

Shirley, sensing Helena's interest, looked up and gave a tight little smile.

Helena walked across. 'Hello, you must be Shirley Beasley? I'm Helena Goodbody, Creative Writing. Welcome to Quorum Thisbé College. I hope they're treating you well?'

'Yes, thank you! Mike Kindersley is very nice to work for. Pleased to meet you, I'm sure,' lisped the girl, tapping her nails on the desk.

'I was talking to the Comstock twins just now and apparently you were all together in the cafeteria this afternoon. May I ask, did you notice anyone sitting at the table near the double doors?'

'I can't say, really. I know hardly anyone at all in the college; I've only been here a couple of weeks.' Shirley was inspecting her nails closely.

'Yes, but did you see anyone at that table, even if you didn't know who it was?'

'Maybe I did, maybe I didn't. I wasn't taking much notice. Those Comstock twins are an absolute scream.' Shirley Beasley paused for a second. 'Why, what's happened?'

'Oh, something has been mislaid, that's all.'

'Sorry I can't be of any help,' Shirley turned away and began to type, her false fingernails making a metallic clatter on the keys.

I need to do more in-depth prying now, though Helena, making towards Michael Kindersley's office. His name does seem to crop up such a lot, and anyway why would a new admin girl mention him at all – it's not as if she's his PA.

Outside the principal's door, Helena heard raised voices from within; one belonged to Isabelle, the other to Mr Kindersley who was also having a coughing fit. 'Aha, perhaps she's confessed about mislaying the briefcase already,' Helena thought, and moved quickly away, wondering what to do next.

She went to the Staff Room, texted Isabelle and sat waiting for her to turn up, which she did twenty minutes later, her face as pale as before but with two red-rimmed eyes.

'Look Isabelle, I know you're upset, but are you telling me the whole truth about the briefcase? I can't find anything out at all.'

'Oh, it's turned up now, Helena; I'm sorry you were troubled. Someone returned it to my locker.'

'Come on now! I think I deserve a better explanation than that. What's going on? Why are you so obviously upset?'

'I'm not upset – oh all right then, I'll spill the beans, and perhaps you could still help me.' Isabelle's eyes began to water. 'The briefcase also contained some private letters. Whoever took the briefcase returned it with the poetry stuff intact but kept the letters.'

'And were the letters anything to do with Michael Kindersley?' asked Helena gently.

'Only partially,' replied Isabelle, avoiding the other woman's gaze. 'I'm being got at – someone is sending me poison pen letters! And I had no idea who was doing it until I realised Shirley Beasley had turned up out of the blue recently. I used to know her five years ago at Quorum Thisbé Academy. There was a dreadful scandal involving the principal and some students, and I had to leave. It can't be anyone but Shirley who's sending me these horrible letters, except it won't do her any good as Mr Kindersley has known all along about my past. I'm just so worried other people might get hold of the letters and read them.'

'I don't suppose you've reported the letters to the police?' Helena knew this was a pointless question.

'No, of course not. I've only told Mr Kindersley and we both agree that the police shouldn't be involved.'

'So, let's go over the facts. We seem to have two mysteries here,' Helena said smoothly. 'Who wrote those poison pen letters – you don't know for sure it was Shirley Beasley – and also, who took the briefcase, and returned it minus those letters. Good grief, it doesn't make any kind of sense.'

That evening, Helena telephoned Theo and went through all the mysterious happenings of the day. She asked for his considered and wise opinion.

'Look for the green-eyed monster,' he advised. 'And now to more important matters: how about our no-strings weekend break in Paris? Shall I book it?'

The next morning, after a dreamless night's sleep, Helena looked for Isabelle at the college. 'I think I've solved the mystery for you,' she announced.

Isabelle was obviously shaken. 'Oh, really? What have you come up with?'

'Well, for a start, your story just doesn't hold water. I think you hid the briefcase containing the poetry stuff – it was never stolen from the cafeteria or anywhere else. And you have not received poison pen letters. You're having an affair with Michael Kindersley, as is Shirley Beasley, although she's been here only a short time. She obviously made a beeline for him to settle some old score with you, and you were so jealous of her and afraid of possibly being replaced in Mr Kindersley's affections that you invented this story hoping to implicate Shirley so that she'd either be dumped or sacked. And this is why you've been so upset because Mr Kindersley wouldn't believe you'd received such letters without the evidence of his own eyes. Naturally, you can't produce the letters because they never existed, and so you pretended they'd been stolen. Your briefcase containing the poetry stuff was quite simply a smokescreen, a vehicle, to make the whole tissue of lies seem authentic – all for Mr Kindersley's benefit. That of course explains why you didn't want the police to be involved. When you realised how deep I was digging for the truth, you changed your tune very quickly and pretended the briefcase had been returned, although my guess is that it was in your locker all along. Have I got that correct?'

'Hmm, no, it's nothing but a tall tale, Helena Goodbody. You should try harder next time,' Isabelle's lips twitched and she averted her eyes.

But Helena was unstoppable. 'Furthermore, when you almost knocked me over in the cafeteria, you had just come from Mr Kindersley's office in a rage because he wouldn't believe you about the poison pen letters and had ordered you to show them to him, which is when you decided on a whim to pretend the briefcase had gone missing and to use me as an unwilling tool in your deception.'

'Huh, what rubbish,' Isabelle said weakly.

Helena continued, 'I won't mention this to anyone concerned, on condition you go straight to Mr Kindersley and confess you were lying. I doubt whether he'll punish you as he is too involved. And it would be advisable to finish your relationship with him – you'd be better off with a faithful man, someone nearer your own age. Anyway, what about the Comstock twins? I could tell by their body language that there's something going on, something in the air.'

'Oh, you guessed. I can't keep anything from you. Well, recently I've been consoling myself with Keith Comstock, if you must know.' Isabelle was attempting a faint smirk now.

'I see! So now you've got a toyboy! But how do you know which twin is Keith? Methinks they're amusing themselves, having a game with you, Isabelle. Taking it in turns, probably. They're incorrigible, a law unto themselves. You should give them a wide berth too, if you have any sense. And now I'm going to make a telephone call.'

'Oh, you're not telling the police?'

'No, of course not. That would be up to Mr Kindersley or, indeed, Shirley Beasley, if she ever finds out you slandered her. Now you should go and sort out your affairs. There's more to life than sex, you know.'

Helena couldn't wait to ring Theo, to let him know that, thanks to his wise hint, she had solved the mystery of the missing briefcase. He was pleased to hear the full story.

'Not bad,' he laughed.

'Not bad – is good,' she said with glee. 'But more importantly, when are we going on our no-strings weekend to Paris? I could do with a nice rest at a pavement café on the Left Bank.'

THE EVENING NEWS

I don't really believe in ghosts, although I've been afraid of them all my life!

Even as a child, I was a clear-headed realist, but still would bury myself beneath the bedclothes, too highly-strung to expose even one finger above the eiderdown in the event some ghastly phantom saw fit to grasp at my flesh. I reasoned it was sensible to hedge one's bets but my intelligence told me I was a fool. So how to explain the strange turn my life has taken? This is a true account of what befell.

During the Great Depression, Rubenstein's Bespoke Tailors rapidly lost custom and all employees were given notice of dismissal. I had toiled there, man and boy, for twenty years and Mr Rubenstein himself gave me the sad news, confiding that he planned to cut his losses and enjoy a well-earned retirement.

Being prudent, I moved into cheaper lodgings and subsisted on bread, cheese and weak beer, but nevertheless my life savings were fast diminishing and I dreaded the looming spectre of the workhouse.

Too proud to join the hordes of shabby cloth-capped men clamouring for work, I would instead spend time in the park or library, returning to my rooms at suppertime. On the way home I invariably bought an Evening Post from the man on the High Street in order to scan the meagre "situations vacant" section.

The newspaper seller had squatted on that same corner for many years. He wore a muffler over the lower part of his face, winter and summer alike, covering a disfigurement sustained in the Great War, so it was said. During our daily transaction, he uttered never a word.

On one particular late autumn evening, a foggy Friday as I recall, a barrel-organ warbled its insistent melody as I made my way along the glistening cobbles, grimly anticipating another evening spent reading by candlelight.

Dispirited by my situation, I avoided previous acquaintances and had gradually become friendless.

Stopping at the newsstand, I proffered some coppers and requested an Evening Post but the old man shook his head and handed over The Evening News. His eyes appeared remarkably luminous, with an amber glow, a strange phenomenon I had never before noticed.

I accepted the newspaper without demur and continued on my way, arriving home with no appetite for my meagre board.

Thinking to scan through the advertisements before eating, I sat in my wing-backed chair by the stone hearth. In spite of the early winter coolness, the grate remained empty, as it had since early March: frugality had become my watchword. I shook out the unfamiliar newspaper and my gaze was immediately drawn to the date at the top: Saturday, 14th November 1931.

Shocked for a moment, I looked again, certain the day was Friday, the 13th November. Could my eyes be deceiving me?

Or was I hallucinating through lack of sustenance? Perforce, I ate a portion of my meagre supper before taking up the newspaper once more but, no, that erroneous date proclaimed itself still. How could it have occurred? I read the newspaper from cover to cover, discovering what would happen between now and tomorrow evening.

Someone has a fertile imagination, I thought; and then my eye was drawn to a report concerning the greyhound races at a local stadium. All the Saturday racing results were listed, winners and odds, together with mention of an unknown man scooping a vast sum on an accumulator bet.

Some devil-driven energy possessed me, and it was a simple matter to calculate such a wager upon which to place the residue of my savings plus any other cash I might obtain before tomorrow afternoon.

An idea occurred! I knew that Mr Rubenstein, my erstwhile employer, carried a wallet stuffed with notes, and so, without a qualm, I waylaid him that evening as he walked home from his gentlemen's club. I shall never forget the horror in his eyes when he turned and recognised me with cudgel poised: I swear it had otherwise not been my intention to kill him.

After a restless night I arose early, and at midday travelled by omnibus to the greyhound stadium where the afternoon was spent risking every last penny in my possession.

By that evening I was a rich man, as the newspaper had reported. Joyfully, I carried off a large sum beyond my wildest imaginings.

I purchased a splendid house and, as the Great Depression eased, went into business as a gents' ready-to-wear outfitter.

I entered local society by dint of contributing to certain high-profile charities and became a well-known figure, a beloved benefactor, eventually being elected to the town council.

Being independent of spirit, I did not feel the need to take a wife in spite of being relentlessly pursued by many attractive ladies.

This was how it should be! I was king of my world, and no woman must be allowed to interfere with it – until Ursula, that is!

Ursula was a plain but wealthy spinster. An idea occurred and I began to pay her court. She was charmed by my blandishments, and a fulsome proposal of marriage was accepted with enthusiasm. I was then free to use Ursula's fortune to invest in a second business as a high-interest money-lender, or, in other words, a usurer. Greed had become my watchword!

At first, our union was happy enough until I began to resent my wife's peremptory attitude, her insistence on organising my life, even to bath times, the correct method of brushing one's teeth and the manner in which I ate my dinner.

Yes, Ursula's disapproving sniff dominated my waking hours and I yearned for former days, for single blessedness: yes, even memories of my erstwhile poverty evoked sweet nostalgia.

I began staying at the office or otherwise avoiding Ursula's company at every opportunity.

Naturally, upon our popular appointment as Mayor and Mayoress, we displayed a united front and were lauded as a totally dedicated, ideal couple.

But even to this day, and purely out of avarice, I regularly stop at the newsstand on the corner to purchase The Evening News, occasionally slipping the old man a florin which he accepts with a nod but without raising his head to make eye contact.

Then I scan the newspaper, heart thumping, but never again have I beheld an incorrect date. Until today, that is – another Friday, the 13th!

As I offered my coins this evening, the old man raised his head allowing those luminous amber eyes to bore into mine and, most unexpectedly, his muffler slipped, revealing his face set in a hideous grin.

With no thoughts of sympathy for the poor wretch, I snatched The Evening News and fled, but some instinct told me that my terrifying experience boded ill.

I hurried home with the sensation of footsteps following on behind.

At one point, I stopped and turned, my heart pounding, but no living soul appeared on the long murky street of wet cobbles, the only movement a skittering of dead leaves and a yellow mist swirling.

Then it was I sensed a hot breath on my cheek and a devil growl beyond my left ear. Every nerve in my body shrieked and I broke into a run.

In two minutes I had gained the house and, slamming the front door behind me, frantically locked myself in the downstairs study in spite of Ursula's strident voice insisting on being advised what ailed me.

*   *   *   *

And now I sit at my desk with The Evening News: the date at the top is tomorrow's…

The banner headlines dance before my eyes and scream in my ears…

MAYOR'S MYSTERIOUS DEATH

Our Mayoress stated to police that her husband locked himself in his study yesterday evening, refusing to open the door. At midnight the Mayoress retired to her bedchamber but was awoken in the early hours by the sound of the Mayor shrieking 'No, no, keep away'.

The Mayoress is adamant no person could have entered the house without her knowledge and she assumed the Mayor was having hallucinations, so summoned the doctor.

When police eventually broke down the door they found the Mayor sprawled in a grotesque position with an unfamiliar muffler draped around his neck and a horrible grin on his face: the ashes of The Evening News smouldered in the grate.

An autopsy will be held shortly but early signs indicate death was due to apoplexy. In the meantime, Councillor & Mrs Antrobus will be deputising for mayoral duties.

*   *   *   *

So here I sit, awaiting the inevitable. I stare at the door heavily bolted, the windows heavily shuttered, the solid chimney breast – could someone, something, perchance enter there?

Oh, how I long for my old life, my shabby rooms, afternoons in the library, bread, cheese, watery beer. Those were happy days, if only I had realised. We do not value what we have until it is gone.

And now, hedging my bets once again, I shall pray for my soul.

You see, I don't really believe in God, although I have been aware of Him all my life.

CHRISTMAS PUNCH

Alone in the crowd – I, Osbert Claude Ramsbottom, sit here in the Market Hall café with a cup of tea, people chattering and laughing around me. I've got nobody I can talk to about my situation.

It all started when I moved into Mr and Mrs Midgley's spare room as their lodger. Oh, it must be nigh on fifteen years ago now. I was employed at the local factory making gasholders. It was a damned good job, I had a great team of lads to work with, plus regular overtime as well, if I wanted it.

I was pretty content going to work of a morning with a good breakfast inside me served up by Mrs Midgley, and coming home on a night to a nice dinner which she would keep hot in the oven if I was working late. Then I would spend any spare time concentrating on my main interest, which is **the bike**. Mr and Mrs Midgley let me keep it in the back yard and I often saw them watching me through the kitchen window, nodding and smiling. I was like the son they never had.

When I wasn't tinkering, I stayed in my room, reading my magazines which were, ofcourse, all about

311

bikes. I had a transistor radio to listen to and didn't much care for television although the Midgleys often invited me downstairs if there was an interesting programme on, but mostly I preferred keeping to meself. On Bank Holidays and that, I'd usually teck meself off into the Yorkshire Dales or summat, any excuse to get on me bike and ride off.

During the week I hardly saw Rita, the Midgleys' young lass, being as how I was out of the house early and, when I got home of an evening, she'd most likely be up in her room doing her homework or out at her dancing class or piano lesson.

We did catch sight of each other at weekends sometimes, but then she was usually off out with her mates and, me being shy, I hardly said a word to her, even on Sunday dinnertimes when we all sat down to eat together, just like a proper family.

Mam and dad live in Manchester, so I didn't go back home much – except at Christmas, of course, or mebbe when I had a week off in the summer holidays. I once went camping with the lads from the factory but I wasn't keen, to be honest. They kept pulling my leg because I didn't much care for all them insects and whatnot. I don't like being teased, especially about things I'm scared of – or about being called Osbert Claude Ramsbottom, come to that! 'What a name to go to bed on,' they allus say!

Then suddenly, Rita Midgley left typing college and got an office job over the yard, opposite the factory.

And when the lads found out we lived in the same house, they used to tease the life out of me until they got fed up and went back to tecking the mickey out of me name.

That Christmas, there was a party in the works canteen and the office staff came to it, an'all. Being shy, I was stood standing by the wall with a half o' shandy when Rita and a couple of giggling workmates rushed up, and dragged me to the fruit punch table. 'Here, have one of these, Ossie,' they squawked, and shoved a glass into me hand.

Well, I don't drink nowt as a rule and this stuff went straight to me head! I started dancing and doing all sorts of daft things, really letting me hair down. Towards the end, I was sort of jiving with Rita when suddenly her feet got tangled in mine and she tripped, nearly falling full length. But I managed to catch her in time with one arm round her chest, the other round her small waist, and I felt her flesh, soft yet firm. By, she was a **grand lass**, definitely not built for speed, what with her big bust, wide hips and that! I had a strange feeling…I wanted to touch her again in her warm, dark places.

Rita blushed and said her mam would be pleased I'd saved her from a nasty tumble, and I mumbled summat on the lines that I'd allus be there to look after her. Her face lit up and she nodded.

And, o'course, we walked home together afterwards, seeing as how we lived in the same house. A lot of catcalls from the lads echoed behind us as we set off across the greasy cobbles down the dark lane. 'Take no notice,' Rita said, as she linked arms. 'Me mam and dad'll be that pleased.'

'Aye,' I said, not really tecking it in, still a bit fuddled by Christmas punch and that.

When we got home, Mr and Mrs Midgley were sitting in front of the TV watching some daft film.

'Mam, dad,' Rita gibbered, 'me and Ossie are engaged. He just asked me and I said yes.'

Mr Midgley took his pipe out of his mouth, said 'Oh, aye,' and stared at us.

Mrs Midgley's eyes glittered. 'It's what we've been expecting, Rita luv,' she said. 'But just think on, there's no hanky-panky in this house, not afore you're married; so Osbert you'll keep to your own room for now and we can all go to town on Saturday to choose the ring.' She paused for breath, but only for a second. 'And I don't believe in long engagements, so we can start making plans as soon as you like…'

After that, I was swept along on a tide of Mrs Midgley's making. I had to spend more time watching telly with them, less on tinkering with me bike. I hadn't really known Rita that well but it soon changed when she prattled on non-stop about her favourite soaps, quiz shows, romantic films, women's magazines, knitting patterns, clothes, makeup, pop music and office gossip: right malicious at times, she was. We hadn't got one thing in common, and the desire I'd felt for her flesh had soon melted away when I woke up with a right sodding hangover from that Christmas punch.

O' course the lads teased me rotten. It was all a big joke to them. 'Teck no notice of 'em,' snapped Rita, 'they're only jealous 'cos they haven't got a fiancey.'

Our wedding day dawned and I just went through with it, because what else could I do? I couldn't wriggle out of it or nowt: I was trapped and that's a fact! Mrs Midgley was not a woman to be argued with!

We went to Scarborough for our honeymoon and Mrs Midgley came with us: she'd booked the interconnecting room.

When it was bedtime, I reached out for Rita (I'd been reading up on what to do) and some of that feeling came back in me loins. But she pulled away. 'Ossie, we can't do it with me mam just t'other side of the wall,' she whispered.

When we got home, I moved into Rita's bedroom, which was full of dolls and lacy, girlie stuff. But it was the same thing at bedtime, and Rita wouldn't let me touch her with her parents in the next bedroom.

I gave up bothering and we had to stay married but celibate, like. But I allus had me bike for company.

About two years later, we managed to get our own little terraced house, one-up, one-down. We enjoyed decorating and buying furniture and soon moved in. That first night in our own home, Rita pretended to be asleep when I got into bed, and so it went. Things had gone on too long for us to change.

People asked us why no kids yet, year after year? I got teased by the lads at work: it made a change from being joshed about me daft name. But I tried to ignore it and o' course I had me bike to tinker with. She was my real companion, never complaining, never staring through evil glittering eyes, never snapping or bossing me around. We were content, me and me bike.

Then last night, after years of so-called marriage, Rita dropped her bombshell. 'I'm expecting,' she said.

'Oh,' I said, and suddenly seeing the light, added, 'is it the Messiah you're having, then?'

'Don't be daft, Ossie,' she snapped. 'Me mam was nagging and prying, I had to try somewhere else – you haven't got it in you, everybody says that!'

'Oh, I see! So everybody's been laughing behind me back?'

'No more than usual,' she sneered. 'And by the way, if you won't own the child, I'll move back home – *then* see what people will say. If you do own it, people'll think it's yours, which would be a good thing as folk wouldn't go on believing you're some kind of a wimp which, of course, you are, *Osbert Claude Ramsbottom* – ugh, what a name to go to bed on!' And she flounced off upstairs.

So – here I sit in the café, alone in the crowd, wondering what to do next. Some people might say I should've strangled her on the spot, but what actually happened was, I had a nightmare that I was strangling her – and yes, I strangled her in me sleep – honest to God!

DEAD LINE

Before fully surfacing from a sweet sleep, the old woman was aware of the strange quality of light penetrating her closed eyelids: there was no sound from the street except for the muffled hiss of a solitary car making its careful way past the house. The woman was instantly wide-eyed and lay there contemplating the ceiling where a brilliant reflection came streaming through a gap in the long curtains.

It was no yellow beam from the sun on a summer's morning, but a pale ambience, filtering through, embracing the room, chilling her nose and cheeks. She could almost smell it, knew that when she padded across the floor in bare feet to look, freshly fallen snow would be shrouding the world outside her window, sparkling, deep and white.

Slowly, the woman arose from her bed and, pulling apart the long curtains, she surveyed the scene below. Blanketing snow had taken on a silvery quality, a reflecting sky glittered above scintillating fir trees, and not a living soul intruded into her vision.

Turning away from the window, she became aware of a young female figure dressed from head to toe

317

in silver lace, reclining on the red velvet chaise longue opposite the bed but, who it was, the old woman could not have said, not immediately, although something stirred in long-lost caverns of memory.

'Hello Silvia,' the figure said, smiling.

'Hello. Have you been here long?' Silvia was suddenly feeling very cold.

'Yes, I've waited quite a while for you: eighty-five years in fact, but of course you couldn't see me then.' The figure moved slightly on the red velvet.

'I'm dead then, am I?' the old woman asked. No wonder she felt chilly.

'Yes, you are, of course you are. I'm glad you're taking it so well. But don't worry too much: you were very brave and fought a long, hard battle but the end was peaceful, and they gave you a lovely funeral with lots of lilies and chrysanthemums, set off with clouds of baby's breath, as you liked to call it.'

'Hmm, the florists did well out of me, then,' Silvia pulled her nightgown closer. 'And I suppose you're going to tell me you're God! I always suspected He would turn out to be a woman.'

'No. You're wrong, I'm not God, not at all. And you've never believed in such a being, not even as a child. Science was always your thing. You cannot decide to play safe and acquire instant faith, just because you're dead. You'll have to do better than that.'

'Oh well, it was worth a try, and I expect I'll remember where I've seen you before, when I can think straight. So, whoever you are - what did you think of me – as a wife, I mean?'

'I detect a note of guilt creeping in there,' commented the figure wryly. 'You did try, I have to give you that – in fact, it took several attempts before you threw in the towel and gave marriage up as a bad job.'

'Yes, three husbands,' Silvia gazed dreamily into the distance. 'All good men in their different ways, each one clever and successful, but not one of them would wash the dishes.'

'You never did learn how to deal with men – they need mothering. Which brings me to the matter of your three children. They all wept bitterly at your funeral, you'll be pleased to hear.'

'That's made me feel better, because maybe I didn't always show how much I cared.' Silvia was overwhelmed by sadness, guilt and regret.

The figure looked at Silvia with compassion. 'It's never an easy task and, after all's said and done, children are for life. I have to say, though, you were a very good grandmother, if nothing else.'

'You seem very cynical for a person in your position! If only I could remember where I've seen you before,' mused the old woman. 'And anyway, what day is this? Is it Tuesday? I've rather lost track.'

'No, it's tomorrow!'

'Nonsense! How can that be? Tomorrow never comes, isn't that what they say?' Silvia pressed a cool white hand to her forehead.

'In life, every day is today. Only when you cross your personal dead line do you reach tomorrow.'

'I see – well, I don't see, actually. None of this sounds feasible to me, but I have no option other than to believe you, and now if it's not too much trouble I'd like to know which place I'm destined for – up or down?'

'There is only one place,' answered the figure, 'but first you must recognise me. Realisation is the only criterion, if that is your desire.'

'You speak in riddles, erm, whatever your name is, whoever you are.' Silvia was irritated. 'This is all new to me – please try to make some sense.'

'I see your temper has not mellowed, even though you're now deceased, departed, passed away, no longer in the land of the living: in a word, dead! That was one of your worst failings – impatience.'

'Hah! You're right about that; but I'm pleased to learn we share the same sense of humour! Well, I suppose I shall have to play this game with you - let's see – you say you're not God. In that case, am I God? Has the whole history of the universe been a figment of my own imagination? No? No, I thought not. Well then, are you my guardian angel?' The old woman watched the figure growing ever fainter, the silver lace turning into snowflakes.

'I never guarded you, but I tried to preserve your underlying good sense. When you had too much to drink or got a bee in your bonnet, I was powerless. Try again, Silvia,' whispered the figure, 'try again.'

The old woman suddenly caught sight of her own reflection in the cheval looking glass.

'I know who you are! You're me!' she exclaimed. 'Me as a girl, an innocent young girl, before all those bad habits took over.'

The figure grew stronger, and arose from the red velvet chaise longue. 'Maybe so, maybe not. Keep your wits about you if you wish to go to your eternal reward.'

'Are you the angel with my face? No?'

The figure shook its head patiently. 'You're getting warmer, Silvia; have another try.'

'Well now, let's see. Are you my alter ego, or my doppelganger, maybe?'

'You're really hot now, Silvia,' beamed the figure. 'Don't burn your fingers on the truth.'

'Hah, I think I've got it – you must be my conscience,' the old woman was smiling, reaching out.

'You've done well, Silvia. You've passed the final test and attained realisation.'

'Well, I never! Do I get a certificate? I always suspected there was only myself to rely on. But I wish you'd made yourself known to me before I kicked the bucket. It would have helped me live a better life.'

'You're missing the point, Silvia. That would not have been playing by the rules of the game. All of *life* is a game, a sort of trial, a daily test on each person's journey towards the dead line, if only they knew it.'

'Yes, I'm beginning to understand, but rather too late, I fear,' Silvia frowned.

'No, it's not too late, never too late for contrition, for realisation.'

Silvia laughed. 'Well, come on then, let's get this show on the road. Where are we going? Heaven, is it?'

'Yes, our own private paradise: a wonderful place where there is no pain, no sickness, no worry. We shall spend eternity there together. Come! Let us go out, go to our reward.'

'Eternity is a long time,' beamed Silvia, 'but I'm glad I'll be spending it with you. What fun we shall have, you and I.'

By way of reply, the figure smiled wryly and looked askance, but Silvia was too absorbed in this newly-found euphoria to notice anything but her own happiness and relief.

And so the old woman and the young woman walked out, hand in hand, into the swirling mists of a place known only as *OBLIVION*...

OFFICE PARTY
(With a nod to Dorothy Parker)

Opening one heavy eyelid, I begin to count those awful brown flowers on the bedroom curtains. Why do I feel so dreadful, so ill? Why is my head throbbing and my tongue rattling around in what I fondly refer to as my mouth but which feels more like the bottom of a baby's pram – all crap and crumbs!? Could this be what they describe as a hangover? It's a new sensation to me.

Then I try to remember the office Christmas party which began yesterday lunchtime. And even though most of last night seems to be a complete blank, I must have got home OK as here I am in my own bed. Mind you, taking a quick peek under the eiderdown, I seem to be naked except for a man's greatcoat and maybe that's why I'm so damned itchy and hot.

I do recall we all downed tools at 1 p.m. and began decorating the office with garlands and tinsel, pushing the desks and chairs out of the way and setting out nibbles, sandwiches, crackers and things. Oh, yes, I do know for a fact we made some fruit punch and I busied myself pouring bottles of wine into a large washing-up bowl but, after that, it's all a bit of a blur.

323

Some of it is coming back to me now – the office wag started playing his maracas and I danced a Spanish flamenco, stamping my feet with a piece of holly clamped between my teeth. I had a sprig of mistletoe in my hair and it seemed the right thing to do to grab Mr Blenkinsop in a passionate embrace and kiss him full on the lips remembering of course to remove the holly from my mouth – or did I? I have a hazy memory of loud cheering in the background.

Oh well, if that's all that happened, it couldn't have been too bad, so I drag myself up, get dressed and crawl painfully into work. But, hmm, why is everyone looking at me and smirking? 'Hi everyone, good party, eh?' I say, uncertainly.

'Yes, it was,' says Sally meaningly, 'and you certainly seemed to be enjoying yourself.'

'Why, what do you mean?' I raise one eyebrow.

'We-e-ell, you were perfectly all right 'til you had that third drink – you proposed to Mr Blenkinsop, poor chap – he was a mite embarrassed.'

'But crikey, is that all? It was only a joke.'

'Oh, Mr Blenkinsop is a good sport, so don't worry, and anyway you calmed down after falling on the floor and seemed perfectly OK 'til you started to smoke that roll-up Dennis handed round. Then you pestered Mr Blenkinsop a bit more, asking him to fondle you.'

'Oh, blimey, is that all, it was only a lark.'

'Ye-es, I'm sure it was! But then you went round and round on all-fours, eating food off the floor, barking and begging to be fed with your tongue lolling out. Poor Mr Blenkinsop, he had to go along with it and feed you crisps and sausage rolls.'

'My goodness, that's nothing – it was only a silly game, you know.'

'Yes, it was very amusing, but after a bit you got up off your knees, whirled around and around, your skirt over your head. You knocked into Mr Blenkinsop and he went flying and ended up full-length. We really thought he'd been injured but he was OK after a tot of brandy. We almost called an ambulance at one point.'

'Oh, dear – but it was only a jape and he wasn't hurt after all, was he?'

'No, he wasn't, not really, except for some bruising to his knees, a black eye and a loose tooth. Then you seemed perfectly fine until you took it into your head to start screaming "Help, help" accusing Mr Blenkinsop of molesting you. He wasn't best pleased when you blamed him for giving you a social disease.'

'But cripes, is that all? It was only a prank.'

'Maybe so, but then you offered to service anyone – everyone – particularly the office boy, the janitor, James, Dennis and Mr Blenkinsop, as long as they formed an orderly queue by the photocopier.'

'Good grief, how funny!'

'Yes, it was, very – and your co-ordination was excellent for a woman so pissed! But the language – where did you learn to cuss like that? As for the janitor, well, we had to haul him off you in the end.'

'Oh, thanks for that – he is quite repulsive. And, anyway, it was only my wicked sense of humour.'

'Yes, I know, you are such a wit – and you appeared to have sobered up 'til you climbed onto a desk, stood up, did a slow striptease but kept your shoes on, and sang "Hard hearted Hannah, the vamp of Savannah" – word-perfect and in tune too. James accompanied you on the harmonica.'

'Oh blimey! That's my party piece.'

'Yes, we enjoyed it – and you seemed perfectly OK until you tumbled off the desk and projectile vomited all over Mr Blenkinsop's new cashmere jacket, and also extinguishing his cheroot.'

'Oh, well, hands up, that was probably a bit much, I admit.'

'Yes, it probably was. The janitor wasn't too happy about having to clean it all up. And oh, before I forget – Mr Blenkinsop wants to see you in his office as soon as possible.'

'Oh my gawd, how exciting - it must be about that promotion I applied for…'

MATRON OF HONOUR

I watched with a sardonic smile as Diana picked up the ornate hand-mirror and viewed herself from another angle, a rueful look on her face.

'Ye-es, I think that will have to do, thank you, Camilla,' she said. 'Now for my nails,' and she flickered her spread fingers at me.

It was obvious that the bride-to-be was very pregnant. The ivory silk dress trimmed with guipure lace was designed in the basque style which displayed her baby-bump in all its glory, while a fascinator of lilies-of-the valley trembled with every movement of her head.

'I'm sure Charles will be overcome with joy when he sees you walking up the aisle,' I said, crossing two fingers behind my back.

'Oh, Camilla, you're such a good friend,' Diana whined, 'you know I'm not looking my best, all blotchy and bloated, but still you make it your business to boost my confidence. It's just a bore, this pregnancy. But Mummy and Daddy can't really complain because, after all, it is their fault – they shouldn't have insisted on such a big wedding then we needn't have waited so long. It's so ridiculous inviting relatives from all corners of the

327

globe. And Charles's people are just as bad, but I suppose it is an important occasion, joining the two families together, you know – it's all part of big business to them, I suppose.'

As Diana twittered on, I calmly painted her nails in pearlised lilac with an appliquéd ivory lily in each centre. Her lipstick was in a shade of lilac to match. The bouquet was a florist's dream of lilies-of-the-valley, gypsophila and lilac rosebuds.

'If it's a girl, I'll call it Lily Gypsy Rose after my bouquet,' she giggled, more like an excited child.

'Surely Charles wants a son,' I said. 'A boy would consolidate the new dynasty and your two families will be happy, especially if you go on to have a second boy – an heir and a spare, you know.'

'Oh, but Charles and I aren't marrying just to please our parents,' Diana pouted. 'Charles and I are madly in love, as I've told you ad nauseam. And it's mere coincidence that the Cathcart-Walkers and Stormont-Grundys are merging their companies. There's strength in unity, you know, Camilla, and the shareholders must be kept happy and on an even keel.'

I made no reply but concentrated on the delicate task of fingernail decoration as Diana continued her wittering. 'You must know how it feels, Camilla – you and Andrew have only been married two years yourselves. I hope the magic hasn't worn off so soon.'

'No, of course not,' I laughed. 'Andrew and I understand each other, we're on the same wavelength, we give each other elbow room, so please don't worry your head about us.'

'You don't mean to say you have an open marriage?' Diana gasped, 'You've never mentioned it before. I'm sure Charles and I would never agree to that sort of thing – it's one man, one woman, as far as we're concerned.'

I didn't bother to respond as I was by now putting the finishing touches to my own toilette, lavishly applying the blood red lipstick to go with my fingernails, shoes, crystal eardrops and necklace.

One hour later at Quagmire Village Church, Charles was standing at the altar with Andrew as the six bridesmaids and I followed Diana and Mr Cathcart-Walker up the aisle to the fanfare of Bach's Toccata and Fugue in D Minor, a rather unusual, nay pretentious, choice of wedding music one would have thought, but which, in the event, did provide a suitably dramatic background to what followed.

Charles turned to greet the bride, but he looked straight past Diana and his eyes met mine. I had no sense of loss or jealousy seeing him marry someone else. I felt confident in his love, confident in the knowledge that Diana was an acquiescent and trusting person, confident I should never have to become a brood mare like her.

Yes, this marriage would keep the Cathcart-Walkers and Stormont-Grundys happy; Diana would be occupied with the new baby and Charles and I could still see each other regularly.

The vicar, Reverend Peter Burgoyne, had hardly begun to speak his opening lines when Diana clutched her belly and yelped in pain. 'The baby, the baby,' she screeched.

She collapsed into Charles's arms, and Andrew helped to bundle her unceremoniously back down the aisle and into the Rolls Royce parked on the driveway outside, to the consternation of the waiting photographers and reporters, all eager to get this society wedding on record and into their celebrity magazines.

After a hurried consultation, the Cathcart-Walkers and Stormont-Grundys decided to postpone the ceremony to a suitable date in the near future, but in the meantime, the reception would go ahead as planned in view of the many friends and relations who had turned up from all around the world

I didn't go to the hospital, not in my ridiculous Matron of Honour corset-dress, and anyway I can't stand hospitals or babies, which I find equally repulsive. I went to the reception instead and was happily mingling, drinking Crystal champagne, chatting up a few likely new men I had spotted in the congregation, when who should appear in our midst but Charles. The band stopped playing as he took his stance on the platform and picked up a microphone.

'Listen up folks!! Diana has had a boy, Nathaniel Charles Hugh Tristram Stormont-Grundy, weighing in at six pounds two ounces,' he announced. 'Please wet the baby's head, and I hope you all get drunk – the bar is free until midnight, so that really shouldn't be too difficult for some of you!'

To the accompaniment of well-bred cheers from the stuffier guests and guffaws from the more raffish element, Charles leapt athletically off the platform and, casually navigating his way through the throng of guests, every one of them wanting to shake his hand and pat him on the back, he made a beeline in my general direction.

Eventually he reached my side and mumbled in my ear, 'Diana's upset and crying: she wanted a girl, wanted to call it Gypsy or some stupid outlandish name! I had to get away, I had to see you.'

He looked around, nodding and smiling as guests called out their congratulations above the background music before putting his lips to my ear once more. 'Look Camilla, there's the bridal suite booked for tonight – no sense in wasting it. I can't wait to rip that bodice off you! Meet me up there later – shall we say 11 o'clock – OK?'

I threw back my head and laughed as if the charming bridegroom had been telling me a funny story and our eyes met fleetingly before we turned away from each other, both wearing beaming smiles, as we began to do our duty and circulate.

Oh yes, I was confident of his love, all right! There would definitely be three people in this marriage.

THE IMPORTANCE OF BEING HENRY

I've always liked the name Henry! To me, Henry conjures up a man who is kind, easy-going and even a bit weak, which means I should be able to assert my strong opinions without much danger of being contradicted – which is nice...

Yes, all my men have been called Henry – I wouldn't have a William or a Sam. Any man with a different moniker does not enter the equation. The trouble is I very often jump in with both feet and put off getting to know the character until later on, because, to be perfectly honest, I believe in keeping a man at arm's length until I have his engagement ring on my finger.

My first betrothed, Henry Quicksand, was a lad of 17. I was 16. I fell in love with him very quickly in spite of his youthful silliness. It was Henry, you see – I simply couldn't resist the name and so I turned a blind eye to his shortcomings and we got engaged.

We booked into The Akimbo Arms for a pre-wedding honeymoon but on the first night when he took his vest off and I beheld his pale body for the first time, my heart sank. His ribcage was protruding and skeletal, a shocking sight for a nervous young girl.

332

Sadly, my revulsion at this unexpected turn of events proved to be an insurmountable obstacle to consummation and I broke off our betrothal immediately. The poor boy was stunned. In hindsight, it was obvious we were far too young for our union to have worked out. I kept the cigar band he had put on my ring finger.

The second one, Henry Bassingthwaite, was 35 when we met. I was 18. I snapped him up immediately and he was in seventh heaven at having acquired such a young girl for a fiancée.

We went to The Akimbo Arms on our pre-wedding honeymoon but on the first night when I emerged from the bathroom attired in a diaphanous baby doll nightie in anticipation of a night of passion, he was already deep asleep – what an insult to an innocent and tremulous young girl!

And so, in spite of the poor wretch offering me the sun, moon and stars, I sent him packing. I kept the ring, although I found out after it turned my finger green, that he'd bought it from Woolworth's.

Henry Krakeborough, that's Henry III, was 20. I was 20. We had the same birthday, which seemed a good omen at the time, but, in any case, I was determined to have another Henry.

We went to The Akimbo Arms on our pre-wedding honeymoon but he lounged about in the bedroom and smoked pot all day. This habit, I realised too late, was why he appeared so laid back – literally. I broke off our engagement as he never did summon up the energy to consummate our betrothal: he probably never even noticed I'd left him. I had to keep the ring as he had tattooed it onto my finger with a rusty needle and indelible black ink.

Fiancé number four, Henry Sukebind, was 23. I was still 20. He was such a calm and serene person, well-groomed with perfectly manicured fingernails, sweet breath, small feet and he adored me.

We went more up-market to The Quagmire Inn on our pre-wedding honeymoon. On the first night he said he respected me too much for anything physical but that it shouldn't stop us from having a happy partnership as he was a dab hand at all kinds of DIY, and he'd assumed that, being a girl, I was a good cook. He cried when I went home to my mother who by this time was keeping a list of my discarded suitors. I kept the ring which he had fashioned himself from a Cola can.

Henry Teagarden, fiancé number five, was 19. I was 22 and now going in for toy-boys. I was thrilled to have a Henry who was younger than me.

As he was unemployed, we stayed at my mother's for our pre-wedding honeymoon but on the first night when he confessed to not owning a toothbrush and wanted to borrow mine, I went straight back to my mum: she was asleep in the next room. He was heartbroken to lose a woman of the world after having bragged to his mates. But little did he realise I was still an innocent, and it hadn't been for want of trying.

I kept the rubber band he had wound round my ring finger.

My sixth fiancé, Henry Clinkbarn, was 18: I was still 22. My toy-boys were getting younger, a trend I found most flattering. Henry was quite childlike and looked up to me, and, being shorter by a head, he had to.

His mother Thelma obviously didn't like her son's choice of life-partner and had a lot of negative advice to dish out on all matters pertaining to our relationship. But I was certain that our pre-wedding honeymoon in The Akimbo Arms would be sublime once Henry and I were on our own.

However, just as we were shedding confetti all over the reception area's threadbare carpet whilst checking in with barefaced cheek as Mr and Mrs Clinkbarn, who should show her orange face but Thelma Clinkbarn, glittering earrings a-dangle under her long frizzy hairdo!

At the sight of her, Henry burst into tears and ran into her arms. You've heard the phrase "and mother came too"? Well, there's a new one – "and the betrothed broke off the engagement and went home to her mum". Not so snappy, I know, but you get the picture! And the ring? It was Thelma's, but I kept it! I know my rights.

I tried again with Henry number seven. Henry Bandicoot was 40 and I was 23. He was mature and level-headed, divorced with a teenage daughter, Arnetta, who lived with him. Arnetta seemed to take to me at once and treated me more like a sister than a potential stepmother. We would go shopping together, we liked the same hip-hop music (much to Henry's feigned but fond disgust), and generally our future as a family looked extremely rosy.

After moving my things into his house in a posh part of Quagmire Village, Henry and I got engaged, but, not wishing to leave Arnetta on her own, we had put our pre-wedding honeymoon on hold until later in the year.

It was on the evening of our engagement, as I was warming up a congealing Chinese takeaway (to be followed by tinned rice pudding and jam) for our special celebration dinner, I saw Arnetta's diary lying open on the kitchen table: I have to confess here that I sat down and read it. The poison dripping from her pen I shall not repeat but it came through loud and clear.

I picked up my bag and made for the door, screaming that the engagement was off and he should ask his spoilt brat of a daughter the reason why. Henry's mouth formed a perfect O as I marched out; Arnetta's face was a study in smug satisfaction.

But, to be perfectly honest, I never did relish being known as Mrs Bandicoot for the rest of my life. I kept the ring, a fine diamond solitaire, bought that very day from Ratner's.

And so we come to Henry Tudor. When we met, he was 34 but looked much older. I was 24. He was a part-time actor at The Quagmire Museum, all togged up as Henry VIII in the Arts Festival living history event. He looked just like those portraits in school history books, although I'd never had much interest the subject until that moment.

We hit it off straight away but unfortunately he won't be free until he's divorced his wife Katherine. She's only given him a daughter when all the time he wanted a son. 'Thou shalt give me many sons, Mistress Anne,' he is fond of predicting as he sprawls in front of the telly. 'Prithee, come sit on my lap.'

My mother is a bit fed up. 'What's he on about?' she says. 'Loads o' kids? Here? I don't think so – we've only got a two-up two-down, and anyway why doesn't he get a job, the lazy sod? No wonder he's so enormous, he eats like a horse and I can't keep buying all this venison he's partial to, and while I'm on the subject, I'm sick to death of being called "wench" and having to clear all these bones off the floor behind his chair – hasn't he any table manners?'

I simply ignore her complaints as I love my Henry so much, but even so I insist on separate beds until we are free to become betrothed because he is, after all, still married to Katherine.

But I do keep nagging him about his divorce which seems to drag on and on for some reason. Anyway, when he does get his decree – it'll be coming direct from the Pope, evidently – Henry has promised to marry me straightaway without worrying about an engagement, and I shall belong to him – body and soul.

But as for "many sons" – over my dead body!

THE AKIMBO ARMS

You can't kiss a girl unexpectedly, only sooner than she thought you would!

Percival Grimpenthorpe had plans as he wiped down the bar of The Akimbo Arms, humming and smiling to himself, thinking of the new barmaid he had just hired. She was a real bosomy type, one to bring the male customers in, definitely. He was sure the girl had already given him a cool appraisal followed by a come hither look, her heavily fringed eyes sweeping him from head to groin, her plump red lips in a pout.

Yes, Percival had plans but he didn't want to push things. He would bide his time – perhaps after her first week he might try something on, see how things developed. And furthermore she seemed to like cats, and, in particular Moggie, his ginger tom. The girl must be a good soul under all that war-paint.

'Oh, so you took her on, then?' Dorinda Grimpenthorpe grumbled, bustling in, untying her apron to reveal a tight black dress stretched around her ample girth, several rows of crystal beads adorning her fairly raddled throat. 'What was her name again – Polly? Well,

I hope to goodness she turns out better than the others, particularly the last one.'

'She will, she will,' Percival picked up a tea-towel and began polishing some Babycham glasses. 'She loves Moggie, so she can't be all bad.'

'What, that mangy thing? Gawd save us! Yes, it is a very good basis for employing anyone – whether they like your fleabag cat or not. Well, on your head be it if she absconds with all the beer-mats like the last one did.' Dorinda grimaced at the memory. 'She can't have been right in the head, that Mavis. At least all the others stole useful things like toilet rolls and soap.'

'Oh, but you always refuse to notify the police about the petty pilfering, and anyway, you think everyone is barmy, Dorinda.'

'Well, that Mavis looked so innocent with it – and so twee, too twee to be true, as it turned out.'

'It could have been worse, my little chickadee. She could have run off with the takings.'

'Well, just make sure you keep an eye on this Polly person then, otherwise there'll be trouble.'

'No problem, dear heart!' Percival smiled without looking up as he carried on with his polishing, wishing his wife had a personality instead of an attitude.

Polly certainly proved to be a man-magnet behind the bar, leaning over provocatively as she served pints of beer. She had an admirably slick line in clichés, too, most of them picked up from various vulgarians of her acquaintance. "Coo, look what's crawled out of the woodwork" and "go home, your mother wants your ears for ashtrays" always went down well and drew loud guffaws from the regulars. Many were the male villagers who turned up to view this new addition to The Akimbo Arms and wallow in her good-natured verbal abuse.

'Good heavens, Percival,' remarked Ralph Grimstone, eyes popping, 'where did you find such an angel of beauty to dispense your foaming ale? And such a ready wit, too! Brains and beauty, a combination not often found in one female.'

'You keep your hands off her, Ralph,' smirked the landlord, 'she's too nice, too classy for an ancient codger like you.'

Come closing time on the Friday night, Percival locked the door behind the last straggling customers and joined his new barmaid who was emptying the ashtrays and wiping them out with a filthy old rag. Percival came up behind and grabbed her round the waist. She stood stock still while he nuzzled her neck. Then she turned and kissed him full on the lips.

When they broke free from the clinch, she said, 'I've been waiting for that, Percival. When can we get together – properly, I mean?'

The landlord was taken aback at her forwardness, her presumption, but also thrilled that he had been right in his earlier assumption.

'Oh, er, we can meet in secret in the old well-house at the bottom of the garden,' he said, rubbing the back of his hand across his mouth.

'I can see you've done this kind of thing before,' she pouted.

'No, no – our previous barmaids have all been right dogs, if you'll pardon the expression. Not one of them has stayed very long – they usually do a moonlight flit, always on a payday, and the last one took all the beermats with her!'

'How funny – all the beermats. She can't have been right in the head.'

'Yeah, that's what Dorinda says – and she came across as such an innocent girl.'

'Well, never mind her – say a time! When can we be alone together?'

And so it turned out that, after a number of torrid weeks of afternoon and evening meetings in the well-house, Polly showed her other side. 'It's so cold in here, and it's so fusty, stinky even, as if something's crawled in and died! And furthermore, we can't keep doing it standing up because there's nowhere to lie down except on the stone floor and there's nowhere even to sit down apart from the edge of the well – honestly Percy, this place gives me the creeps. How long has the well been blocked up? Are you sure there's no dead dogs rotting away down there? Anyway, I'm fed up of it. When are you going to divorce that old bag and marry me?' And so she moaned, on and on and on…

'Hmm, I think you only want me so you can be landlady of The Akimbo Arms,' Percival grimaced. 'I can't see Dorinda ever agreeing to a divorce, we've been married for twenty years. Can't we just carry on like this? I could try to come up with a better meeting place.'

'But all this cloak and dagger business, hole in the wall stuff, I can't stand it, I shall have to rethink my plans very carefully.'

'Oh, please don't leave me, I do love you,' Percival whined. 'I couldn't stand the trauma of going through another moonlight flit…'

'Oh, so you did do it with the other barmaids,' began Polly, eyes flashing beneath her thickly mascara'ed lashes. 'I suspected as much – I suppose it's a perk of the job with you landlords, even in a spit-and-sawdust place like this.'

'No, no, of course not, how could you even think such a thing. It's you I love, and we-e-ell, I'll see what I can do about Dorinda. It's just that I never even believed in divorce until shortly after I got married! But, yes, I've definitely changed my mind now, thanks to you, my darling, and of course Dorinda is past her sell-by date, I agree. You've done much more for the business than she ever did, my love.' Percival clutched Polly to him as if he never wanted to let her go.

'I'll keep you to that, you old bugger. Now let's go indoors and get warm, I'm bloody frozen.'

That evening, Percival began praising Polly to his wife. 'She's so good for the business,' he wailed. 'I think she deserves a little extra this week, don't you?'

'Oh, so you're at it again, are you?' was Dorinda's response. 'Another pash! You just can't be trusted with these barmaids! Don't worry, dear heart, you'll get over it – she'll be just like the others, no doubt, doing a moonlight flit one day after she gets paid. We shall have to nail everything down in case she walks off with something valuable.'

Percival met Polly the following afternoon in the murk of the well-house with the fanciful news that he was working on Dorinda and hoped she would soon agree to a divorce because she had said she was fed up of the hard slog of pub work and really only wished to retire, as long as she had a good settlement package.

'Well, that's better than nothing, I suppose,' was Polly's mealy-mouthed response. 'I shall just have to be patient, that's all, until it's all been worked out, and hopefully the ugly old cow won't get too generous a settlement package! But I won't wait forever, you know, just remember that.'

'I know, my dearest! Now come here and let's carry on from where we left off…there should be a bonus in your pay packet tomorrow!'

The next day passed in a haze of anticipation for Percival who could think only of his well-house tryst later that evening! How lovely was his gorgeous Polly, always ready for it, not having to be cajoled, coerced or persuaded into it like all the others, Dorinda in particular. What was it Dorinda often said to annoy him? Oh yes, he remembered: it was "when love turns to champing jaws at the breakfast table" or something on those lines. No romance in her soul, no understanding of the male libido. The nearest he got to his wife these days was when their underwear met in the washing machine!

Polly was going about her business behind the bar in her usual efficient way, acting out the charming and seductive barmaid, jollying up all the regulars and she even had a beaming smile for Dorinda as that lady handed over her weekly pay packet.

'There'll be a small bonus for you this week,' grated Dorinda. 'Come and see me in the office before you go to bed: I need some help with the accounts.'

'Oh, thanks, yes, OK,' Polly smirked, slipping the packet into her handbag under the bar. *Honestly, that ugly old cow obviously doesn't hold any grudges, agreeing to a bonus! Ha, some women are so stupid. Unless the old gargoyle is trying to ingratiate herself, hoping to squeeze out a more generous divorce payout, because she must realise that I hold the whip hand now – well, she won't get a penny more out of Percival, not if I have anything to do with it, so sucks boo, whatever the hell that means!*

Tipping the wink to Percival that she would be late for their tryst as she would be busy mollifying his wife, Polly got on with her work with more sparkle and vivacity than usual. Things were working out just fine!

Come midnight, Percival made his way to the well-house to wait for his ladylove, all het up with passion. He smoked a cigarette as he perched on the edge of the well and looked up through a hole in the roof at the glittering stars. *What a wonderful time they could have together, how they would enjoy each other's company in secret for the rest of their days if only Polly could be persuaded not to keep insisting on something more legal, like marriage! Surely he could keep her happy with regular bonuses – paid out of his own pocket, if necessary!*

As he waited with increasing impatience, a shiny object caught his eye on the ancient flagstones. He stooped and picked it up. It was Moggie's collar tag in the form of a bell. What the…? The cat wasn't allowed in the well-house, not that any danger remained since the well had been covered in with stout wooden boards some years ago, but still…

By half past midnight, Percival was beginning to feel worried! Where was Polly? He retraced his footsteps over the long pathway to the kitchen door of The Akimbo Arms.

He looked everywhere, all through the house, all through the pub, with no sign of his darling girl nor his beloved Moggie.

He found the door of Polly's room unlocked and went in and was shocked to the core to see that all her clothes and belongings were gone.

Surely not another moonlight flit, not his lovely Polly, not after all those promises they'd made to each other, not that he'd actually been sincere about his side of things, he knew he'd never divorce Dorinda, but he had truly believed that Polly was genuine in her pleadings for a lifetime together…

Hmm, women! You just couldn't trust them, they were always after the main chance!

*   *   *   *

Dorinda was sitting up in bed wearing her smug "I told you so" face when he reluctantly entered their bedroom.

'I can't find Polly and I can't find Moggie, either,' Percival wailed. 'I've found his bell: look, here it is, I wanted to fix it back on his collar.'

Dorinda smirked. 'Hmm, yes, that Polly, she's another fly-by-night! I *did* try to warn you, and all I can say is, it's a pity you hadn't nailed the cat down this time…'

GOING SPARE

It was there on the bristly doormat this morning – I knew what it was immediately, recognised the official brown window envelope. I tucked it into my handbag meaning to read it once I got to work. I could hazard a guess at the contents, and was in no hurry to see it writ large in black and white.

The bus arrived early for a change, and I had a mad scramble to get the correct fare out of my purse.

Once at the office, settled at my desk, I felt for the envelope but it didn't seem to be there.

I upended my bag onto the desk, and out tumbled several credit cards, loyalty cards, cigarettes and lighter, two lipsticks, tube of makeup, comb, perfume, spare knickers (just in case), spare tights (ditto), used tissues, new tissues, an old envelope, address book-cum-diary, purse, two squashed chocolates, pen, pencil – but no letter! Where the hell was it? The silk lining of the bag had a long tear and I felt inside and underneath, but found only another old sweet wrapper, a pencil sharpener and an ancient toothpick. No letter! No sign of it…

I was worried then, I couldn't concentrate – oh why hadn't I opened it at home and left it there on the hall table like any reasonable human being? I was so stupid, couldn't do anything right: maybe that's why I'd ended up in this mess in the first place.

I planned to telephone them as soon as I had five minutes to spare but not today, not with this Fielding account to wade through and a deadline looming at 5.30. Tomorrow, yes, I would definitely ring them then – after all, I couldn't be absolutely sure what was in the letter, was merely making an educated guess, but at the same time I could not risk simply ignoring the possibly serious outcome of playing dumb. I had to start being more accountable and responsible for my own actions!

And being more responsible included making time to eat a proper lunch. I therefore disciplined myself to abandon the desk and its huge workload for ten minutes and, hurrying to the canteen at 1 o'clock, I took my place in the queue.

The new man from Accounts was in front with his tray, and he turned round, beaming at me with such lovely teeth that I smiled back in spite of my preoccupations.

'Hello there, I'm Mike, new boy on the block – trying to remember as many names and faces as possible – how to make friends and influence people, you know the type of thing,' and he laughed engagingly.

'Yes, I've seen you around, Mike, welcome to the madhouse, and I'm Ginny – hope you'll enjoy working here: it's not so bad.'   I couldn't help noticing he was extremely attractive in a boyish way.

Anyhow, when I paid for the ham salad plus pot of tea and turned round with my tray, Mike beckoned me to a seat at his table for two.

'I can't stay long,' I began, but he was so amusing and lively that I really forgot my worries and actually laughed several times at his witty comments.   I envied his positive take on life.

Suddenly the arrow of time bored itself into my consciousness – I had taken far longer than ten minutes: to be precise, fifteen minutes, and, rising to leave, I began to make my excuses.

'I hope we'll see more of each other,' was his parting shot.   *You're not kidding*, I thought! He would certainly pull me up by my boot-straps, give me a new lease of life. I already felt better, more on top of things.

So I passed the rest of the day in a less negative frame of mind, and decided definitely to ring them tomorrow, put the thing straight, find out exactly what was required. Yes, that was it, that's what I would do!

Anyway, by the time I got home that evening, my mood had changed: I was jumpy and anxious, felt myself panicking, going spare, unable to unwind, willing tomorrow to dawn so I'd be able to make that phone call, and maybe see Mike in the canteen.

I changed out of my smart office suit and high-heeled shoes, took off my earrings and all my makeup, did a deep-condition of my hair with vegetable oil and, suddenly feeling the need for food, lots of food, I made for the kitchen with all speed, on a desperate mission to raid the refrigerator.

When the doorbell rang, I stood stock still, almost didn't go to the door, almost didn't open it, what with my shining moon face, hair spiked in greasy tendrils, tea-stained tee-shirt and baggy old tracksuit bottoms! Furthermore, I held a chicken leg in one hand, a cigarette in the other.

But, with some manipulation, I did manage to open the door and, cautiously peering round, I beheld a beautiful young man holding my brown envelope and beaming with his perfect teeth.

'I found this at the bus stop and thought I'd deliver it personally – could be important – huh, is that you, Ginny?' he said, peering first at me, then at the name on the letter. 'Oh, I see, your name is really Virginia – I *never* made the connection – I could have handed you this at lunchtime had I known you were one and the same.'

He stared at me curiously. 'By the way,' he said, 'have you done something to your hair? It looks nice…'

Well, imagine it if you can! Embarrassed wasn't in it – I didn't know which way to turn – whether to put the chicken leg or the cigarette in my mouth, and in the end I just waved them both at him.

'Oh, Mike,' I beamed, 'what a relief – thank you so much – erm, do you fancy a chicken leg? I've got one going spare...'

KISSY

I was snuggled in my cage having a bit of a nap, being somewhat tired and shagged out after a particularly long squawk, when something disturbed me and I awoke with a sudden start.

I couldn't see Mummy at first until I hopped down from my perch and onto the little platform leading to the cage door.

Then I saw her – she was lying on the carpet, face down. Well, I thought, she must be tired and shagged out, too. Perhaps it was having to listen to my long squawk that did it for her. Poor Mummy, she usually sleeps in her bed, not on the floor. She must have been really, really exhausted.

I flew down and landed on her shoulder and began nibbling at strands of her long brown hair, a little game we often played that usually amused her immensely. She would laugh and laugh, then purse her lips at me and croon, *Kissy love Mummy, kiss kiss,* and silly things like that.

But this time she didn't do anything, just stayed where she was. Poor Mummy must be worn out with looking after me and Daddy, I thought.

Hopping carefully to the other side of her head, I saw her face in profile against the carpet. *Kissy love Mummy*, I shrieked.

There was some red stuff coming out of the side of her mouth and I suddenly noticed the mess it had made on the floor. I'd never seen such a thing. Mummy wore red stuff on her lips, I knew that: I watched her put it on every morning, but she had never put it anywhere else, not to my knowledge…

I pecked at the red stuff but it was (*squawk*) too *salty*: it made me thirsty! I flew back into my cage for a drink from my little bowl. The water turned pink and cloudy for some reason and I really needed some fresh.

I swooped back to Mummy and tried to wake her with *Who's a pretty bird?   Ha ha, come on Kissy, Mummy love Kissy* – some of the words she'd taught me and loved to hear me repeat. But she stayed still. Mummy is so deep asleep, I thought, it would be a real shame to disturb her.

I really needed a drink by then so I flew into the kitchen and saw the washing up bowl full of water. A quick dip of the beak and (*squawk*) it was too *soapy*! Mummy always used far too much Fairy Liquid: she did tend to be extravagant, in my opinion.

Then I noticed the dripping tap which Mummy was always saying needed a new washer. *Tut tut* she'd go, *this tap really needs a new washer*. Luckily, Daddy had never got around to seeing to it, and so I was able to have a nice long drink which did quite revive me until I began to feel rather peckish.

Once again I flew back to my cage and ate some seeds and nuts and nibbled on the cuttle-fish bone for a bit, and then I sat there on my swing trying to think, wondering what to do next.

I decided it would be a good idea to hit the little mirror with my head for a while, which I did, and then I rang my bell for good measure, but nothing seemed to throw any light on my current predicament and, although I racked my brains for minutes on end, no other course of action presented itself.

But I suddenly noticed that my perch had red claw marks on it which quite upset me, goodness knows why, so I flew back down and sat on the carpet by Mummy's head. *Kissy love Mummy, kiss kiss*, I squawked, pecking her lips gently, but instead of the lovely greasy scented taste of the red stuff she used, there was a horrible smell of something else, stale and sour.

It was growing dark by then, so I decided to stay on the floor by Mummy's head and I fell asleep nestling into her lovely long hair. I was in the middle of a nice dream, all about being set free in a field of sunflowers and millet sprays, when I heard Daddy's key rattling in the front door.

After a few seconds he came into the room, switched on the light, rushed over and dropped to his knees by Mummy, and lots of water came from his eyes and he made roaring noises in his throat. Then he got up quickly and tapped three times on the telephone.

Very soon, some men dressed in green came and took Mummy away but I don't think *they* could wake her up either, because they never brought her home again, or it could be they liked her too much to give her back. I can understand that! *(squawk)*

Poor Daddy! He will sometimes sit on Mummy's chair of an evening. I fly down and perch on his shoulder, trying to cheer him up. *Kissy love Mummy, kiss kiss*, I say over and over.

And it's so strange because Daddy lets the water come from his eyes again, *every* time. I've tried gently sipping a drop as it rolls down his cheek, just to help him out, you know, but *(squawk)* it's still far too *salty* for this old bird.

FIRST IMPRESSIONS

These are for you, he says,

handing me chocolates, flowers and champagne.

And he's so charming all through dinner.

I like your natural beauty, he croons.

Gosh, he knows how to treat a lady -

I actually find his pot belly quite endearing

and the precise way in which he corrects my

replacement of the salt and pepper, and how he chews

his food the recommended 36 times whilst explaining

the reasoning behind it...

I have to admire a person who cares so much about

details! It certainly makes a girl feel more secure...

And when he tells me all about his ex-wife, it's really,

really interesting, not at all boring!

Evidently, she didn't understand him – a right bitch she

was and so vain, too...the poor chap, having to put up

with that kind of thing!

Can I see you again? he murmurs, brushing my cheek

with dry lips.

Oh, yes, please – I'd like that!   >>>>>>>>>>>>>

(look out, folks – here comes the rhyming bit…)

Could it be love at first sight!?
Can't wait for tomorrow night…

*   *   *   *

These are for you, he says, handing me a gift bag
containing a pair of the highest killer heels you've ever
seen, black fishnet stockings and a suspender belt, plus
a voucher entitling me to a day's stay at a beauty spa
for a complete makeover!

Thank you, I say, that's very generous; but I thought
you liked me for myself?
Oh, yes, he laughs, throwing back his head and
displaying all his gold fillings. *Yes, I do! I do!*

However – there's always room for improvement…

AT THE CEMETERY GATES

Valerie wore her pink frilly dress set off with white plastic handbag and matching high-heeled shoes for the office Christmas party which was to be held at Quorum Thisbé Town Hall.

Her mother hadn't been happy about letting her go as it finished so late. The girl had to promise to stay with her friend Cheryl and make sure they caught the late-night bus, which would drop them at the Cemetery Gates, and then it was only a fifteen-minute walk down Akimbo Lane to the safety of home.

'I've heard of girls going missing at night in town,' her mother said, wearing her worried face.

'Silly Mummy, we'll be quite safe. Mr Quigley won't allow any funny business at the office do and the bus stop is only around the corner from the Town Hall.'

'Well, yes, I suppose so.' Valerie's mother frowned and looked doubtful.

The two friends looked forward to the annual social event with much excitement. They had practised applying makeup for weeks and eventually settled on red lipstick for Cheryl and a demure cyclamen for Valerie. Both girls sported circular patches of rouge on their cheeks and bright blue eye-shadow.

Came the day, the 7 o'clock bus dropped them in Quorum Thisbé town centre. Mr and Mrs Quigley were waiting on the Town Hall steps to greet arrivals who were then ushered in towards the cloakroom where they deposited coats and powdered noses, eventually emerging with the expectant air of butterflies breaking free from the chrysalis.

The ballroom was crowded and hot, a hum of voices swelling under flashes of light cast by a revolving glittering mirror-ball.

Very soon, the band began to play an old-fashioned waltz and a few mature couples took to the floor, dipping and gliding to the sedate strains of Sid Strudwick's Strutters playing a strict-tempo version of "In the Mood". The younger people seemed reluctant to dance: boys congregated on one side, some clutching pints of beer, warily eyeing-up the girls grouped opposite under the wrought-iron balcony as if taking shelter.

Cheryl suddenly squawked, 'Oh, come on – let's groove,' and she put her handbag on the floor and began gyrating around it. Other giggling girls joined in, but Valerie held back shyly.

After a while Cheryl grew bored and pointed out a boy. 'Crikey, Valerie, look at his quiff – cor, it's Graham from Accounts, with his brothel creepers and drape jacket – he'd never dare turn up to work dressed like that! I'll go ask him up, we've got to show the oldies how it's done.'

Cheryl approached the boy and chatted to him in her vivacious way. *Honestly,* thought Valerie, *she's so forward – I could never do that.* As she watched, Graham took Cheryl's arm and led her to the bar where he bought her a drink, some sort of spirit, Valerie thought, although she could not tell exactly what it was.

Very soon, the band struck up with "Blue Suede Shoes" and the youngsters took to the floor, jiving and bopping. Valerie looked on, tapping her foot, but recoiled in distaste when Mr Quigley came over bringing a lad from Despatch.

'Now you two, don't be square, get with it,' he commanded, and walked off grinning, having done his duty by the two wallflowers.

Valerie knew the boy by sight – Cheryl always referred to him unkindly as "Owlie" because of his huge horn-rimmed glasses and beaky nose.

Valerie was obliged to spend the rest of the evening with the boring boy. They jerked about self-consciously to the music, but she hated it and felt increasingly worried about the time as Cheryl seemed to have disappeared from view.

At the end of the dance, having managed to evade Owlie's persistent offers of a date or at least a lift home on his motorcycle, Valerie ran for the last bus, hoping against hope to see Cheryl at the stop.

In the event, there was no Cheryl, only two other passengers already seated on the lower deck, one elderly man sitting at the front, and a middle-aged woman in a glazed-straw hat sitting halfway down. Many late-night carousers were pushing and shoving, clattering upstairs to the top deck, so Valerie took a seat downstairs behind the woman in the hat.

'Fares, please,' sang out the conductor, a cheeky grin on his face.

She was relieved to be on her way home, but the whereabouts of Cheryl worried her, as did the prospect of walking along Akimbo Lane alone and in the dark.

Valerie sat in a reverie, thinking about the evening, a big disappointment. *Honestly, that Owlie, wanting to take me out – as if!* She would avoid him at the office in future. Some lads actually believed they were God's gift…

Suddenly, interrupting her train of thought, a voice said, 'Have you had a good time tonight?' It was the elderly man who had turned to stare at her. She nodded politely, averting her head to gaze at the impenetrable darkness outside.

'So, where's your boyfriend? You must have one. Surely he should see you home? It's quite late to be out on your own, you know.' The man persisted until she turned and shook her head, not daring to reply.

'And I think I know where you live,' he continued. 'You're Mrs Hagstone's girl, aren't you? I don't think she would like you to be walking down

Akimbo Lane alone at night. I could escort you, get you home safely, if you wish.'

Valerie shook her head and turned to look through the window, now rain-streaked. Her heart sank – not only a fifteen-minute walk down Akimbo Lane in the dark, but in heavy rain, with no umbrella and now this old man pestering her, maybe following her all the way home!

It was agonising trying to ignore the man's torrent of questions. Then he started to leave his seat to move nearer. This was too much for the woman in the glazed-straw hat. She called out in a stage whisper, 'Just leave the girl alone, won't you, or I shall have to report you to the conductor.'

'Why? I ain't done nuffink,' the man muttered, evidently hurt, but staying put in his original seat. 'I was only being friendly to the youngster – she looks so scared to be out on her own.'

'Well, you're not helping, so stop bothering her,' the woman replied. 'Honestly, these people!' she said confidentially, turning towards Valerie. 'I've seen him on this late-night bus before, trying to chat women up – I think he's likely harmless, but still, it makes you uncomfortable, doesn't it, dear, specially when girls have gone missing – probably runaways, if you ask me! By the way, aren't you Mrs Hagstone's girl?'

Valerie nodded, and the woman continued, 'yes, I've known your mum a long time; I remember you as a kiddie, but goodness, how you've grown.'

Valerie smiled, and the woman responded. 'You're a proper young lady now,' she chirped. 'Don't you live down Akimbo Lane?'

Valerie nodded again, so relieved to have met a nice lady, an acquaintance of her mother's no less, that she almost sobbed. 'Yes, but I'm scared of walking down there on my own, especially now,' she whispered, nodding meaningly towards the old man. 'I promised to stay with my friend, but she went off with a lad she knows from work.'

'Oh, a bit flighty, is she, dear? Left you on your lonesome? A bit mean, I call that. And you certainly shouldn't be going down Akimbo Lane on your own at night. Look, I live just by the Cemetery Gates – my son is groundsman. You come back with me, and he'll give you a lift home.'

Valerie settled back in relief and beamed gratefully at the woman. The elderly man had evidently lost interest and was gazing out at the lashing rain which appeared to be increasing in its intensity.

'Cemetery Gates,' sang the conductor, 'last stop before the junction.'

Several passengers clattered down the stairs and staggered away noisily into the darkness. The elderly man took hold of Valerie's arm and said, 'I'm here to escort you home, if you wish, Miss Hagstone,' but the girl shrugged him away, shaking her head. The man hobbled off, muttering to himself as he disappeared through the rain in the direction of Akimbo Lane.

Valerie and the lady stepped onto the pavement, the conductor rang the bell, and the bus sped away with a squelching sound.

The two companions hurried, huddled together, towards Cemetery Cottage, a mere fifty yards away from the bus stop.

'That old man is such a nuisance,' said the woman. 'I really ought to report him to the police – pestering young ladies, it's simply not on.'

The cottage was in darkness. 'He's not back yet,' said the lady. 'I expecting he's still checking the cemetery for tramps – shouldn't be too long.'

With a majestic gesture, she removed her glazed-straw hat as if it were a coronet and placed it carefully on the hall-stand. Then turning to Valerie, she added, 'Well, how about a nice cup of tea while we're waiting. You just sit down in the lounge through there, make yourself comfortable.'

Valerie sat in a soft armchair, closing her eyes with gratitude and exhaustion. Then she heard the front door open and whispered voices in the hall, then a burst of raucous laughter.

'Good,' she thought with relief, 'her son's back and he sounds very jolly; I'll be home in five minutes if she doesn't insist on the tea.'

The woman came in carrying a tray and set the cups and saucers and a plate of biscuits on a side table.

'Actually, I'm not really wanting any tea just now,' the girl began timorously. 'Erm, I'm so sorry, but if your son wouldn't mind giving me a lift home, I'll be off. My mother will be worried…'

'Oh, you must be chilled to the bone, I can't let you go without something warm inside you,' smiled the woman engagingly, picking up a large ceramic teapot decorated with red and blue flowers. 'What on earth would your poor mother think of me if I let you go home frozen? And anyway, we still have to wait…'

'Wait? But wasn't that your son who came in just now? I'm sure I heard someone laughing…?'

'Oh yes, that was my son, he likes a good laugh, but, as I said, he checks the graveyard for tramps every night, and when he gets home he has to clean all the grave soil off his boots, have a wash and change his clothes. You wouldn't want him giving you a lift home stinking of dead people, now, would you?'

'No, no, I wouldn't,' murmured the girl weakly.

She looked around the room and was astonished to see many dead, stuffed animals, large and small, cats and dogs, mice, rats and hamsters, and even a snake, displayed on the mantelpiece, on the shelves, the sideboard and other surfaces.

'Aha, I see you're admiring my son's handiwork,' laughed the lady. 'It's a hobby of his: taxidermy, it's called – have you ever heard of that? And he's always busy with one thing or another, either here or in the graveyard. He collects random human bones, too, when he finds them lying about. Oh yes, there's never a dull moment in this house, I can tell you!'

She offered Valerie a biscuit on a plate, but the girl shook her head and shuddered. She stared at the woman who smiled and raised her eyebrows. 'Anything wrong, dear? You don't like biscuits? Oh well, never mind, but come on now, have a sip of your tea. The sooner you drink up, the sooner you can get home to your poor mother. I did add some cold water to your cup so you wouldn't be waiting for it to cool down – I hate drinking tea too hot, don't you, dear? It tends to burn the tongue, I find – yes, very painful it can be, hot tea.'

The girl instinctively did as she was told and picked up her cup with a shaking hand. Then she drank deeply, greedily, gratefully, suddenly realising with surprise that her mouth was as dry as a bone.

MIDNIGHT SUN

Scene: Breakfast-time in a family kitchen in the year AD 2115. Fifty-something Roy and Faye sit at the table:

Roy: What's for breakfast, love? I'm famished this morning, more than ready for my fry-up.

Faye: Oh sorry, Roy. We're fresh out of bacon and egg pills. What can I tempt you with instead? There's toast and marmalade tablets, boiled egg with soldiers pills, muesli capsules. Take your pick.

Roy: You sure you're looking in the right drawer? Oh, never mind – I'll have the muesli, I suppose.

Faye: Rightie ho, love. Here – catch!

Roy: Thanks, love. *(chewing and slurping appreciatively)* Mm, yum! Very tasty - *and* healthy! But, love – where's Neptune? He hasn't shown his face yet. Still in bed, the lazy monkey.

Faye: Yes, he's watching a re-run of his favourite dream – you know, the one about going on holiday.

Roy: I'll give him "going on holiday" if he doesn't come down soon.   He'll have to suck his breakfast on the way to school. How many times have you called him this morning?

Faye: Oh, don't go on at him, love! Let's try this – *you* try hacking into his dream machine and *I'll* send him an extra-sensory thought wave. Here goes: 'Dear Neptune, get out of bed this minute – I won't tell you again, cheers, Mummy xxx'.

Roy: OK, love, I will, but thinking about it, I reckon the lad could have a point, we *will* have to start planning our holiday soon. How about Antarctica – it's lovely and warm in December, or Tesco Island, nice and soft on the feet, or the Sahara Lakes?

Faye: Nah, Antarctica is far too hot, Saraha Lakes are too cold, and Tesco Island is too plastic-bag-squishy and just as wet as it is here – although not as cold, I'll give you that. Anyway, we're living on an island, so where's the novelty in going to a similar place? We want somewhere different – drier would be nice.

Roy: How about a flight to the Moon, then, love? It's very dry there. A bit expensive but we could probably stretch to a week for the three of us.

Faye: The three of us? What about little Tsunami? We couldn't leave her behind.

Roy: Oh, she's only three – too young to appreciate a foreign holiday – wouldn't your mother have her? Just for a week?

Faye: What are you like – talk about the memory man! As you well know, my mother's still on her way back from Mars. She won't be home for another five years or so and then it'll be the compulsory euthanasia when she clocks her 75th birthday shortly afterwards. So we can't depend on her to babysit, unfortunately.

Roy: Oh yeah, I remember now – she's a right gad-about, your mother. Hmm, who can look after little Tsunami, then, if we go to the Moon for a week?

Faye: Little Tsunami can come with us. It would be good for her particle physics studies – I must say she's taken to them like a duck to water.

Roy: Yeah, you're right, but only because I've taken the trouble to teach her. That useless playschool hasn't progressed much beyond differential calculus.

Faye: Well, I did complain to the playschool, but they have to go with the lowest common denominator, apparently. It's not very fair on the bright kids, that's all.

Roy: Yeah, you're right there, love. And by the way, changing the subject, just look at the sun streaming in – it's nearly midnight – Neptune will be late for school.   There's no excuse, it's only one morning a week. Surely he can drag himself away from that holograph recorder for a few hours. He'll have the Dream Police after him if he's not careful.

Faye: Oh, Neptune's a good boy, he wouldn't dream *anything* subversive. Anyway, he's always going on about actually joining the Dream Police when he grows up.

Roy: Don't give me that, love – the lad wants to aim high, not low. I'm hoping he'll do well in his String Theory exams and go to Ben Nevis Beach University.   Then he can follow me into the profession.

369

Faye: Yes, I suppose so – although I don't think he
        wants to work in The Sixty Four Euro Shop with
        you, Roy.

Roy: And what's wrong with working in The Sixty
        Four Euro Shop, may I ask?

Faye: Oh, nothing at all, it's a good solid career if
        you're clever enough to be taken on – but don't
        go on about it, love. Neptune's only 24 – he
        won't be going to university for another three
        years yet. There's plenty of time to decide about
        his career. He could change his mind again and
        again – you know what kids are like.

Roy: Yeah, you're right as usual, love.

Faye: Let's concentrate on planning our holiday. I
        don't want anywhere too hot, too cold, or too wet.

Roy: By Hades, there's no pleasing you! Now where's
        that lad? Faye, you're the mother, give him a
        shout.

Faye: *(calling up the stairs)* Oi, Neptune – *lo-o-ove*,
        get up *now*, this very minute! Oi! Are you getting
        up or not? Look, I should warn you – we need
        your advice about booking a *holiday*!

Roy: Ho ho, that did the trick, I can hear definite movements from above! You're a clever gal, Faye – clever and beautiful. Come here and give us a kiss.

Faye: You keep your distance, Roy Cohen Mahmood Patel Chang, and get ready to take your son to school. Now here's his breakfast pill, his lunch tablet, sou'wester and wellies, and, oh yes, I've packed his snorkel and flippers.

Roy: Snorkel and flippers?

Faye: Yeah, snorkel and flippers! And an extra bucket for baling out. You know, we really ought to trade in that ancient rowing boat – I feel so embarrassed whenever it sinks. Now – a lovely motor-boat would be nice, to keep up with the Hussein-von-Stottlemeyer-Shantung-Joneses. I feel that embarrassed: we're the only family on Pennine Island who hasn't moved with the times.

The End

Lightning Source UK Ltd.
Milton Keynes UK
UKOW04f2137100715

254920UK00001B/20/P